# CHASING GHOSTS

## A Quentin Strange Mystery

by

Dean Cole

www.deancolebooks.com
www.thequentinstrangemysteries.com
Twitter: @DeanColeWriter

*The boundaries which divide Life from Death are at best shadowy and vague. Who shall say where the one ends, and where the other begins?*

Edgar Allan Poe, *The Premature Burial*

## - CHAPTER ONE -

# *A Murder of Crows*

HILDERLEY MANOR LOOMED through the windscreen of Kat's Mini, nimbus clouds swirling above its balustrade roof, crispy leaves strewn across its gravel drive. A murder of crows loitered on the lawn, some cawing and batting their wings, others pecking the grass, hunting for worms drawn to the surface by the recent rainstorm. The place couldn't have looked more bloody haunted if it tried.

I stepped out of the car and shivered as the autumn chill hit my face. Kat got out too, frowning up at the house as she took a long, slow drag on her Marlboro Light.

'Jesus,' she said, carelessly flicking the ignited tip into some nearby undergrowth. 'Who lives here? The Addams Family?'

I smiled but it was a ghost of one. Now we'd arrived, the willing participants of a ghost hunt inside one of Britain's most haunted buildings, I was starting to get cold feet. The enormous house looked spooky enough in broad daylight, what horror would it become after midnight?

Come on, Quentin, I reassured myself. You're braver than that. You've watched horror films back to back, home alone with the lights off, then gone to bed without so much as a second thought.

You once slept in a graveyard, drunk, admittedly, and too off your face to find your way home, but waking up to find you've been using a gravestone as a pillow would have traumatised a lesser man. And there was that time you did the Ouija board with that large girl from school, Melissa Dandridge, in that derelict building behind the cinema all the kids were too scared to enter. You were eleven then. A child. You're twenty seven now. A man. It's a spooky house in the remote countryside of Northern England. What's the worst that could happen?

I tried not to ponder that question as I shut the passenger door, catching a glimpse of my reflection in the window. My mop of brown hair was all over the place. My skin had the pallor of a vampiric creature from The Twilight Saga. The round specs made me look like a cross between one of The Beatles and a senior Harry Potter. The only positive was the specs were doing a grand job of concealing my sleep-deprived eyes. It wasn't just the prospect of three nights inside Hilderley Manor that had been keeping me awake in recent days.

Kat whistled, striding to the boot of the car. 'I'll give it to the guys back at the office. I can count on them to send us to one of the most morbid places in the northern hemisphere.' She cast the house a suspicious look under her heavily-pencilled eyebrows. 'I just hope there's booze in there. And they better let me smoke, or else.'

As she retrieved her case, I wandered over to the iron gates, great fortress-like things that appeared to be keeping something in instead of out. I lifted my specs and let them perch atop my ruffled fringe. Longsighted, I could make out the building's most prominent features: the innumerous mullioned windows covering its facade, black vines snaking up the aged stonework, the decorative trim over the front door, gargoyle-like and crumbling with years of weather damage. An impressive edifice, Hilderley Manor managed to look both inviting and intimidating at the same time.

The windows reflected the storm clouds above our heads, leaving only my imagination to picture what awaited us inside. Something I'd seen in a period drama on TV most likely, with dark walls, draughty corridors and cooks and housemaids buzzing about the place like worker bees. I forced myself not to imagine more. My mind would conjure all manner of horrors if I thought about it long enough and I'd never get past the gate, let alone the front door.

Specks of rain alighted on my cheeks and a low rumble across the sky heralded more thunder. The tempestuous weather we'd had on the way here was making a reappearance. As if sensing this the crows took off in search of safety, their screeching caws splitting the sky as they vanished over the tall hedges that bordered the manor.

In their commotion I didn't see the elderly man who had emerged from the side of the building. Actually, 'elderly' was being kind: shrivelled as a prune and gnarled as a tree he must have been a hundred if he was a day. He stood there, a shovel in one hand, staring at me unblinkingly. Even from this distance I could tell the look on his haggard face wasn't welcoming. A shiver tickled the nape of my neck, and this time it wasn't because of the autumn weather. Did he know something we didn't? Was his uninviting reception a portent of unfavourable things to come?

I had the urge to turn around, get away from this place while I still had the chance. But as I was contemplating just that, a weird feeling came over me. A feeling I was being encouraged to reconsider, beckoned even. A gust of wind stirred the undergrowth, furling the hem of my blazer and blowing dry leaves past my feet. A superstitious person might have said that gust of wind was a ghostly whisper. I wasn't a superstitious person, though. Was I?

A hand suddenly grabbed my shoulder.

'BOO!'

I spun round so fast my specs fell off my head and slid to the tip of my nose. Kat's baby blue eyes, so at odds with the raven curls, scarlet lipstick and power suit-clad slim figure that defined her, flashed wickedly back at me. 'Are you going to stand there gawking at that place all day, or are we going to find ourselves some ghosts?'

My heart was still drumming beneath my ribs as she dropped my rucksack in my arms. She had something else for me. She lifted it in front of my face the way you might confront a boisterous puppy with a slipper it had half eaten.

'What is this?'

'My camera,' I said nervously.

'That is not a camera. It's a relic. You're working for a newspaper now, Quentin. The days of snapping goofy photos of your friends to stick in grubby albums are over. We use state-of-the-art equipment at the *Gazette*.' She dipped her hand inside an enormous handbag. 'This,' she said, presenting me with what I instantly recognised as a digital single-lens reflex camera, 'is a camera.'

I stared in awe at the camera presented before me. It was a professional model and easily in the higher end of the price range. 'For me?

'Yours to keep for as long as you're working for us,' said Kat, dropping it on top of the rucksack. 'When — *if* you go, then we want it back. Deal?'

I nodded, still ogling the unexpected gift. I could only dream of owning such an impressive and expensive piece of equipment with my measly income.

I caught Kat before she was about to toss my old camera into some nearby shrubbery. 'Don't! It's got sentimental value.'

Kat twisted her face as if questioning how anything so hideous could have sentimental value, but, mercifully, dropped it on the rucksack with the DSLR. 'And don't break that camera,' she said sternly. 'We don't insure against carelessness. If you do, the cost will be immediately deducted from your pay.'

Speaking of pay ... 'Erm, Katrina —'

My partner rolled her eyes. 'Please, Quentin, I won't tell you again. Do not call me Katrina. I'm allergic to the name for numerous reasons we shall never discuss. It's Kat. Just Kat. And always Kat.'

'Sorry. Kat. Got it. It's about my first payment—'

I paused, noticing her looking at my chest with a look somewhere between a grimace and deep pity.

'Did you have to wear that outfit for your first assignment?' she asked.

I lowered my chin, eyed my shirt and blazer nervously. 'Why? What's wrong with it?'

'You look like someone from the last century. No, the century before that.'

'I thought it looked smart,' I said. 'You know, professional.'

'If your name is Albert Einstein, maybe.' Kat shook her head wearily. 'Remind me to take you shopping when we get back to Cricklewood. I know some great stores there for boys. I'm thinking ... modern man-boy from the city.' She assessed me the way one might envisage which decor they wanted for their living room. 'In the meantime we'll just have to hope people think it's a new trend.'

'What if I like what I'm wearing?' I said defiantly, then knew instantly I'd said the wrong thing.

'If we're going to be working as a team for the foreseeable

future I require that you keep up with my standards,' Kat replied firmly. 'This job means everything to me. And appearances, today, are almost everything.'

'Sounds a bit shallow if you ask me,' I muttered.

Kat's mouth fell open. Mascara laden lashes fluttered as she came dangerously close. 'Listen up, buttercup. There's an entire world of people out there trying to get noticed. The competition has never been higher. You have to be multifaceted to stand out. No, you have to be bloody Superwoman! I'm not just a journalist. I'm a hustler, an actress, a mentor, I know how to market, network and I still look this good doing all of it.' She tugged at the lapel on my blazer. 'That's why I can't be dragging around someone who looks like they've just stepped out of a Tardis.'

Did she miss bitch off that list? I might have asked, if I didn't envision getting a knock about the ears with that handbag.

Her face turned from stern to threatening. 'I'm also an absolute dragon if someone pisses me off. So,' she said, the perfected smile returning, the way a chameleon changes its appearance in an instant, 'you're not just a photographer. You're an assistant and a stylish, suave gentleman from the city. What are you?'

'A photographer, an assistant and a stylish, suave gentleman from the city,' I intoned reluctantly.

'Now we're getting somewhere,' she said, picking lint off my blazer like a solicitous mother.

But as another rumble of thunder caught our attention, I couldn't help but wonder, just who was Kat trying to impress? Couldn't she just interview people, write her article and let me take some photos? Which, after all, is what we were being paid to do. Since arguing with her was likely futile — if not a genuine hazard to my safety — I decided to keep that little sentiment to myself.

Finished with her lecture she took off, shouldering her way

through the gate, a Burberry suitcase on wheels dragging behind her.

Struggling to push my specs up my nose with my luggage laden arms, I watched her stride up the driveway, her heels crunching the gravel, curls bouncing around her shoulders, completely ignoring that I'd been about to ask her something.

But then it wouldn't be the first time Kat would pay no attention to what I had to say. And she'd pay a tall price for it, too.

If I'd been many years younger I might have stuck out my tongue. If I'd been of an uncouth disposition I might have spat in those billowing locks of hers. But I was neither of those things. All I could do was wonder, depressingly, how long her previous partner had survived. I sighed as I stowed both cameras in my rucksack. One week into my new job and I was fast learning my role in this newfound partnership. I was the apprentice and Kat was the boss. Would it be a match made in heaven or a match made in hell? Only time would tell.

The elderly man was no longer standing there, as if he'd vanished like a spectre. The sky was getting darker, the day drawing on. The house seemed to have grown taller all of a sudden, formidable. With the clouds no longer reflected in the windows, I could see right in. Kat's words resounded in my head: *'are we going to find ourselves some ghosts?'*

I didn't tell her I thought I'd already found one: the misty figure I'd just seen looking down at me from one of the second floor windows.

\* \* \* \* \*

You could hear the echo coming from inside as Kat rapped the knocker on the heavy, engraved front door. When it creaked open, a squat, rosy-cheeked woman with her hair in a bun poked her head out. She raised a hand to shield her eyes from the daylight.

'Katrina Brannigan and Quentin Strange,' said Kat, proffering her hand in an exaggerated professional manner. 'We're here for the ghost hunt?'

I cast Kat an indignant glare. So Katrina was fine as long as it was coming out of her own mouth? She paid no attention to me as she waited for the woman's response.

'Ah, yes,' said the woman. 'Come in, dears. Come in.'

She had a friendly Scottish accent that conjured images of wild thistle and lochside castles. In fact, everything about this woman, from the expertly polished shoes on her tiny feet to her neatly buttoned cardigan, was welcoming. She ushered us through the door with a warm smile, her cheeks like apples.

At least someone's pleased to see us, I thought, the Grim Reaper from outside still playing on my mind.

The building was surprisingly warm for its size; the ceiling was so high your eyes automatically went upwards to see if there was a ceiling up there at all. It felt at odds with how dark and gloomy the place was, like we'd stepped into an underground cavern.

The smell wasn't unpleasant, but it wasn't exactly pleasant either. I was pretty certain no dead bodies were festering beyond the large double doors leading into the main rooms, but there was definitely something stale navigating the air. It was mixed with the smell of furniture polish, fire wood and vegetable soup cooking somewhere in the distance, reminding me what it was like to have things cooked from scratch instead of reheated in a microwave or delivered in boxes by strangers. A refined bachelor I had not been of late.

The front door closed behind us and the woman appeared in front of us again.

'Just the two of you, isn't it?'

'That's right,' said Kat. 'We're from the *Cricklewood Gazette*. I'm a journalist. Quentin, here, is my photographer.' The possessive *my* didn't go unnoticed. 'We're putting together an article with the help of *Pluckley Ghost Hunters*. Is the team here?'

'I'm afraid they're running a little late,' said the woman, 'but it'll give you time to get settled in while you wait. I'm Mrs Brown, the housekeeper. You can call me Elspeth if you like.'

Elspeth. I tried to say the name in my mind. I've got a bit of a lisp, albeit barely noticeable. I'd be sticking to the much more manageable Mrs Brown. I didn't say this out loud, though, offering Mrs Brown a courteous smile as she rang a small bell, presumably to let others know we'd arrived.

Kat, a heavy smoker, wasted no time alleviating her anxieties. She planted her hands on Mrs Brown's shoulders and affected a fawning smile. 'Elspeth, you little Irish munchkin, please tell me I can smoke in this fantastic building of yours?'

The little woman blinked, taken aback by the boldness. And the fact she'd been called Irish when she was very much Scottish. I'd known Kat only days, but could already picture what it was going to be like introducing her to people, the way you might show off an exotic pet — it could be dangerous if pushed, but show it respect and everyone should be OK. Right now, Mrs Brown looked anything but OK. She looked like someone staring into the maw of a tiger.

'Sorry, angel, but this is a public building. We have a strict no smoking policy,' she replied. She corroborated this by pointing to a no-smoking sign on the wall.

Kat responded to this unwelcome news with a strained smile before turning to me, the ingratiating act vanishing in an instant. While Mrs Brown was brushing the creases out of her shoulders, she leaned in to my ear and whispered, 'If there's a smoke alarm in the room, you can cover it while I lean out the window.'

I had to admire her tenacity. Though I can't say I wasn't secretly pleased I wouldn't have to spend the weekend breathing in her toxic, second-hand cigarette smoke. A perennial hypochondriac, I like my air — and my lungs — free from pollution, thank you very much.

Done with the preamble, Mrs Brown led us deeper into the hallway. Our footsteps were muffled by a sumptuous rug covering most of the stone floor. I glanced around, taking in the large, open space around me. My imagination was right: it was as if we'd stepped back in time several decades. Aged portraits in gilded picture frames adorned the dark wood walls, their eyes appearing to follow us as we walked. An elaborate chandelier hung from the sky-high ceiling, though not a single one of its bulbs was lit, the only source of light coming from the candle-like sconces in the alcoves. A large bifurcated staircase dominated the space, its hard edges and carved spindles adding to the grandeur of it all.

'Your room's on the second floor,' trilled Mrs Brown. 'Follow me.'

She trotted up the staircase, her polished shoes rapping the ancient wood. Kat followed first, looking flustered as she struggled to extend the handle on her suitcase to carry it up the steps. As I brought up the rear, my eyes strayed to a dark corridor off to one side of the hallway. I had a disturbing feeling someone was watching me. Was the creepy bloke from outside loitering in the shadows? Seeing nothing there I shook the thought away, but I was quick to catch up with Kat and Mrs Brown after that.

After ascending another flight of stairs we were led down a long, spacious corridor. The walls up here, like downstairs, were covered with dark panelling and a well-worn runner the colour of blood lined the floor. Mrs Brown halted in front of an open doorway and gestured for us to enter.

'I'm afraid yours is the smallest room,' she said. 'It used to accommodate lowly staff many moons ago, but it's reflective of the price and with recent decoration I think you'll find it pleasant enough. Bathroom's along there, two doors on your right.' She crossed her hands in front of a well fed midriff. 'Right then, I'll leave you to it. Come down to the lounge when you're ready. It's the large room on the left. If you need anything in the meantime, don't be afraid to ask.'

Then she was walking away as swiftly as she'd brought us up here. We stood at the threshold of the room like two forsaken children as the tread of the little Scotswoman's shoes tapered down the corridor and she became even more diminutive than she already was.

Kat stepped inside the room first and I followed. It was clean and tidy, with a fourposter bed, a coffer, a changing screen, mahogany furniture and a large paned window. Despite the size of the window, the room, like the rest of the house, was gloomily dark. Kat solved this by striding to the bed and switching on the bedside lamp. Chintz fabrics and gleaming wood lit up all around us.

A pleasant smell perfuming the air caught my attention. My nose hunted it out to a bowl of potpourri sitting atop the heavily-grained surface top of a nearby dresser. Standing next to the bowl was a clear vase filled with white lilies.

*White lilies …*

The room seemed to disappear as the flowers, their ivory-coloured petals, their sweet fragrance, triggered a memory …

*Multiple wreaths arranged on top of the coffin. How beautiful yet tragic it looked for someone so young. White for peace. For light and love. For purity …*

'God, it's even worse than I imagined.'

The memory ebbed away as Kat's voice pulled me back to the room. 'Sorry?'

'The room. I've seen less depressing funeral parlours.'

'Oh,' I said, still distant. I took another glance at the space around me. It didn't look depressing to me. I've always felt an affinity with old things. They're out of their time, forgotten. Sort of like me.

'Still, we're only here for the weekend,' said Kat. 'And it was dirt cheap compared to prices down south.'

She dropped her handbag on the floor and fell backwards onto the mattress, her body carving a dent in the perfectly fitted linen. She remained there, spread eagle, staring dreamily up at the roof of the fourposter. In a more dignified fashion, I walked over to the coffer at the foot of the bed and pulled off my rucksack. It was only then that I noticed something wasn't quite right.

'Wait, why is there only one bed?'

'Because we're sharing.'

I felt my stomach lilt. 'Sharing?'

'They didn't have any rooms with separate beds.'

Sweat prickled my hairline. Sharing a bed? With another person? A female person? Seeing the growing horror on my face, Kat rolled her eyes.

'Hun, do you honestly think I don't know about your preferences?'

'My preferences?'

'You're gay, Quentin. Anyone can see that.'

I blinked. Looked around me as if I'd just been outed to Hilderley Manor's ghosts.

'There's nothing to be ashamed about,' said Kat, heaving

herself into a sitting position. 'Who isn't gay today? Or at least a little bit. I did an assignment on sexual orientation. Apparently nobody's fully straight or gay on the sexuality spectrum. Hell, I'd consider women myself if it meant I never had to meet another guy like any of my exes.'

'I'm not ashamed,' I said. 'I just … didn't think it was that obvious. And I'm fussy about sharing my space. It's a hygiene thing.'

Kat got up and walked over to the dresser mirror. 'In fairness, I do have exceptional intuition,' she said, tilting her face to admire her bone structure. 'But you made it more than obvious when we first met that you bat for the other team, or whatever that phrase is.'

'How?' I said, my voice shooting higher than I'd intended. I cleared my throat. 'How?'

'I was wearing a low cut top and your eyes didn't once stray to these,' she said, peeling back the lapels of her coat to reveal her cleavage bursting through a low buttoned shirt. 'Let's face it, what straight guy is going to resist a peek at these beauties?'

I looked at aforementioned bosom, which Kat was now plumping admiringly. They were indeed an impressive pair of appendages, like two small watermelons squeezed tightly together in a slingshot. But I was too busy trying to figure out what she'd seen in me that was so 'gay' to give them much attention.

Sensing any answer eluding me, I walked over to the window. The weather was growing wetter outside, drizzle scattering the window panes with tiny water globules. I stared at the well kept grounds below, at Kat's Mini parked in the distance, and shivered. The temperature seemed to have plummeted the higher we'd ventured up the building. Or was it just this room? I touched the ancient looking radiator under the window, flinching when I discovered it was stone cold. I pulled my blazer tighter, drew in a breath, released it. The window misted opaque. The bedside lamp, reflected in the window, silhouetted my head and shoulders onto the frosty glass. It would make a great stylistic shot if this were a scene in a Gothic horror film, I couldn't help noticing.

Kat, a true Southerner, began mimicking Mrs Brown's Scottish accent. '*"I'm Mrs Brown, the housekeeper. You can call me Elspeth if you like."* I had a teacher at primary school who sounded just like that, you know ...'

But I wasn't listening as I watched thunderclouds swirl in the sky, more crows seeking refuge in the canopies of leafless trees. A storm was brewing. Or was the sudden cold feeling something more worrying? My thoughts drifted back to the misty figure I'd seen standing at the window. Had I really seen it? Or was it just the creepiness of the place messing with my imagination?

'... and she had this huge mole on her face that made her look like a witch —'

'Think we'll survive the weekend?' I interrupted.

Kat snorted. 'Don't be a drama queen. Ghosts don't exist. And this weekend will prove it.'

I stared at her reflection in the window, watched her walk over to the bedside table and pull open a drawer, no doubt looking for freebies or valuables she could pillage.

At the same moment the elderly man reappeared down on the driveway, the shovel replaced with a tattered broom.

'I don't know,' I murmured, as I watched him hobble to the edge of the lawn and start sweeping a sea of dead leaves. 'Who knows what's going on in this universe? Who are we to say this supernatural stuff is just a figment of people's imaginations?'

'Pffft, I should have known you'd be into this nonsense too,' said Kat, sliding the drawer shut and searching the cupboard beneath. 'But despite your award winning photography skills, some floating dust and smears on a lens isn't proof the afterlife exists.'

I spun to face her. 'They weren't smears. And that dust? They're called orbs. Look it up. In fact, I'd have thought a 'multifaceted' journalist like yourself would have done that already since you're about to write an article on the subject.'

Kat's eyes drifted up to me from the other side of the fourposter as she shut the cupboard carefully. 'So there is fire lurking beneath that meek veneer of yours.' She squinted her eyes, an almost proud grin curling her painted lips. 'Calm down, Cruella, it's called an opinion. We're all entitled to one.'

My gaze remained steadfast. Ordinarily a pacifist, I was surprised by the tetchiness Kat and her jibes were able to draw out of me. Either that or the last few weeks' lack of sleep was finally catching up with me. I softened my tone. 'What were you looking at the photos for, anyway, if you're such a sceptic?'

'Josh showed everyone in the office. He's obsessed with anything supernatural, especially now we're extending our monthly print magazine to cater to a more diverse readership. He was jumping around the place like he'd won the lottery when he saw your little offerings. Can't say I thought much of them myself, but you certainly fooled him.'

'They're not fake,' I said, irritation returning to my voice.

Kat hauled her handbag onto the bed and started rummaging inside. 'Yeah, yeah. Keep your mop on. Who cares if they're real, anyway? You got a job at the *Gazette*. That's all that matters, right?'

I felt annoyed at Kat's lack of respect. I had been lucky to get the job at the *Gazette*. I was searching for jobs when I spotted the advert: *Photos wanted showing evidence of ghosts or ghostly apparitions.* I'd been photographing orbs and other anomalies around my apartment for months. Just days before I saw the advert

I happened to capture my most intriguing shot yet. A face. Or something like a face. It was a smoky shadow the shape of a person's head and shoulders, positioned in the corner of the bedroom as it appeared to look directly at the camera. But the editor at the *Gazette*, Josh Mendy, hadn't only liked the apparition in my photo. He said I had a great eye for framing a shot and drawing the viewer's attention to its most important features. That's why he'd offered me a job.

And there were other things Kat didn't know. There was more than just anomalies in my photographs making me wonder if another world running parallel to this one we couldn't see really did exist. For months strange things had been happening to me. I'd heard voices, felt presences, seen inexplicable lights and shadows; I'd experienced precognition, picturing entire events or conversations before they happened. And then there were the dreams. No, not dreams, those scenarios created by the subconscious, your brain trying to process what you've been doing and thinking about during the day. These were something deeper. Memories. And they felt so real, like I was right there experiencing them all over again. Add to all this me getting the job at the local paper, which had brought me to this godforsaken place on a rainy day in mid-October, and the more everything started to feel less like coincidence and nearer to fate.

Kat finished retouching her lipstick then squirted herself with perfume. She stretched out her hands, unceremoniously cracking the bones in her fingers. The sound made me wince. 'I'm going downstairs to bring Petunia up the drive and have a smoke,' she announced. She waltzed to the door, bending to sniff the lilies before slipping out into the corridor. The remaining tension appeared to leave the room with her.

In her absence I felt a strengthening of my resolve. Whatever was happening to me had to be more than my imagination, whether it was the work of a supernatural force or not. Hundreds of photos taken throughout my life had never revealed such strange and mysterious things. I'd barely been able to predict the weather before, let alone the future. And the dreams. Surely it wasn't normal — possible, even — to dream your past exactly as it had happened all those years ago?

I couldn't ignore these things any longer. Better yet, maybe Hilderley Manor's ghost hunting team could help me make some sort of sense of them? After all, what do you do if you suspect you're being haunted? I couldn't exactly call the Ghostbusters.

*But ghosts, Quentin. You're talking about ghosts*, the critical voice inside my head whispered …

I pushed my doubt away and walked over to where I'd left my rucksack. I carried it around to what I was going to claim as my side of the bed. I unzipped one of the side pockets and pulled out the brown labelled bottle tucked discreetly behind my spare glasses. I stared at the small white pills inside. Pills that were supposed to calm my nerves and stop my obsessive thoughts, to sedate what my doctor had called my 'overactive imagination.'

I debated taking my daily dosage. The pills gave me unwanted side effects: nausea, bad headaches, loss of libido — even if my sex life was as active as an extinct volcano. But they did reduce the intensity of the visions. Somewhat. I thought again about the misty figure standing at the window. A creation of my mind or something more? The lines between reality and my imagination were blurring more and more. Maybe that's what the pills were meant to do.

I opened the bottle, poured one of the white ovals onto my palm and chucked it into the back of my throat, swallowing it dry. I wasn't willing to discover what else this haunted place had in store for me. For the moment, at least.

Thunder rumbled outside, grabbing my attention. I returned to the window. Kat had reached the ground and was striding down the driveway, thumbing her phone and puffing on a cigarette, Petunia (her Mini) patiently awaiting her return on the other side of the gate like some oversized pet. The old man had stopped sweeping the leaves and was staring up at the window, watching me. His expression was even less inviting than it was earlier. 'What is your problem?' I might have shouted out. If I hadn't been raised to have better manners when it came to strangers. If I didn't sense something sinister lurking behind those rheumy eyes of his.

# - CHAPTER TWO -

# *White Feathers*

AFTER WE'D UNPACKED and freshened up we headed downstairs to meet the others. A young man in catering uniform standing at the entrance to the lounge fitted us with stickers that had our names written on them in black marker. Kat looked down at hers, which had been adhered to her left breast. 'Stickers with our names on? What do they think it is? Nursery school?'

Entering the lounge, it was easy to pick out the ghost hunting team who would be escorting us around the manor over the weekend. There was four of them, each wearing a black shirt with their logo, *Pluckley Ghost Hunters,* emblazoned on the front. It was designed in a serif font with two neon eyes peering out of the letter *O*. Obvious, but effective. The foursome were assembled near a large open fire, peculiar looking equipment scattered over the antique furniture around them.

'That's them,' said Kat, producing a notepad from her bosom. 'Just as weird as I expected.'

She jotted in the notepad, presumably taking notes on what she was observing.

I assumed the other people in the room were our fellow guests. A young, attractive and well-dressed couple stood at the opposite side of the room, their hands all over each other as they admired a collection of photographs hanging in frames on the wall. She was petite and stunning, with the dark hair and eyes of Asia. He was equally beautiful — of Greek descent I deduced at a glance — and impressively muscular. The girl was holding what I thought was a fur accessory, until a second glance made me realise it was a small fluffy dog.

Another woman was milling about a table ladened with food and beverages. I say milling; she was more like a fish feeding off a coral reef as she made her way through tureens, bowls and sandwich-filled platters. She was as colourful as a sea creature, too. A halo of wild gold hair bordered her heavily bronzed and painted face, and her large frame was draped in mounds of multicoloured fabric. Accessories of all sorts — rings, jewels, wrist bands and necklaces — hung off her like Christmas tree decorations. I had a hunch there was something different about her ... something mystical.

One of the ghost hunters, a bloke with thick-rimmed glasses and a peppering of grey through his black spiky hair, stepped forward authoritatively when he noticed Kat and I had entered the room.

'Welcome, folks,' he said. 'I'm Giles. And this is my wife, Annie.' He coiled an arm around the slim woman with shoulder length hair standing beside him.

The attractive couple peeled themselves away from the photographs, shuffling up behind Kat and me as we moved closer to listen to what he had to say.

'I'm the lead investigator of *Pluckley Ghost Hunters* and Annie is our location researcher,' Giles went on. He gestured to the only other male of the foursome. 'That's Norman, our parapsychologist.'

Norman, a giant of a bloke who was a generation older than Giles and had not a single hair on his shiny, tanned head but made up for it with a silver beard that grew down to a beer-belly waist, gave us a curt nod then went back to fiddling with his camera, blowing dust off its lens.

Giles then gestured to the last ghost hunter, a woman who was the youngest of the group. She was full figured, with mahogany and orange highlighted hair and a cherubic face. There were at least two piercings in it. 'And that's Carrie, our team sensitive.'

Norman ... as in Psycho's Norman Bates? Carrie ... as in Stephen King's Carrie White? Annie ... Annie Wilkes? Is it just me or was there something in that?

As Carrie offered a demure smile, I stared at each of the ghost hunters in turn, the flickering flames of the fire gilding the shoulders of their black shirts. I never imagined such a fascinating group of people existed. But then, until recently, I never really imagined ghosts existed. *Could* exist, I reminded myself. Unless *Pluckley Ghost Hunters* could definitively prove otherwise over the coming days, the jury was still out on that one.

'We're just unpacking the rest of our stuff, then we'll run through the weekend's schedule,' said Giles, checking his watch. He nodded at the table where the halo-haired woman was still working her way through the food, paying no attention to us. 'Help yourself to snacks and refreshments. We'll be stopping for a proper meal at seven, but that's a good few hours off and this ghost hunting business can be hungry work.' He laughed at his own joke then resumed helping Annie, Norman and Carrie with their equipment.

I glanced to my side, expecting to see Kat there. But she was already at the table appraising the alcoholic beverages. I had no appetite and no desire to drink. The coffee I'd had when we stopped at the motorway service station, combined with my morning pill, had made me queasy. Or was that just my nerves contemplating forthcoming events? It looked like the young couple weren't hungry either. They'd moved on to admiring a stag's head that was surmounted over the mantelpiece. Or at least he was; she looked horrified by the hideous thing.

A born recluse, any social setting of more than four people was my worst nightmare. But I had been challenging myself recently to confront that fear. Swallowing down the urge to find a corner to hide in, I decided to introduce myself.

'Hey,' I said to the guy, proffering my hand.

Respectfully, he removed a pair of designer shades before shaking it. His grip was so firm it felt like he might crush my knuckles into bone dust. He looked even more ripped close up, with rugby player shoulders and veins protruding from his neck. Umber eyes glanced at the sticker on my chest. 'Nice to meet you, Quentin. I'm Matthaios. That's Math-a-os. Nobody can pronounce it, though, so call me Matt.'

Matthaios. Definitely Greek. So I was right.

He snaked his arm around the woman. 'This is my girlfriend, Ash.'

Ash showed me a cosmetically enhanced smile. She was strikingly beautiful, with perfect waves in her hair and flawless skin the colour of rich coffee. You'd have thought she was attending an expensive dinner party looking at her attire, all revealing garments complemented with twinkling jewelry. 'Say hello to Cottonball,' she said.

The little creature looking up at me did indeed look like a ball of cotton, though a pair of black round eyes and a matching snout amidst all the fluff gave away it was very much a canine. The shape its mouth formed when the tongue was hanging out looked like a permanent smile.

'He's a two year old Pomeranian socialist, Gemini vegetarian, and a little bit OCD,' Ash said. She leaned forward and lowered her voice to a whisper. 'But we try not to mention the last part when he's listening. He's a little bit sensitive about it.'

I smiled at Cottonball, about to give him an affectionate scratch behind the ears, but thought better of it.

'It's a good job the housekeeper is a dog lover,' said Matt. 'Pets are strictly not allowed, but she's overlooking it because Cottonball's so small.' He bent down to look the tiny dog in the eyes. 'This place probably has rats bigger than you, doesn't it, buddy?'

'And he's as good as gold. Aren't you, poppet?' Ash cooed, making kissing noises with her large pouted lips. Cottonball wriggled in her arms, wagging his tail and trying to give his mummy kisses in return for the compliment.

I'll confess I was starting to feel a little envious of the adorable pooch. Cottonball wasn't only cuter than I'd ever be, he had a far more interesting bio — and probably more money, too, judging by that diamond encrusted collar he was wearing.

'Is that your girlfriend?' Ash asked.

'Girlfriend?' I followed her gaze and saw Kat humming to a silent song and guiding speared olives into her mouth. 'Oh. No, that's Kat … my business partner.'

I'm not your rainbow flag waving type of gay, eager to point out that the world consists of a mixture of sexual orientations (and opposite sex friendships) and just because a guy and girl are together it doesn't automatically mean they're a couple. So I didn't bother correcting Ash's innocent assumption. In fact, arguably the most socially awkward human being in the United Kingdom, talking about my love life with strangers felt about as comfortable as having my intimate areas waxed — not that I knew how that felt. I changed the subject swiftly to stop them probing further.

'This your first ghost hunt?' Then I wondered: are regular ghost hunts even a thing?

'Yeah. A treat for Ash's birthday,' replied Matt. 'She loves all this spooky stuff. Don't you, princess?

Princess? I couldn't help raising a brow at that little term of endearment. I noticed the watch on Matt's wrist that must have cost a small fortune. And the flashy sports car out front had his name written all over it. Call me sceptical, but I had a feeling it wasn't just Matt's handsome Greek looks that Her Royal Highness Ash found so alluring.

'Happy birthday,' I said.

'It's not until next week,' Ash cooed. 'We'll be in Rhodes then, visiting Matthaios's family. This weekend's just the appetiser. Matthaios is the sweetest. It's been nothing but surprises for a whole month.' She stood on tiptoe and kissed her lover's neck. Matt made no attempt to conceal how pleasurable he found this, his dark lashes fluttering with arousal.

I cleared my throat, shuffled uncomfortably in my brogues. Public displays of affection had a way of leaving a sour taste in my mouth. Were frisky lovers the ones to blame, though? Or was I just feeling the pangs of my non-existent love life?

'Oh, I'm so excited about this weekend, though,' enthused Ash when she'd finished stamping her DNA over Matt's neck. 'I wonder if we'll be using the Ouija board? I hope my aunt Rosamie comes through. She might have a message for me about the future. A baby maybe? Marriage?'

Matt's olive complexion turned a little paler at the mention of children and marriage, but he tried his hardest to look like he shared his girlfriend's enthusiasm. I couldn't say the same. Every time I thought about what the ghost hunters had in store for us I got the sensation of snakes writhing around inside my belly.

'Ooh look, they've got kombucha,' said Ash, dragging Matt by one of those impressive triceps towards the table.

I expelled a sigh of relief when they'd gone. Any longer and they might have started pulling each other's clothes off.

Left alone, I decided to take a look at some of the photographs and paintings dotted around the flock covered walls. One of the paintings depicted Hilderley Manor in a previous era, the faded oils enhancing the creepiness inherent to such old buildings. I squinted through my specs, studying the intricate details. I scanned through the rows of windows, searching for our room. Somewhere on the right wing of the second floor, wasn't it? Yes, there …

I swallowed, felt a sensation like icy rags being dragged across my back. What were the chances? The chances that our room happened to be the same window I'd spotted from the driveway, the same window in which the misty figure had stood, staring down at me. And there it was again, watching over the grounds of the manor in that same eerie way. Like it was waiting for someone. At least I think it was a figure. Could it be a smudge? I leaned forward for a closer look, but then spun round sensing a presence behind me.

The halo-haired woman was standing there, her shamrock-green eyes wide and twinkling. Fumes from the lacquer in her golden mane were so strong they made my eyes water. Every colour under the sun seemed to adorn her face and body, giving her a psychedelic effect. My eyes were drawn to a conspicuous teal crystal attached to a chain around her neck, its shiny surface reflecting the chandelier light above our heads.

'Good afternoon, Quentin,' she said.

Startled by her sudden appearance, it took a second to

remember I was wearing a sticker with my name on it. I searched her chest for her own sticker but discovered she wasn't wearing one. 'You're not a guest?' I asked.

She shook her head. 'Esther Hill, psychic medium and spiritual catalyst. I do freelance work, helping paranormal investigators like the lovely crew here with my ... special abilities.'

I had no idea what a spiritual catalyst was, but my ears pricked at the word medium. Those that claim they can communicate with dead people.

'You might have seen me online?' she said, bumping her hair with her palm to give it more volume. The bangles on her wrist rattled like a child's play toy. 'My following has really taken off over the last year. I make regular videos and attend workshops all over the world. Thousands have heard the messages I've been blessed enough to channel from our higher source. It seems people can't get enough of the spiritual path these days. Wouldn't you agree, Quentin?'

The spiritual path? Our higher source? I had no idea what Esther was talking about. I was about to ask her if she could clarify what a spiritual catalyst might be when, out of nowhere and for no apparent reason, she reached out and removed my specs. She leaned closer to study my eyes and her smile broadened.

'Ah, a seeker.'

'Sorry?' I said.

'You're a seeker. I can see it in your eyes, amid your pain. You're searching for answers. It's why you're here, isn't it?'

Goosebumps broke out across my limbs. I swallowed the thick lump that had lodged itself inside my throat. I wanted to tell her that she was wrong. I wasn't seeking anything. I was here with my journalist partner to take some photographs, photographs for the article we were making. But if that was true then why was I having such a visceral reaction to a perfectly innocuous question?

'We're all on the path, even if most of us don't know it,' Esther said. 'You can't escape it, Source. It connects everything that is, ever was, and ever will be. Those of us that suffer the greatest tend to be called towards it the most, though.'

I shivered. Everything about Esther Hill, from her striking appearance to her dreamy voice, unsettled me. There was nothing malevolent about her, but she gave off a palpable energy that made me hazy and spoke as if she was the omniscient narrator in this fairy tale we mere mortals called life.

She cocked her head like a curious puppy as she continued to study me. Was she trying to read my thoughts? I might have known if I'd been able to see her eyes. Since she was still holding my specs, all I could make out was a fuzzy mass of hair and bright colour. I opened my mouth to speak, but whatever I was about to say fizzled on the tip of my tongue before it had chance to escape my lips.

'You've lost someone you cared about deeply,' Esther said, handing back my specs. 'They're never the same the eyes, after losing someone they love.' She sighed ruefully. 'How precious young eyes are, so unscathed, so fearless, the way they glow with wonder and expectation. Then the harshness of living in this world hits and they become dulled, always wary, always longing for what they lost, always fearing the next blow. Nothing like the death of a loved one to turn your world on its axis. Right, Quentin?'

I opened my mouth but again nothing came out. I was too stunned to speak. Could this extraordinary woman really see inside my mind?

Her eyes strayed to my shoulder. I looked down and saw a small white feather had alighted on my blazer. I glanced up at the ceiling, expecting to find an avian creature up there. But there was nothing above me other than the lounge's sky high ceiling with its decorative molding.

Esther pinched the feather between her thumb and forefinger, held it up to the light and studied it with a dreamy fascination. 'White feathers are a sign of angels, you know.'

I swallowed. Finally finding my voice, I replied, 'They are?'

'Looks like someone wants to let you know they're watching over you.'

We were suddenly interrupted by Kat gliding up beside us, a glass flute filled with a sparkling beverage pinched between her fingers. She looked to me and then Esther for an introduction. But Esther, either still stuck in the other world in which she lived or feeling suddenly unsociable, maundered off, not bothering with goodbyes, still enthralled by the feather.

'Who's *that*?' said Kat, when Esther was out of earshot.

'A psychic. She's part of the ghost hunting team.'

'Which part? The hunters or the ghosts?'

'I'll admit she's a little eccentric, but I think she really is psychic,' I said in Esther's defence. 'She was telling me things. Things she couldn't possibly have known.'

'I'm not surprised. She's probably picking up messages from Mars, size of that hairdo.'

The tension from my unusual encounter lifted. I giggled. Kat did, too. We were like two school friends who had found themselves the bystanders at this novelty gathering. In that moment I felt an affinity with Kat for the first time since we'd met. Regardless of her bossy demeanour, here, in Hilderley Manor, this foreign place full of strangers, she was at least someone familiar.

'Heads up, looks like there's another one,' she said.

I traced her gaze and saw a dark haired man getting fitted with a sticker at the lounge's entrance, the shoulders of his grey trench coat slick with rain. He turned to reveal a handsome face not much older than mine with a smooth brow, aquiline nose and stubble-defined jawline. A sophisticated quiff combed into his hair must have been set with plenty of hair product since it had survived the rain and the motorbike helmet in his hand. The genes were as Irish as mine were English.

He stepped inside the room, sweeping rain from his face. Which wasn't a particularly friendly face. Not hostile as such, more … disillusioned. Those Irish eyes, blue as winter skies, assessing the room's inhabitants as they trailed from side to side, said they'd seen it all before and were still wondering what the point was. I could read the name on his sticker from feet away: Will.

Then something awful happened. My heart fluttered. Not the way hearts do in romance novels, when a character sees someone they're magnetically drawn to in a completely awesome and inexplicable way, something more than just physical attraction, a connection, like tuning a radio dial to the correct frequency. It was more of a flicker, a flame reigniting after having lain dormant for a while. And it was awful because I hoped that part of me had been stuffed down for good, as buried as the dead rumoured to haunt the very grounds I was standing on. No good came from that fragile part of my soul being exposed to the light. Do our shadows live on like ghosts, echoes waiting for the right moment to be heard once again?

Will's eyes met mine before I had chance to look away and pretend I hadn't noticed him. A smile that was difficult to interpret tugged at one side of his lips before he made a beeline for the ghost hunters, making gestures like he was apologising for being late.

'That's right. Five,' said Kat.

'Sorry?' I replied, watching Will as he shook hands with Giles.

'The booking was for five guests, remember? That's you, me,

Barbie and Ken over there and the new guy.' She pulled out her notepad and, struggling to hold the flute and write at the same time, scrawled this down. 'Five guests ... the Freaky Foursome ... and the crazy psychic woman. That makes ten.'

'Right, five,' I muttered distantly. 'I mean ten —'

Kat tittered. I flashed her a nervous look. The smirk she was wearing told me all I needed to know. She'd seen me staring at the new arrival and her journalistic mind was busy putting two and two together.

To disguise the heat flooding my cheeks I pretended to take interest in the painting I was looking at moments ago. But something was wrong. My insides froze. The misty figure in the window — the smudge — had vanished. The blood left my cheeks as fast as it had filled them.

# - CHAPTER THREE -

# *Twin Flames*

THE FIRST HUNT commenced two hours later, following a detailed explanation of the weekend's schedule from a nervous looking Carrie. Inhibited, with a tendency to blush at the slightest thing, the youngest member of *Pluckley Ghost Hunters* suited her title of Team Sensitive, whatever that was.

It was Friday night, meaning there'd be two more hunts over the weekend before we headed home Monday morning. It also happened to be the thirteenth of October, making it unlucky Friday the 13th. Never a good omen when you're about to go hunting for the dead. I told myself that was just Western superstition, but it didn't stop my nerves tightening like elastic bands as dusk evanesced into night.

The storm that was brewing earlier was now in full rage, howling and battering rain against the windows like a banshee wailing to be let in. We bustled out of the lounge, torches like headlights on the hallway's stone floor. The team and Esther led the way, Matt, Ash (carrying Cottonball in her arms) and Will following close behind, while Kat and I brought up the rear. With the torches and the atmospheric weather I couldn't help feeling like a member of the mystery solving gang from Scooby-Doo. The only difference here was if we did encounter any supernatural creatures they wouldn't be the cartoon variety.

Kat, in her more practical ensemble of short-sleeved shirt and pencil skirt, her hair up, handbag brimming with accessories and perhaps a set of nunchucks for anyone who might defy her, appeared nonchalant about what lay ahead. Which I guess made sense, her being a self-professed sceptic and all. In fact, preparing for the evening she'd seemed more concerned with choosing an outfit that would 'give off the right impression' and had spent at least twenty minutes deciding if she should go for something 'white-collar' or 'sportif'. It certainly wasn't the ghosts she was trying to impress. It was incredible how many clothes she'd managed to fit inside that case of hers and I wouldn't have been surprised if it contained a separate outfit for each of the multiple personas she took such pride in. Her lack of fear, however, did help to balance my own anxieties somewhat. If it was genuine nonchalance and not bluster.

As I walked, new camera in hand, I noticed her rubbing her arm and grimacing. 'What's the matter?' I whispered.

'This nicotine patch is useless. It's doing nothing for my craving.'

'You're wearing a nicotine patch because you can't smoke for two hours?'

She lifted the sleeve on her other arm to reveal *another* patch adhered to the skin beneath.

'Two?' My voice shot up a key. 'You'll poison yourself!'

Hearing us, Matt glanced over his shoulder to investigate. A curt nod and a smile satiated his curiosity, and he looked ahead once more, continuing to lead the way. Kat dismissed my concern with a wave of her hand, as if she'd been censured for something as harmless as eating one too many biscuits.

'Hun, no one ever got a waistline like mine eating food. And nicotine is the only thing keeping me from stuffing it in my face.' She flicked her hair and continued to rub the patch.

Maybe she'd developed a superhuman tolerance after years of inhaling her poison. Maybe she'd be dead herself before the night was out.

Approaching the stairs, I spotted the staff who looked after the manor, slipping into coats and scarves as they headed off home for the evening. Mrs Brown, fitting a bucket hat on her head, spotted me staring and waved. I waved back, trying to catch a glimpse of Dracula amongst their group. Hopefully he'd be joining them, not lurking around the manor overnight like a bad omen. But there was no sign of him.

As we moved higher up the building, there was an almost tangible feeling of anticipation between the ghost hunters. Their camcorders followed our every move, ready to catch any paranormal activity — orbs, shadowy figures, footsteps and other noises, Norman informed us. My senses became heightened. The team carried an air of professionalism that was quite impressive. You couldn't be in their company and not feel that the activity they spoke of was as commonplace as any other occurrence. It was both unsettling and intriguing.

The tension really accelerated when Annie, the location researcher, a woman who liked to talk a lot, started telling us about previous ghostly happenings reported to have occurred in the manor — random guffawing believed to be the disembodied voices of barons and lords, cooking smells wafting from the kitchen in the middle of the night, guests hearing whispers in their ear as they lay in their beds, and, most ominously, a woman in a black dress who had been seen and heard multiple times marching purposefully up and down the corridors, cackling maniacally. As if that wasn't terrifying enough, it was believed witchcraft, including the dark arts, had been practiced near the property for centuries. Maybe that wasn't too surprising, a building steeped in as much history as this one, until she told us that crows had been found nailed to trees in the dense woodland behind the manor — and in the not-too-distant past.

She was telling us about a demon dog regularly seen and heard around the grounds, that had a vicious growl, red eyes and a foaming mouth, when I forced myself to tune out. My own experiences over the last few months might have given credence to the possibility of an afterlife, but the tales Annie was telling us were simply a scare tactic. And it worked. Once you started associating the stories with the house, the imagination began to run rampant. Every little noise, every shadow, became something more sinister. Was that scratching noise along the corridor a pesky rat or the demon dog scratching to get inside? Was the creak beyond that doorway the lady in black, ready to come marching out and scare the life out of you?

As much as I reminded myself all this stuff was just local myths, the acts of creative pranksters and the fantasies of vivid storytellers, my skin was still covered in goosebumps and my hair was standing on end by the time we reached the second floor.

Things only got weirder when we were led into a room filled with children's paraphernalia. There was a tale that surrounded this room, too, involving a possessed doll and a young girl it had purportedly tormented, but I tried not to listen to Annie as she embellished every chilling detail to a bewitched-looking Ash.

'Everyone gather in the middle of the room,' Giles instructed us, and we did, forming a circle on a large oval rug decorated with flowers, animals and the letters of the alphabet.

Kat, who had been diligently jotting in her notepad, rapped me sharply on the forehead with her pen.

'Ow. What'd you do that for?'

'We're not at a museum. Stop daydreaming and start taking photos.'

With a scowl I switched on the camera. A play around with it earlier had helped me figure out the basics. I peered through the viewfinder and searched for a suitable shot.

Perhaps for nostalgia, or some odd custom I didn't want to know about, the room had been kept to look like a nursery. Though it was obvious no modern day child could have resided within its walls. An old rocking chair neighboured an equally outdated crib, conjuring images of translucent beings rocking back and forth as they read stories to children that no longer lay there. Toys that looked like they belonged in a museum, most probably Victorian, were dotted here and there: a wooden horse, a carousel, a rattle and a Jack in the Box; each one as crude as the last, the large sizes impractical for the tiny hands they were crafted for. And, most worrying of all, a collection of pot dolls in Gothic dresses sat in a neat row on top of a painted dresser, their black, lifeless eyes appearing to take interest in the room's visitors.

I took photos of all of these then flashed Kat a resentful smile, though she didn't notice, too preoccupied with checking her phone and rubbing her nicotine patches.

'We're going to try and contact the dead,' said Giles, like this was everyday business for him.

Kat tittered. I jabbed her with my elbow.

Contact the dead. My heart rate picked up a pace, through excitement or fear I couldn't work out which. For the next few moments, with keen interest, I watched the hunters carry out a series of actions they'd clearly done many times before.

Norman unpacked equipment from a heavy looking holdall

and Annie and Carrie carried it to various positions around the room. Esther Hill was either deep in thought or getting into some sort of meditative trance. She stood in the middle of the circle, eyes closed, hands clenched in fists by her sides, brow corrugated with concentration. Every so often she'd lift her head or tilt one ear over her shoulder as if straining to hear what someone had just said. Was she already picking up messages from the other side?

'That's a REM pod,' said Giles, pointing to a gadget Annie had just placed on the floor by the door. 'It emits an electromagnetic field. If energy disturbs that field it'll let us know by emitting a series of loud beeps. It could indicate a spirit has entered the room. The K-II meter Carrie is holding will hopefully light up in response to specific questions.'

I twirled my head to locate Carrie. She was moving around the room lifting a device akin to a remote control in the air, as if she was trying to make it interact with the ether. I'd just taken a photograph of her doing this when I became aware of the woody, spicy scent of a man's aftershave.

Will had sidled up beside me holding a small tape recorder. It was a retro model, not the modern devices and apps most people used these days. The sight of it made me long for my old camera, which was hidden at the bottom of my rucksack out of Kat's reach. Old, familiar things have always given me comfort in uneasy situations. And the current situation was definitely making me uneasy.

He switched on the recorder and dropped it in the chest pocket of the black shirt he had on under the trench coat. Was he a journalist, too? A novice ghost hunter? Whatever he was, my attempt to study him furtively had failed miserably. He was regarding me with thin, suspicious eyes. I glanced away, pretending to look preoccupied with the options on my camera. What was it about the handsome devil that brought about such a disagreeable reaction in me? Mercifully, it looked like the ghost hunters were finished with their preparations, providing a welcome distraction from discovering the answer to that question.

The team gathered around us, a sudden seriousness about their manner. Norman, who had resumed filming us with his camcorder, circled the group, shooting us through his viewfinder like a paparazzo.

'Out of my face with that thing!' Kat snapped, as the camera brushed in front of her. 'You're like a bloody mosquito.'

Norman backed away swiftly.

'Ready, everyone?' said Giles.

We nodded. Annie moved over to the door. From behind me there came a flutter of electric blue flashes. I turned to catch a glimpse of the storm outside the window, a lightning fork splitting through black roiling clouds followed immediately by an earthshaking rumble. The storm was right above us.

'Ready, Esther?' said Giles.

Esther raised a hand as if asking for a moment, then nodded. On her cue, Annie switched off the lights.

The room was plunged into darkness. It took a minute for my eyes to adjust to the black. Gradually I could begin to make out the faint outlines of the others. Then torchlight came on, affording more visibility, along with more lightning that lit up the room intermittently with electric blue flashes. The ghost hunt had begun.

A palpable anticipation hung in the air as we waited to see whatever it was Esther was about to do next. I jumped when she suddenly spoke out loud.

'If there are any spirits here could you please make your presence known?'

Not a single breath punctuated the silence as everyone waited for a response. None came. Esther persisted.

'Could you please give us a sign? Make a noise? Touch one of us? Could you move something in this room?'

I imagined cold hands reaching out of the darkness and groping me. The Jack in the Box springing open suddenly and giving me a fright. A possessed pot doll finding its feet, jumping down, walking across the floor and tugging at the hem of my trousers. But again nothing happened. Until —

A knock. Three times.

Ash gasped. The ghost hunters uttered excited whispers. Kat didn't sound so sceptical anymore as she leaned in to my shoulder and whispered, 'What the hell was that?'

Esther, unperturbed, continued. 'Thank you for making your presence known. Now, could you please let me know that you can understand my questions? Please knock once for yes and two times for no.' She paused. 'Are you a male?'

We waited. And waited. Then, amazingly, from out of nowhere came two inexplicable yet very distinct knocks.

'Thank you,' said Esther. 'Are you a child?'

Two more knocks.

The K-II meter Carrie was holding began to flash erratically from cold blue to hot red. As she discussed something with Annie in ghost hunting jargon, I caught a glimpse of Kat trying to catch what they were saying. She transcribed what she was hearing in her notebook, aided by a light bulb in the tip of her pen. A woman prepared for all eventualities. But her conviction appeared to be waning. The apprehension in her frown belied the confident, tenacious woman who had swept into the manor, absolutely certain ghosts didn't exist. Was she starting to have doubts?

Two knocks, twice, to each question — a quick mental calculation told me the knocker was an adult female. Instantly I thought of the lady in the black dress. Then I remembered that I'm a rational human being and there had to be some logical explanation for what I was hearing. And yet — something about the energy in the room felt authentic. I searched the shadows for any eerie faces that might be lurking behind me. A voice made me start.

'OK, hold up. How do we know it's not one of you lot doing the knocking? Making sure we get our money's worth so we'll tell everyone how great your weekends are? You could easily stage something like this. Is that why you've turned off the lights? Is someone out in the corridor? The room above this one?'

Will had spoken. His voice was slightly gruff, perhaps from smoking, but resonant and distinct, defined by the short vowels of the regional accent. Through the gloom I could see torchlight twinkling in his eyes. The challenging stare he was giving the ghost hunters didn't waver as he waited for a response.

The team didn't appear offended by this sudden outburst, as if they'd heard the accusation before. Quite willingly, a couple of them lifted their hands like surrendering criminals, proving they weren't holding any contraptions or gadgets, that their hands weren't near any surfaces it would be easy to give a crafty knock. Will strained his eyes to check them like a suspicious detective.

'There's no third floor, either,' said Norman. 'The space above this is the attic. And we've been warned by Mr Crouch, the caretaker, that it's strictly out of bounds to guests. You can ask him yourself.'

'You'll just have to trust us,' added Giles.

Will eyed the shadowy faces around him, but offered no apology for the accusation. Which was pretty brazen considering he'd only just met these people and was already calling them out as potential frauds and liars. It was clear the handsome man in the long coat wasn't one to mince his words.

'It must be real,' said Ash. And Cottonball, perched in her arms, tilted his head and let out a small whimper as if in agreement.

'Amazing,' said Matt.

'It's dangerous,' said Kat.

'No,' said Esther. 'We're completely safe. This is an old energy that remains firmly rooted to this building. These old buildings are rife with them. It will only interact with us when we're in its domain and we won't be bothered by it once we've left the building.'

'On personal hauntings,' piped Norman, and you could hear the genuine curiosity in his voice, 'do you believe it has something to do with a person's psyche, as in their psychological state?'

'It can affect it,' said Esther. 'People who are depressed, neurotic, suffering from any form of mental distress, are much more susceptible to negative energies. Sometimes, if the energies vibrate at the same frequency, the entity can use that person's energy to interact with the physical world. A despairing wail could make a light bulb pop. But an explosion of rage could make the entire electrical system in a building go out. As most ghosts have a negative imprint due to unfinished business, it makes sense that your classic hauntings happen around someone who is experiencing mental difficulty.'

'That's what happened to us the other week,' said Ash. 'One of the bulbs on my vanity mirror blew out. Practically brand new it was, too. Wasn't it, Matthaios?' She gasped suddenly, clasping her hand to her chest. 'What if I'm getting the same depression my uncle Jerome suffered from?'

'And it's the same in cases where people lose someone?' Will asked Esther, ignoring Ash's dramatic interjection. 'I mean, it's not unusual for people to report seeing a loved one shortly after they've passed. Am I right?'

I detected a hint of cynicism in his voice. He wasn't so much interviewing Esther, but testing her answers for validity. Maybe he was a member of the secret service, and the ghost hunters were being investigated for deception or something equally nefarious. I noticed that he'd spoken with his chin lowered to his chest, as if conscious of the distance between his mouth and the tape recorder stowed inside his shirt. Was that a clue he was involved in a clandestine operation? Whatever he was he certainly knew how to steal the limelight, and captivate an audience. Everyone was hooked, waiting for Esther's response.

'If a person yearns hard enough for someone they truly loved and lost, they can manifest remnants of that person's energy, sometimes mentally, sometimes physically, which is all the same. After all, reality is ultimately what the mind perceives. It's usually only for a short time, though, following a loved one's death, when a part of their energy is still firmly rooted to this world. Such experiences can bring great peace for the bereaved, and show them for the first time that there really is more to this reality than most of us think.' Esther paused for effect. 'But there are some hauntings that go even deeper.'

More thunder cracked above our heads. The circle of eyes blinked in the torchlight.

'Oh?' said Will.

'Souls have contracts with each other before they incarnate in this world,' Esther went on. 'We call some of them twin flames. Twin flames are not just soul mates, they are the same soul. They are there to help the other become their highest, truest self. A haunting from a twin flame is the deepest sort of love.' She smiled as if this was the most delightful thought.

The northerner didn't look convinced. 'You expect us to believe that souls exist before they incarnate into a physical body?'

'Why not?' said Esther, unfazed by the handsome young man's cynical stare. 'Souls are of a higher dimension, it is no great feat for them to enter and exit the third dimensional reality at will. And they are more than eager to take part in the human journey for the growth and expansion it will create.'

'The human journey?'

'Love, loss, pain, happiness, life, death ... the whole gamut of human emotion,' replied Esther.

Will studied her through the torch-lit darkness for a long moment. 'You're saying souls want to experience all of that? Including pain and death?' He scoffed, looking at the rest of the group as if hoping to see his own doubt reflected there. But the eyes peering through the gloom just blinked. 'Well, where's the logic in that? Why would something already dead incarnate in a human body, then go through a lifetime of tribulations just to die again?'

Esther grinned sagely. 'Only a logical mind would say such a thing. And you, my dear, possess a fine example of one of those. But it takes more than a logical mind to understand how the universe works.'

Will had lost his tongue all of a sudden. As if she'd expected this, Esther continued.

'We live in a world of duality. Day, night. Male, female. Life, death. Love, hate. Good, bad. It is this duality, this contrast, that creates expansion in the universe. How can the universe know black without standing in the perspective of white? How can it know true love without knowing the agony of heartbreak? How can we develop empathy for another's plight without experiencing suffering for ourselves? Contrast, and all the pain that comes with it, is not an option of this life, it is preordained.

'Source, however, which is where everything originates from, is non dual. It is oneness. It can only witness, not experience. And Source is everything. It is the stars as much as it is your soul. It sends forth a part of itself in human form, remaining present as what is known as the higher self. Every time you reach a preference, Source says, 'Ah. That's what I am.' Because it's only from the human perspective that Source can see itself.

'For thousands of years humans have been forgetting this part of ourselves and never more than in recent decades. We got lost in the human ego, the dark side of our nature. The wars, the millions of murders committed in the last century proves that. But these are great times. We're being called to remember that the higher self is always with us, to remember that we are all oneness, all pure love. Your higher self is always with you, always calling you to remember what you are. Your deepest pain, your anger, hurt, hatred, jealousy — it's an alarm bell, reminding you what you are not, that you have lost yourself. When you understand this you can see that no death is in vain. You see that every painful experience, every heartache, every tragedy, creates a desire for something better, it creates a calling back to love.

'All you have to do is come back to love, to what feels good. The billions of souls currently on the planet are part of the great awakening, each and every one of us. Life as a human on our planet, from the impartial perspective of Source, is a beautiful dream. That, my friend,' Esther said, looking at Will, 'is how souls exist before, during and after we die. Don't be so flippant the next time you hear a strange noise in the middle of the night. The way a small mind lashes out at what it doesn't understand, it dismisses what it can't see as fanciful.'

'You could have just given me the abridged version,' said Will.

My mind swirled as it tried to make sense of Esther's words. It was the last thing I'd expected to hear, and yet a part of me sensed I had been given an insight that felt strangely familiar.

No one else seemed to have a response to this profound and extraordinary explanation. In fact, Esther had bewitched the occupants of the room into a stunned silence. Even the ghosts had gone quiet. As if sensing this, Giles, clearing his throat, said, 'Well, let's get back to a little reality, shall we?' And I sensed that the leader of *Pluckley Ghost Hunters* was a much more pragmatic investigator of the metaphysical than the woman hired to assist him on this weekend.

Norman had moved over to the rocking chair and was setting up a tripod in front of it, Annie standing over him, lighting his workspace. Giles carried a large, wooden box over to them.

'We're going to do an experiment,' he said. 'Inside this box is a haunted artifact, a bible owned by a priest several hundred years ago that is believed to be cursed. The haunted attachment could make it exhibit activity or trigger activity from other spirits inside the house. Whatever happens, we hope to catch it on our thermal imaging camera, which will be trained on it overnight. A warning, though. Nobody touch it. It's believed that whoever does becomes affected by the curse.'

And with that ominous message he opened the box. Everyone craned their necks to see what was inside. Using a grabbing device, Norman retrieved from inside the box a tome that was as thick as a house brick. Pinched between the claws of the grabber, like a bone in a dog's mouth, the bible was guided through the air and dropped on the seat of the rocking chair.

Everyone listened as Norman told stories of the various paranormal activity his camera had captured over the years. Everyone, even Will, listened intently, intrigued by what he was saying. Everyone, that is, except for Kat.

Looking to my side, I spotted her missing from where she was standing moments ago. My eyes searched the gloom, landing on the door just in time to catch a glimpse of her handbag slipping out of it.

* * * * *

I sprinted through the front door in pursuit of her, but once outside it was obvious my chase was fruitless. Kat was gone. Not a shadow. No scent of perfume. Not a trace.

Collecting my breath, I scanned the grounds around me. The moon had emerged out of the darkening sky, gilding the tops of the encroaching trees and casting groping shadows on the gravel drive. The storm had calmed for now, leaving a glistening lawn and earthy aroma in its wake. Hunching my shoulders against a fresh breeze, I heard footsteps behind me.

Will was coming out of the door, a cigarette bobbing between his lips. He strolled past me, propped one foot against the wall, lit the cigarette and released a plume of smoke that blew high into the humid air. Partly silhouetted in the moonlight he resembled a film star from a bygone era, or someone equally adept at snaring your attention.

Keen to share the high I was feeling, I pushed my shyness aside and said, 'Wasn't that compelling what we just heard up there?'

Will tilted his head and regarded me for a long moment. Distrust flashed in his eyes, which wasn't entirely surprising. Given the way he'd spoken to the ghost hunters I hadn't expected geniality.

'It was interesting, I'll give it that,' he replied curtly.

'You sound sceptical,' I probed.

'When you've witnessed as many of these as I have you're not so easily taken in by the showmanship.'

I knitted my brow, disheartened suddenly. 'D'you think it was a trick?'

He shrugged, blew out more smoke through puckered lips. 'Ask me again when the weekend's over.'

My shoulders sank, my enthusiasm deflating. As if on cue the rain started up again, battering the roofs of the cars parked on the drive and forcing me into the door's recess. I scanned the manor grounds once more in a vain attempt to conjure Kat back into existence. Maybe she could offer a balanced perspective on events. Maybe she could assuage the worry now circling around my brain that the ghost hunters were taking us for fools, that spirits didn't exist, that I really was going crazy.

Water dripped from the trim over the door and landed on my specs. I wiped it with my sleeve and sidled closer to Will.

'Are you an expert on the subject?'

'Fiction writer. When I'm not doing the day job, that is.'

A writer. So that explained the journalistic level of interest in everything. It explained the way he bordered the edges of the group with his recorder, present and yet not quite present, like a shadow, absorbing information he was sure to make a commentary on later. A member of some secret service? What the hell was I thinking?

'Do you write about this stuff?' I asked, nodding at the house as if the building itself defined the supernatural. Which, in a way, it sort of did.

Will nodded. 'I'm here to do some research for my work in progress. In particular, Esther Hill. I've been following her work for a while. Once you get past the woo-woo frills, some of the stuff she has to say on consciousness and non-duality is fascinating. She isn't your average psychic. She's leading the field, breaking through misconceptions, exposing our broken systems and causing one hell of a stir in the process. And people in their droves are listening to what she has to say. Her message is resonating. I was lucky to get a booking for the event at such short notice. She's a sought after name in the new age field right now. I'm still feeling her out, though, checking if she's the real deal before I believe what she has to say.'

Just who did this man trust?

'What about *Pluckley Ghost Hunters*?' I asked.

'They've picked up a lot of stuff from TV, those popular ghost hunting shows you see on satellite and various self publishing platforms. Oh, and that's how they're making their profits by the way. Expect to see yourself in a future episode.' He sucked on his cigarette. 'The equipment they're using, though pricey, is easily obtainable online and isn't scientifically proven to confirm the existence of ghosts. But then no such test exists. It's up to us to make what we want of the phenomena. The knocking we heard earlier was compelling, if it wasn't a stunt.'

He spoke with the confidence of someone who knew what they were talking about, not just someone who had researched the subject but someone who was genuinely interested in it. Those people who really know their stuff. His analysis of the team made my doubts about their authenticity return. I wondered what else he might know, and was just about to ask him when I noticed those blue eyes of his appraising my outfit.

'Who'd you come as, anyway?' he said.

The comment caught me off guard. Suddenly I didn't feel so amiable towards the straight talking northerner. There was no malice behind the words, but I was in no mood for such frivolity after the evening's events. I felt spooked, a touch delirious and I was becoming increasingly convinced Kat had run off into the countryside and might need me to call a search party. I was also fast getting tired of people commenting on my choice of outfit, even if I wasn't doing myself any favours by dressing like a character from one of Sir Arthur Conan Doyle's novels.

Looking at Will standing there, too gorgeous to be real, a grin curling a pair of very kissable lips, I felt the urge to strike him sharply on the nose. Or at least retort with some witty quip about his own outfit. But he made the clothes he wore look good, not the other way around, and that hair probably looked photoshoot ready when he rolled out of bed in the morning. Plus, I'm about as violent as a guinea pig. Instead, pathetically, I edged to the other side of the door and pressed my back against the wall, adopting a look comparable to a sulky adolescent, arms crossed and staring pointedly ahead.

If I'd expected an apology, I certainly wasn't going to get one. Will released a small laugh. Silence followed before he spoke again.

'Want one?'

I cast him a sideways glance under my sulky brow and saw he was proffering a half empty packet of cigarettes. Half empty because I've always been a half empty not a half full sort of person. I was feeling pretty pessimistic about how this interaction was developing, too.

'Don't smoke,' I replied shortly. 'And neither should you.'

I hoped he hadn't heard the crack in my voice. I might have looked defiant on the surface, but inside I was feeling deep insecurity. An insecurity that, as much as I hated to admit it, was as raw as it had been at school. Nothing helped me forget the taunts and threats from the schoolyard bullies, or the resentment I felt at myself for never fighting back. As I stood there, hunched and shivering like a defeated street dog, more water from the building's brickwork dripping on my face, it took a well practised endurance to stop myself from bursting into pathetic sobs.

'It was a joke, you know,' said Will.

I cast another moody glance at the floor, avoiding his gaze.

Persistent, he said, 'It's the way I roll.'

This time I did meet his eyes. But I was frowning.

In response to this Will shook his head, looking confused that I didn't appear to be on his wavelength. 'You know … the way I banter. I like to joke now and again.'

I really had been out of the social loop for too long. I began to feel conflicted, that awkward feeling where you have a loyalty to your original reaction but you're not so sure about it anymore. 'Well, maybe you need to find some better jokes,' I replied, immediately cringing at how petulant I sounded.

There was another moment of quiet, where for a second I was worried it was him contemplating acts of violence towards me. He flicked the burning tip of his cigarette into the air, which landed a few feet from Matt's flashy sports car, scattering orange sparks across the gravel. Then he sauntered over.

I braced as he stopped a few inches in front of my face. Rain had landed on the sticker on his chest, making the black ink streaky and illegible. He peeled it off, scrunched it in his palm and flicked that, too, into the night air. Had no one ever taught this man the etiquette of not littering?

'Names, clothes and looks don't make a person, mate. You offend me by assuming I'm shallow enough to give a shit.'

Aftershave, spearmint gum and cigarette smoke emanated from him. Despite my aversion to the toxic cancer sticks, it made for an oddly alluring concoction. I searched his eyes, trying to read if he was being genuine or not. It was hard not to get lost in them. This close up he was impossibly handsome; the lips were full and defined, his teeth were white, clean and straight despite being a smoker; his olive skin would have made the prettiest women envious it was so smooth and unblemished.

'I couldn't care less what you're wearing,' he reiterated. 'In fact, I think you look ...' he creased his brow as he searched for the right word, 'spiffy.'

I frowned. 'Spiffy?'

'Yeah, you look just like this old granddad I used to have.'

The lips curled mischievously. And the anger reignited in my belly ... but then dissipated. A playful glint in Will's eyes showed the cheeky spirit lurking within his psyche. I had seen that look somewhere before. In the eyes of someone special. Someone who never would have set out to intentionally upset me. Suddenly I could see how oversensitive I was being, see the funny side of this rather unusual greeting. I could see how isolating myself, living in books and films instead of the real world, capturing life as photographs instead of friends and experiences, had kept me out of touch with the nuances of social interaction. I smiled, even if it was a wary one.

'The name's Anderson. Will Anderson.' He proffered groomed digits for me to shake.

I did, at least, get the James Bond reference. I shook his hand. 'Quentin Strange.'

'Strange ...'

'Don't even try it,' I said.

This time Will smiled. He winked, said, 'Later, squire,' then sauntered back inside the manor, as casually as he'd drifted out of it.

I watched him stroll across the giant hallway, whistling as he took in the scenery around him. Reaching the foot of the stairs, he stole a glance over his shoulder. I averted my eyes. But too late. Will Anderson the writer knew very well I had been watching him.

'It's like The Amityville Horror house in there, that's bloody why!'

Kat's voice snatched my attention as it tore through the breezy night air. I craned my neck and saw her storming down the side of the estate, one hand pressing her phone to her ear, the other pinching a half smoked cigarette. The wind had blown her hair about her face, giving her the appearance of someone wild and disorganised, a far cry from the immaculate professional she worked so hard at portraying herself to be.

'Well make sure he calls me first thing!' she yelled into the phone, before ending the call with a firm jab of her thumb.

She flicked the burning tip of her cigarette into a nearby bush, making a crow burst out of it with an angry squawk before taking flight. Then she was making a beeline for me, her face as thundery as the skies were moments before.

'You, come with me,' she snapped. 'We're finding other accommodation.'

'Sorry?'

'There is no way I'm sleeping in there tonight.'

'What? Why?'

'There are ghosts in there, Quentin. Ghosts!'

'We came to a haunted house to take part in a ghost hunt. What did you expect?'

Kat threw up her hands. 'Frauds. Charlatans. Those crazy people off the TV with gold bouffants who pretend to be possessed or kick over a chair when the cameras aren't looking to make it look like a ghost did it. Not that *Exorcist* nonsense we just saw up there.'

'You don't know it was real,' I said, swallowing down a growing nervousness.

'You've changed your tune!' she barked. She eyed the house

warily as if expecting to find a spectre looking down at her from one of the windows. She lowered her voice to an almost whisper. 'No. Something isn't right about this place, I can feel it.'

My stomach was churning. I felt certain we'd witnessed something incredible and genuine, regardless of what Will had said. And I had a feeling Hilderley Manor had even more incredible things for us to discover if we could hold out a little while longer. I had to persuade Kat to let us stay the night.

'Think about the article,' I said. 'Imagine how much better it'll be coming from a more subjective angle, now you'll be writing it from personal experience. It'll be a much more intriguing read. You'll probably get twice as many readers.'

Kat contemplated my words very carefully, her wide eyes still heedful of the house, which towered over us like a forbidding spectator.

'You really think that would draw more traffic to the article?' she asked. You could see her brain ticking over, picturing the many hits her online article might accumulate.

I nodded fervently. 'People who like to read about the supernatural love the suspense, they love the thrill of the scare. They want you to be as fascinated and open-minded as they are. Think of yourself as the conduit through which they will experience this haunted, mysterious place standing before us.' I adopted the tone of a mentor delivering sage advice. 'If you be brave for your readers they'll return the favour by giving you the hits you crave.'

It took Kat maybe three seconds to deliberate this enticing thought. Drawing a deep breath and flicking a strand of hair from her face, she said, 'Well, I guess if I'm going to become a serious journalist I have to get used to being in the war zone at some point.'

She threw her shoulders back and marched through the front door like a soldier heading into battle. A second later she was back.

'Oh, and thanks,' she said, peering around the door frame. 'I wouldn't have thought it, but you're actually quite persuasive. You should develop that skill more. It could come in handy if we're still working together after the weekend's over.'

She disappeared again, leaving me standing alone in the drizzling rain to mull that over. I guessed it was a compliment, coming from her.

Duper's delight curled one corner of my mouth. So it wasn't just taking photographs I was good at after all.

# CHAPTER FOUR

# Full Moon

THE LAKE AT night is as beautiful as an oil painting, black trees surrounding it like sentinels, moonlight shimmering on the surface of the rippling water. A soothing chorus of crickets fills the air, as if a sea of them spreads for miles across the vast open wilderness.

'Come on,' says Elliot.

We interlace fingers and wend our way through the long grass shooting out of the peaty earth. When we reach a small, weathered dock jutting out from the bank of the lake I see what it is he's been so keen to show me on the journey up here: a rowing boat sitting in the water, a rope securing it to the dock.

'We're going in that?' I ask, my insides clenching.

'The moon's full tonight. Just wait until you see it from the water.'

Elliot abandons me at the edge of the bank and climbs inside the boat, heat flushing his cheeks, eyes twinkling with eagerness.

I cast the dark woods we just came out of a wary glance. We're so far from town, from the safety of civilisation. Anything goes wrong and it'll be a while before someone comes all the way out here to find us. I look again at the boat and get hit with another pang of unease. No, not unease. Something more disconcerting. A foreboding. But is it a worry worth heeding or just unwarranted fear?

'What are you waiting for?' says Elliot. He's finished unfastening the boat from the dock and is beckoning me with a wave of his hand.

My stomach contracts as I consider rejecting his wishes. This is his gift to me, a romantic gesture for my seventeenth birthday which is just around the corner, and I don't want to hurt his feelings. How could I justify spoiling such a touching offer for the sake of a petty fear?

Against my better judgement, I push my fears away, steel myself, and climb inside the boat.

Elliot propels us into the lake like an accomplished rower, the oars making gentle lapping sounds as the boat glides effortlessly across the water. My fingers grip the wooden bench my buttocks are glued to as I snatch glances over the port side of our water vehicle. Thoughts teem through my mind. How deep down does the water go? What creatures lurk beneath the glistening surface?

'I don't know if this is a good time to tell you that I can't swim,' I say.

'I know you can't swim,' Elliot replies with a soft laugh. 'That's why we're in a boat.'

He stops rowing when we reach what looks like the middle of the lake. He nods at me to look skyward. I follow his gaze and my jaw slowly falls open. He was right. The moon is a sight to behold from this spot, a glowing marvel in the middle of the star-filled blackness.

Elliot lets go of the oars and leans back, breathing deeply as if he's drinking in the beauty around us. His enthusiasm for nature is one of the things I love most about him, even if I'm not half as agile or intrepid as he is when exploring it. I've watched him monkey up trees, scale craggy rocks and dive off high precipices into uncertain water. It isn't just the longish hair he's constantly tucking behind his ear and the v-shaped torso that give him the nickname Tarzan. Staring at him now, his face awash with peace, I get the sense that if he were to keel over and die at this very moment it'd be exactly how he'd like to go.

I shiver at the morbid thought, glancing over my shoulder at the distant bank. It's almost invisible in the dark, obscured by mist rising off the water, creating the illusion that we're farther away from the safety of land than we probably are.

'Why do you make me do these crazy things?' I mutter.

He chuckles. 'Because I enjoy watching you face your fears.'

I throw him an indignant look.

'Each time you overcome one challenge it makes you that little bit braver,' he says. 'I don't like seeing you afraid.'

His words surprise me. I had no idea he felt that way. Suddenly I feel guilty for all the times I whined like an annoying younger brother, for admonishing him whenever he did something dangerous and daring. Even if it was only because I was worried something bad would happen to him.

'I love feeling fearless,' he says with a sigh, as a nocturnal bird hoots softly in the sentinel trees. 'There's something about being close to death that makes you feel truly alive. When you're playing it safe, life feels dull. Like you might as well be dead if that's all you're ever going to feel. But knowing you could die in the next second reminds you how precious life is, it reminds you that the simple act of being able to breathe is the biggest gift there is.'

I regard him as he stares dreamily up at the sky, half of his face bathed in moonlight, the other in shadow. A memory comes to mind. Once when I was younger, riding my bike along a rugged dirt track, I fell off and landed flat on my chest, knocking the air clean from my lungs. Lying there, struggling to breathe, alone and defeated in the muck, the pain so intense I was convinced I'd broken a rib, I knew the desperation to be in any situation other than this one was going to kill me. If the pain didn't get me first, that is. But then my attention fell on an ant marching across the dirt — a six-legged, treacle coloured creature no bigger than a pea — and a peace I find hard to describe to this day fell over me. The pain washed away. My vision became still and crystal clear. I knew that if I died in that moment, none of that would matter. Because I'd been lucky enough to be alive, to witness this marvellous little creature, a miracle. Is that the same feeling he's talking about?

'I'm going in the water.'

Elliot's voice snaps me out of my reverie. He stands, starts kicking off his shoes and pulling up his sweatshirt.

'Elliot, don't. It's dark. It's too cold.'

'It's perfect.'

'You'll freeze your balls off in there.'

He continues to undress, ignoring me.

'Elliot, please.'

Down to his underwear now, he starts removing those too. I avert my eyes in embarrassment; it isn't the first time I've seen him naked, but not in the way people might think.

'Let's hope there aren't any sharks,' he says with a wink.

And before I have chance to respond he does a cannon ball dive off the side of the boat. There's a deafening splash as his body hits the water, spraying my clothes, my hair, both lenses of my specs.

My heart hopping in my throat, I scoot to the side of the boat and peer anxiously into the frothy blackness. There's no trace of him where his body hit the water. Anxiety burgeons as I wait for him to resurface, seconds feeling like minutes. I edge closer still to the side of the boat, trying to blink him into view through my water-dotted specs, willing him to break through the water's surface.

'Elliot!?' My voice reverberates in the frigid air, reminding me just how alone we are out here in the middle of nowhere.

The only response is the chorus of the crickets, which sounds less soothing by the second, more like some haunting, chanting taunt. Why the hell didn't I listen to my intuition?

Still no sign of him. I feel the blood drain from my face. 'Elliot!'

Then, suddenly, an explosion of water and laughter behind me. 1 twirl to find Elliot heaving his glistening body back inside the boat, *hair plastered to his skull, his face beaming with mischief.*

*My nerves uncoil. My breath releases. I can feel my heart beating once more. 'You fool!' I shout. 'Cold water's dangerous. Mum told me it can kill you in minutes if you go into shock. What if you hadn't come back up and I wouldn't have been able to help you because I can't swim?'*

*He's laughing as he drops inside the boat. Water drips off his body and starts pooling at his feet.*

*'I already told you, I do a breathing technique every day that I learnt from this Dutch athlete called The Ice Man.' He demonstrates by breathing so deeply I can see his diaphragm expanding. 'It helps train your mind and body to withstand cold temperatures.' He shakes his hands. 'Whoo! It's especially cold down there tonight, though!'*

*I shield my specs from more flying water, gripping the bench with my other hand as Elliot's weight rocks the boat. I reign in my anger, something I've been learning to do. Ever since the therapist told me that anger is just a cover emotion for fear. And we should listen to our fear, she says. She also says we should apologise when we've reacted out of anger, or the other person will go off and make their own assumptions about why you acted that way.*

*'I'm sorry I snapped,' I say. 'It's just —'*

*'I know,' says Elliot, snatching up his underwear. 'Your mum worries. And it makes you worry, too.'*

*In the nippy air I feel my cheeks redden once more. It's hard not to feel embarrassed about my problems, especially around Elliot, someone so brave and carefree.*

*The elastic on his underwear snaps against his skin. He bends and gropes the bottom of the boat for his sweatshirt. But as he struggles to find where he shed it, he loses his balance, and his foot slips on the puddle that has pooled beneath his feet. It's like slow motion as I watch him, arms flailing, fear dawning on his face. Failing to regain his balance, he reaches out to grab the side of the boat.*

*And that's the fatal mistake.*

*The full weight of his body hits the wood with bone-cracking force, almost overturning us into the lake. I steady myself by grabbing the seat, wincing at the sound of his skull making contact with the sharp edge of the wood, like a hard-shelled fruit hitting concrete from a great fall. Unresponsive, limbs hanging loosely over the side of the boat, a crimson rivulet emerging from the crown of his lolling head, Elliot slips into the water. I reach out to grab his leg, but it's as if a beast from the depths has him in its maws and is dragging him under with greedy force.*

*I grip the edge of the boat and start snatching at the air in a vain attempt to seize him before the water takes him. But it's no good. His body floats away from the boat as if it's being carried by a nonexistent current. I stop and stare in horror at his face floating just above the water a few feet away. His eyes are dead and still, his mouth gaping open, allowing water to pour in, where it will find his lungs. His head begins to submerge until all I see is the tips of his pale fingers just below the surface, as if they're reaching out for me, someone who can't swim, to save him ...*

I woke with a start, my heart pounding like a cantering horse, my body soaked in sweat. It took a moment to remember where I was, but then it slowly came back to me. That soft rumble and whistle wasn't the wind, it was Kat sleeping on the pillow beside me. The antique furniture around me wasn't a hallucination, it was the contents of the manor room I was staying in for the weekend.

A dream. No. Not a dream. A memory. And not just the fragment of a memory, those faded films that loop like broken records in the recesses of our unconscious. This felt so real I could smell, taste and touch every part of it, as if I was right there again, that night on the boat, a decade ago.

Was it a malfunction in my brain? Were the pills affecting the part of it that stored memory? Or was this something unexplainable? The same something that had made me predict that car wreck on the M1, the day before it happened. Sensed Aunt Muriel's brain tumour before the doctors had given the official diagnosis. The thoughts swirled like leaves in a gust of wind and disappeared before I could catch them ...

I lay there in the stark quiet of the darkened room, staring at nothing. As unsettling as it had been to relive Elliot's fatal last moments, the dream had brought about a morbid comfort. I had him back for a moment. My handsome Tarzan sitting beneath the enchanting moon, the way I wanted to remember him. And then he was gone again.

A dull feeling that had become a familiar friend since that fateful day crawled into my soul and decided to curl up there. The years hadn't made the longing wane. If anything, they only made it stronger. I wanted more than ever to hear his voice one last time. To take back the words I said but never meant and replace them with the ones I never got to say: 'I love you.' They hadn't erased the shame. The shame I felt for being useless, responsible for his death because I wasn't brave enough to jump into the water and save him, even if it would have led to both of us ending up dead. Or the horror I experienced lying in that boat for forty eight hours before the emergency services finally showed up, shivering and in shock, Elliot's dead body floating in the water.

Would the pain ever go? Did I want it to? Something about it felt comforting, familiar. It kept us connected. Forgetting, being healed, seemed selfish.

I dabbed my still moist brow with the back of my hand. The background silence of the room was unbearably loud. I rolled my head to one side and stared at Kat. Moonlight from the window dappled her face and chest, which was rising and falling with each intake of breath. She continued to slumber, her eyes concealed behind a silky eye mask embroidered with the words *Diva Sleeping*. Any reservations about sharing the bed with her had gone. She provided an unexpected comfort against the isolated feeling brought on by this haunted and remote place. Even if my presence didn't offer her the same consolation, evident from the steel-pointed umbrella sitting ready on her bedside table in lieu of a weapon.

My eyes drifted up to the window. The moon was shining as full and bright as it had done that night on the lake. Squinting at its blurry edges through my unspectacled eyes, another memory came to me. There had been a full moon the last time I woke after having one of these 'dreams.' A coincidence or not? Anything seemed possible in the wake of the evening's ghostly events. They had made the weekend take on a different tone, plunging every belief I held into question. Had I really witnessed authentic evidence of spirits, though? Had those knocks proved there really was a link between this experience and another one we couldn't see? Could I really believe what Esther, the all seeing woman who talked so expertly about souls and the universe, had revealed to us in that torch lit nursery room? So many questions, I thought, rubbing my temple as I sensed a headache coming on. And I thought the pills were supposed to *stop* me overthinking.

Aware that I needed to use the bathroom, I pushed myself into a sitting position and fumbled for my specs. I slid them on and peered through the gloom, hoping they wouldn't reveal any unwanted visitors lurking in the room's shadowy corners. Careful not to wake Kat, I eased myself out of bed, wincing as the mattress springs protested. I tiptoed over to the door, pulled it to as quietly as I could and slipped out into the corridor.

The lights were off in the house, making it difficult to see as I crept, barefoot, along the blood-coloured runner. The place creaked and echoed in the quiet, the tall ceilings and hard surfaces amplifying the slightest noise. The weather had calmed considerably, but a low, eerie wind still whistled outside. A tree swayed through a far off window, the branches casting finger-like shadows that danced up and down the panelled walls.

I regretted not grabbing Kat's lighter. The bathroom was near impossible to find in the dark, especially since each door looked the same as the last. Had Mrs Brown said it was two doors on the right? Or was it three? I should have grabbed a shirt, too. With the central heating turned down and no warmth rising from the lounge's open fire, the air was practically refrigerated. My bladder was about to burst and my toes felt like they'd been sitting in ice water when I did eventually find the right room. I slipped inside and pulled a dangling light switch, squinting as a bright bulb buzzed into life.

The decor of the bathroom was as antiquated as the rest of the place, with chequered floor tiles and a claw-foot bathtub. A steady drip echoed from the toilet cistern. I don't know if the fixtures were authentically old or modernized versions designed to stay in keeping with the age of the place, but out here alone, at this ungodly hour, that was the least of my concerns. The only thing I cared about was making sure the lady in black wasn't in there, ready to lash out at me for interrupting her private business. Relieved to see no sign of her, I tiptoed over to the toilet.

But as the moments passed I couldn't help but fret over how at mercy I was to the manor's disembodied residents, standing there in my boxer shorts, urinating. The shower curtain was drawn shut, just like you see in scary films, that scene where the killer or demon face is hiding behind there, about to jump out. My neck prickled with unease as I avoided looking at it. I tried to reassure myself it was just my mind playing tricks; there was no one, no thing, in the room, only me. But how could I be certain when just hours before I'd heard the supposed sound of ghosts knocking on the walls? An eddy of fear continued to whirl around my stomach as I finished my business and shook off.

Keeping a watchful eye on the bathtub, I hastened to the sink to wash my hands. The plumbing gurgled into life as I twisted the taps. A large mirror provided a clear view of the shower curtain as I soaped my hands. No one was standing there. Why then did it feel like eyes were boring into my back?

A scene began to play in my mind: a decaying hand sliding out from the side of the curtain, the pale, purple-nailed fingers gripping the fabric — until a noise downstairs snapped me back.

I dried my hands swiftly and opened the door, stood there listening in the gloomy silence. The boards beneath my feet creaked, but other than that it was dead quiet. Then a loud crash came out of the silence. Sharp and clangy, like kitchenware hitting hard flooring. Adrenaline flooded through me and I froze statue-like, hairs standing to attention. When my feet began to move again, I was heading in the opposite direction of where the racket had sounded from, fleeing back to my room — but then I paused.

Curiosity got the better of me. Was this the paranormal activity Hilderley Manor was so famous for? And what if I could witness it for myself, erasing months of doubt over whether or not what I'd been seeing and feeling, this apparent supernatural phenomena, was real or not?

I ventured over to the staircase, stopping at the summit and peering down into the dark hallway. No spirits lurked in the spacious gloom below. Steeling myself, I began down the steps, my bare feet falling quietly upon each polished step, trying not to make a sound, trying not to slip and break my neck. A thought occurred midway: I should go back and get the camera. How would Josh Mendy at the *Gazette* react to a photo of a ghost captured in the infamous Hilderley Manor? But I didn't want to risk missing something I might never get to see again, didn't want to risk waking Kat and facing her wrath.

When my feet reached the cold stone floor of the hallway, another noise came out of the darkness. I jumped, spinning my head to the right. It had come from there, down the corridor leading to a part of the house I hadn't explored. My pulse accelerating, I moved towards it, like the foolish character in the scary film who goes off to investigate a strange noise when anyone with half a brain can see they're going to end up paying the price for it. Was I going to end up paying a price for my curiosity?

A door was ajar at the end of the corridor. A dim light spilled out of it along with a cold draught that snaked along the ground and nipped at my bare feet. My footsteps slowed as I moved towards it, each step becoming more tentative. My ears pricked to detect the slightest noise. More movement came from behind the door. The flicker of a shadow caught the light. I braced, reaching out my hand to push open the door — when all of a sudden it swung open.

'Jesus!' a voice hissed, and a body barrelled toward me brandishing a heavy bottle. Mercifully it was lowered before being brought down on the crown of my skull.

The figure holding it grew into focus. Will Anderson was glaring down at me with a look somewhere between anger and deep relief. He uncoiled his breath.

'I thought you were a flipping ghost.'

I swallowed. Unclenched. Felt my heart decelerating from its runaway rate. 'I thought you were.'

We stood in the light of the doorway, uncertain what to do next, our fear thawing.

'What was all the noise?' I asked.

'Came down to get a drink.'

I stared at the bottle in his hand. Wine. A very large and considerably empty bottle of wine, I noted dubiously.

'Well, what are you waiting for?' Will said, edging to the door.

'Sorry?

'I think we both need a drink after that scare.'

He vanished through the door and a second later there were sounds of cupboards opening and glasses tinkling.

I don't drink, I thought. But I followed him through the door anyway.

* * * * *

The kitchen was a practically antediluvian affair with a charcoal stove and copper-ware hanging from racks on the walls. A window looked out at a jungle of garden bushes and potted plants which were swaying in the flourishing wind.

Most of it was just for show, Will informed me, as I sat across from him at a large oak table, my hands crossed in front of my privates. To represent what the manor looked like in a previous era. Hilderley Manor wasn't just for ghost hunting tours and people looking for convenient accommodation, he explained. It was a popular tourist attraction for history enthusiasts and educational school tours — even if the school kids were more interested in its haunted reputation than its historical past.

Suddenly the creepy non functional nursery made sense. As did the juxtaposition of everything looking like it came out of a Sherlock Holmes mystery but functioning like any other modern lodging.

I took another sip from the glass of wine Will had poured me. It was a tentative sip; the hypochondriac in me was well aware of the risks of mixing alcohol and prescription medication. Inevitably, even with my specs fixed firmly to the bridge of my nose, the room was turning blurry and my head was feeling drowsy.

It appeared Will, too, was affected by the beverage. He was looser, more animated, pointing out the room's features with sweeps of his arms like he was the manor's tour guide. The disenchanted look had washed from his eyes, and instead they possessed an almost childlike glint of wonder and enthusiasm.

Through the moody light provided by the candelabra light fitting above our heads, and the heady fumes of the wine, I studied the self-assured northerner sitting across from me, who was swaddled in a tartan dressing gown and guzzling wine from the bottle like it was cranberry juice. His eyes bore the dark circles of a person who is often up past midnight. Light creases on his forehead and between his eyebrows were evidence he spent a lot of time concentrating. I found myself transfixed by both his peculiarity and those classically handsome looks that made it hard not to stare.

'I know what you're thinking,' he said, noticing me staring.

I said nothing.

'You're thinking, that's not a writer: look at him, he drinks, smokes, has that thick northern accent — he doesn't even speak grammatically correct.'

I was actually thinking of telling him about the dream, and the other happenings that made up my odd life. But for some reason I couldn't bring myself to say the words out loud. I'd kept them to myself up until now, not even telling the doctor who had prescribed the pills, instead describing my symptoms as excessive worry, hallucinations and vivid nightmares. 'I think I see dead people' isn't something you want to say when you meet someone for the first time. Not if you don't want to be ridiculed, accused of lying or, worse, locked up in the modern equivalent of a mental asylum. But surely Will Anderson, the supernatural writer, wouldn't be so judgemental?

'I probably wouldn't have guessed you were a writer if you hadn't told me,' I replied honestly.

'Don't you find that fascinating?' There was a slur in his voice — and no wonder since he'd nearly drained the bottle and was already eyeing up the cupboards for another one. 'People probably look at you with your glasses, your nice voice and that ridiculous getup you wear, and think one thing. They look at me and think the opposite. In fact, they probably think you're the writer. They picture you sitting at a bureau, a real old-fashioned one, knocking off reams with your quill like you're goddam Poe or someone. They look at me and think … what?' He appraised his reflection in the window. 'Male model? Actor? Escort? Yet they'd be wrong about both of us.'

I didn't know whether to be insulted or flattered by that comparison. Watching the handsome wordsmith ponder over what he'd just said, I struggled to reason what could have spurred such a random revelation. As if sensing my bewilderment, he elaborated.

'What I'm saying is, people always have their own version of who you are in their head. And you can't blame them. I mean, what else have they got to go off? But even if they get to know you, do they really know you? What if you're putting on a pretence? What if they are? It begs the question, can anyone ever really know us other than ourselves?'

Was this what they called an existential crisis? Or was he just drunk? I looked dubiously at my own glass. Was I? I wasn't prepared for such a profound and mind bending statement at — I glanced at the clock on the wall — nearly two in the morning. I did, however, now fully understand why Will was a writer. If his musing was even a tiny insight into how his brain worked then it was no wonder he felt the need to get the thoughts out of his head and onto pages. He'd have probably gone mad by now if he hadn't.

'I can't say I've thought about it much,' I said. Though I'll confess I wasn't being entirely honest there. I had thought of such things. I just didn't like to dwell inside my mind for too long. It's like peeking inside Pandora's box: you know if you lift the lid too far, there'll be no going back.

'I have,' he said with a sniff. 'And I've come to the conclusion that the world only exists based on what we believe it to be. Life is a one man show, my friend. A one man show.'

'Is that what you like to read about? Philosophy?' I asked, hoping to steer the conversation back to something more comprehensible.

'I'll read anything if it's got words on it. Except maybe romance. Not snubbing it, I just don't believe in happily ever afters.'

This was a view I did share. A non-fiction reader myself, it was science, quantum mechanics, politics, art and photography that lined my bookshelves. Save for that introspective phase in my teens when I thought fiction might hold the answers to why the world was so dark, messed up and confusing. Hours and hours were whiled away one cold winter with Clive Barker, Stephen King and James Herbert paperbacks. The only romance I'd invested time in had ended in tragedy in the middle of a lake. Maybe that's why I avoided them.

'Reading anything good at the moment?' I asked.

'I am, actually. A book about negative emotion. It talks about how we numb them with addictions — prescription medications, drugs, sex, video games, shopping, dopamine hits we get from likes on social media. The author explains how it's all a distraction, a plaster for a society that's never felt more lonely and disconnected. It's facing our emotions and understanding why we're so screwed up that leads to our ultimate freedom.'

A nice, uplifting read, then, I thought sardonically.

I sipped more wine. 'How's the research for your own book going?'

'I'm hoping to probe Esther Hill tomorrow. Figuratively speaking, that is,' Will added with a wink. 'The woman's harder to get alone than the prime minister. She's either getting the ghost hunters to run around her like skivvies or making calls to her management team. The fame has gone to her head. It's a ghost hunting weekend for Christ's sake. The writing, well, that's another story.'

'Oh?'

'Good old writer's block. Haven't had a workable idea for weeks. Which is a problem when your publisher's breathing down your neck and the deadline's inching closer by the second. I thought this place might give me some inspiration, get those creative juices flowing so to speak. But so far nothing.'

'What's it about, this book of yours?' I asked, interested.

'It's about a parapsychologist torn between his own scepticism and the evidence he uncovers when investigating reported hauntings. It's the second in my Jack Reid series. I plan to write seven in total. My working title is *Portent*, I know that much. But I usually discover the title after I've written the story, buried somewhere within the paragraphs of its pages.'

'Parapsychologist?' I raked my brain. 'That's like Norman, right?'

'Yeah. They study near-death experiences, precognition,

telepathy, clairvoyance, psychokinesis … the list goes on.'

'Don't all parapsychologists believe in ghosts? I mean, isn't that the point of being one?'

Will necked another swig from the bottle and shook his head. 'Many of them are trying to disprove paranormal claims by finding logical explanations for them, only concluding that they're unexplainable after eliminating the obvious first. My protagonist, Jack Reid, does this. I thought it would create enough conflict for a story if the main character was a sceptic, but the occurrences in his investigations constantly make him question that scepticism.'

The conversation we'd had hours earlier floated back, making me question if Will, himself, was a sceptic. Was writing the protagonist in his books his way of exploring his own doubts about the subject? Or was it, as Esther Hill had cheekily pointed out, that logical thinking brain of his coming at the topic from an objective angle?

'I'm boring you with this writerly talk, aren't I? Feel free to tell me to shut up. Hell, I bore the knackers off myself half the time.'

'It's not boring,' I said sincerely. 'It sounds like a good story.'

For the first time I saw a softness emerge in Will's face. And, if I wasn't mistaken, a touch of scarlet had reached the tips of his cheeks — though that could have been the drink.

'Cheers, squire,' he said with a wink.

A brewing wind rattled the windows. There must have been an opening somewhere, because a draught leaked in, brushing my bare skin, making my nipples harden and goose pimples erupt across my limbs. Even my privates shrank reflexively. I lifted my bare feet off the cold tile floor and placed them on the chair's footrest. Will noticed this.

'You look freezing,' he said. 'Here, take my dressing gown.'

He stood and, a little unsteadily, walked around the table,

shedding the dressing gown off his shoulders. Chivalrously, he held it open for me to slip my arms through. The warmth from his body, held in the fabric, extinguished my chill as the gown cascaded over my bare skin. The garment smelled of stale aftershave and cigarette smoke, but I couldn't help feeling touched by the kind gesture. Did everyone get the same treatment, or had I done something to deserve such courtesy?

'I'd have grabbed something to wear but I didn't want to wake Kat,' I said.

Will fell back into his seat. I blushed at the sight of his bare chest, a smattering of dark hairs growing in between the nipples. The man was attractive before, but that was nothing compared to what he looked like underneath his clothes. He drained the last vestiges of wine from the bottle at the same time as keeping his eye on me. There was a tattoo etched along the inside of his right forearm, an illegible scripture most likely containing some deep meaning. When he'd finished drinking, he said, 'She's pretty, your girlfriend.'

'Oh, we're not — I mean — I'm — Kat's ...' Blood suffused my cheeks. I gulped my wine to try and conceal my chagrin. Could I have sounded any more moronic?

Whatever Will's thoughts, his expression didn't betray them. Or was I right in thinking that cheeky grin had returned to his lips for the briefest moment?

'Don't worry, mate. I'm messing with you. Anyone with eyes can see you're gay.'

'What —'

Exactly what did people see that made my sexuality so obvious to them? I didn't walk around wearing a rainbow badge. I wasn't effeminate, flamboyant or overtly groomed in any way that could indicate I was trying to attract the eyes of another man. I don't think I even knew *how* to groom. In twenty seven years I had never plucked an eyebrow. I had gone nowhere near a tub of moisturiser. And I treated my hair like one of those 'grow your own' grass heads you get for kids: I just watered it and hair sprouted out in all directions. Not that I was afraid of people knowing about my sexuality, as Kat assumed. But privacy is sacred in this social media age where everyone is too willing to share every detail of their life. I like to retain at least some mystery.

Will got up and started searching for more wine, whistling as he peered in doors, pushing aside pots and jars. A slave to my male visual brain, when he stood on tiptoe to search a higher shelf I couldn't resist snatching a furtive glance. In just his boxers and crew socks, much of his smooth olive skin was on display. The buttocks, squeezing together beneath the fabric of his underwear, resembled a ripe peach. He had what your standard gay dating application would rate as an average-to-athletic physique — not that I was familiar with such applications. Not that familiar, anyway. Maybe he lifted weights, played a sport or visited a gym regularly. Maybe he was one of those blessed souls born with lucky genetics that made you look great whether you worked at it or not.

I felt inadequate by comparison. My whole life I have been cursed with a body as thin as a rake. My twenties had filled me out a little, but when I looked in the mirror it was hard not to see the scrawny teenager I used to be. Hard not to see the unappealing baby face: the eyes bereft of hope, eyebrows like two upside down smiles etching a permanent expression of forsakenness into my forehead. Which, as an adopted illegitimate child, I technically was. Forsaken, that is. Where had that face come from? My mother or my father?

I was thinking that it's a good job I have a large penis or I'd have nothing positive going for me, when Will returned to the table, fresh bottle of wine in hand. He dropped down and popped the cork like an expert. I eyed the shadowy corridor beyond the doorway nervously. I hoped no one was going to steal downstairs for a midnight snack and discover us. I didn't think Mrs Brown would take too kindly to her stockpile of alcoholic drink being consumed so flagrantly. He offered to refill my glass but I reclined.

'Are you usually up this late?' I asked, feeling much warmer now thanks to the dressing gown.

'I'm a writer. Staying up into the middle of the night is part of the job. Even with writer's block. Just because I'm not producing words, that doesn't mean I'm not using my noggin to figure stuff out. I find some of my best ideas come in the early hours, actually. Something about the moon focuses my mind, clears space for my imagination to run wild.' A picture of me sitting with Elliot on the lake drifted into my mind, but I forced it away. 'A little juice helps to loosen the cogs, too.'

I raised an eyebrow. A *little* juice?

The light above us flickered suddenly. The wind made a ghoulish howl as it blew through the crevices in the exterior door. The dream niggled at my mind still. The misty figure I'd seen standing in the window. The painting in the lounge. The knocks on the walls we'd heard only hours earlier.

'Have you always been interested in the supernatural?' I asked.

'The afterlife, the unknown … it leaves so much to the imagination. As a fiction writer who wouldn't want to go there?'

'Have you ever seen one? A ghost?' I waited carefully for the answer.

'I've seen things. Couldn't say for certain if they were a ghost, though.'

'Like what?'

Will looked at me, then at the wine bottle, picking the label with his thumbnail. He was recalling a memory. And it wasn't a good one. I knew because I recognised that look, was used to dwelling in the darker corners of my own mind. I looked at the bottle. Was alcohol the vice he used to numb out his own uncomfortable feelings?

'You have seen something, haven't you?' I prompted.

As if coming back to the room suddenly, he took a deep breath and shook his head. 'Ghosts aren't real. Spending your time chasing them is a waste of time.'

'You're the one who writes about—'

'Yeah, well, it doesn't mean I have to believe in them, does it?' he replied shortly.

A quiet ensued. Outside, a gate creaked on its hinges then slammed shut. Branches scraped the window.

'Have to say that what Esther was saying about us all being connected by the same Source was interesting, though,' he said, his voice softened again.

'Yeah,' I agreed.

'Ever tried this? He reached his arm across the table and placed the palm of his hand on the back of mine. A shiver ran the length of my arm in response to the sudden touch. 'Close your eyes.'

I did.

'Do you feel that?'

I concentrated on the sensation of his hand on mine. In seconds there was another sensation. A heat felt like it was flooding out of Will's hand, through my skin, into the flesh, the veins and the bone. 'Wow,' I said, smiling.

'Jesus,' Will hissed, tearing his hand away.

I started at the abrupt interruption and flipped open my eyes. Will was staring at the window, his eyes wide with fear. I followed his gaze and saw the caretaker, Stan Crouch, standing outside, looking in at us. I pushed away from the table, an instinctive reflex, the chair legs squeaking against the floor tiles.

The old man was wearing a raincoat that shadowed half of his face, but there was no mistaking that same cold, impenetrable stare he had given me when I first arrived. He watched me for a second longer before turning and vanishing into the turbulent fronds. There were sighs of relief from both of us.

'God, he creeps me out,' I said.

Will said, 'There's a cottage at the bottom of the garden. Saw it from one of the upstairs windows earlier. Must be where he lives.'

Brilliant. I wasn't sure which was worse. The ghosts residing in the walls or that Grim Reaper lurking at the bottom of the garden. It'd be a small miracle if I managed to get any sleep tonight.

The mood in the room felt even colder than its draught suddenly. I stood, removed Will's dressing gown and laid it on the table. 'Thanks for the wine,' I said. 'Even if it wasn't yours to give.'

Will looked surprised to see I was leaving. 'Any time.'

I left the kitchen, walking back down the shadowy corridor, my head dizzy. But it wasn't just the wine that was affecting me. It wasn't just the caretaker with his weird stare. Will was getting into my head. And it felt as good as the warmth that had flooded from his hand into mine.

# - CHAPTER FIVE -

# *Robins and Butterflies*

THOSE DAMN CROWS wouldn't stop squawking when I woke up next morning. One of them even started pecking at the window, rapping the glass like an annoying parent refusing to let you sleep in. I don't know why, because I'd never felt any animosity towards the common bird before, but the ebony-feathered creature with its beady eyes and clawed feet gave me a deep sense of unease. It was as if it was trying to tell us something. Warn us, even. The way it tap tap tapped, threatening to break the glass. It finally got the message when Kat's heel went sailing through the air and ricocheted off the pane with a reverberating rattle, even gave us an angry squawk as it flew away.

'Wretched thing,' huffed Kat, swinging her legs off the bed and slapping down her eye mask.

She stood and stretched, her silky nightie cascading down the back of her pale, shapely legs. In the soft light pouring through the window you could see just how attractive she was, her skin as fresh as a raindrop, her body as lithe as a ballerina's. There was a delicacy about her reminiscent of a china doll. Pity the same couldn't be said of her manner.

My body was nowhere near as graceful this dreary morning. It ached like a creaky antique, something that always happens if I don't get at least eight hours sleep. To make matters worse the wine had disagreed with my system, making my head throb as if I had a bird of my own in there, trying to peck its way out. I should have known it would, having been abstinent since that time I drank too much at one of the two parties I've ever attended and ended up passing out in that graveyard. I had to face it: when it came to alcohol I had the tolerance of a newborn. I knew I'd be desperate to crawl back to bed come noon, not that Kat, my drill sergeant, would be having any of that.

'Hurry up,' she ordered. 'I'm starting my interviews today. When I'm finished you'll need to take some group shots of the Freaky Foursome.'

As she rummaged through her belongings, I yawned and stretched out my legs, my feet looking like mole hills beneath the plush duvet. It was the first time I'd slept in a fourposter, and this one with its ornate posts, sheltering roof, even a curtain for those private moments, made me feel so protected I was reluctant to get out. Maybe I was harbouring a subconscious memory from my childhood crib. Though if the rumours about my infant years were true then protective environments had been no part of them.

Kat pushed herself up from the position she'd adopted on the floor. She had retrieved from her suitcase a bathrobe, a towel and a collection of toiletries that could fill a small store shelf. 'Up, Quentin!' she reminded me, carrying them to the door. Then she vanished into the corridor with an energy that should never be allowed in the early hours of the day.

Reluctantly, with a long groan, I sat up and reached for my specs. I pulled open the drawer in the bedside table and felt around for my pills. I unscrewed the bottle and was just about to pour out my morning dosage when a thought stopped me. Something Will had said during last night's conversation niggled at my mind: *'we numb them with addictions — prescription medications, drugs, sex, video games, shopping, dopamine hits we get from likes on social media.'*

What if the anxiety the pills were supposed to suppress had something important to tell me? What if the dreams did? How long would it be before the pills began to suppress those as well? I tilted the bottle, listened to the pills rattle, debated. Would it be worth the withdrawal symptoms? Had I, deep down, known they were never the answer all along? I resealed the bottle and stowed it back in the drawer, deciding the risk was worth it. There'd be no more running from my own ghosts. Hilderley Manor's, however, could be a different matter.

When I met Kat in the dining hall for breakfast, it was obvious from the look on her face I hadn't done enough in the ten minutes it had taken me to get ready to conceal how rough I was feeling.

'Are you ill?' she asked.

'I got up last night to use the loo and bumped into Will,' I replied, sliding into a seat. 'We got chatting and I ended up having a drink.'

She pursed her lips thoughtfully. 'Then you're probably dehydrated. Here,' she said, pushing a tumbler and a jug of water across the table. 'Make sure you drink at least two glasses. Have you been sick?'

I nodded sheepishly, remembering my visit to the bathroom before creeping back to our room. I hadn't needed Annie's creepy tales or my vivid imagination to scare me that time. It was like my very own horror film, that vomit scene from The Exorcist. But I don't think it was the wine alone that caused the sickness. The entire evening had been a shock to my system.

'Then you'll need something sugary. Vomiting causes

hypoglycemia. Have a pain au chocolat.' Kat pushed a plate of pastries under my nose. 'It'll also soak up the rest of the alcohol still floating around your system.'

Nurse Brannigan certainly knew her stuff.

She poured tea into a cup, watching me concernedly. I did as she recommended, pouring myself some water and downing the glass in a few gulps. I nibbled the pain au chocolat, but knew that what I really needed was to fill my stomach with a substantial meal for the first time in days. When the caterers arrived I didn't hold back.

Breakfast was a full English. I polished off two rashers of bacon, a slice of buttered toast, three sausages, a fried egg, mushrooms, two large tomatoes and a generous helping of baked beans, washing it all down with a cup of strong coffee. Almost instantly I began to feel better. Kat, a vegetarian, had beans on toast, cutting it into delicate triangles while she scrolled through her tablet, checking emails and her Twitter account, courtesy of the manor's inclusive Wi-Fi connection.

'Meat's as bad for you as it is for the planet, you know,' she said, not looking up.

'So is smoking.'

Her eyes narrowed dangerously, but thankfully at that very moment we were interrupted by a young woman with kohl-rimmed eyes and her hair in a chignon wheeling a trolley over to the table.

'Anything else?' she trilled in a melodious Welsh accent.

Any more food and I'd have probably burst. I shook my head courteously while Kat eyed up the tomatoes and mushrooms on the trolley. Dabbing my mouth with a napkin, I leaned back and observed the tranquil atmosphere in the room.

Barbie and Ken, as Kat had dubbed them, were sitting at the

table in the bay window, Ash feeding toast to Cottonball while Matt guided a fork-speared piece of egg into his mouth. Esther Hill and the ghost hunters were conversing across a large table in the middle of the room. Well, the hunters were; Esther was busy applying blusher in a hand mirror, sucking in her cheeks to locate her cheekbones. A few of the other tables were occupied by unrelated guests also staying in the manor over the weekend. That left one person conspicuously missing amongst the hum of voices and scraping cutlery.

'I'm going for some fresh air,' I said, but Kat barely noticed as her pot of Earl Grey was refilled.

My eyes protested to the stark morning light the moment I stepped outside. The fog of early morning had lifted, the skies had calmed for now, but dull clouds foreshadowed more bad weather to come. All that remained was a light drizzle, which dampened my face but didn't warrant a trip upstairs to fetch my blazer. I pulled my fingers into my jumper sleeves and headed around the building to investigate the manor's rear garden, more pesky crows surveilling me from high in the trees as I trundled through mulch and leaves blown about during the evening's storm.

The garden was an impressive expanse of land, with sprawling lawns, trimmed hedges and a fountain positioned in the middle of it all. At the far end stood the cottage Will had seen from one of the upstairs windows, a miniature abode with a stable door, leaded windows and red and gold ivy spreading unchecked over its face. So that's where Mr Crouch resided when he wasn't creeping around in the middle of the night, spying on the manor's guests.

I halted at the top of the steps that led to the gravel courtyard, inhaling deep lungfuls of fresh morning air, which was flooded with the scent of the garden's flora. I entwined my fingers and stretched out my arms, squeezing out the stiffness in the muscles and sinew. It was only then that I noticed Will sitting on a bench near the fountain, the canopy of a leafless oak sheltering him from the drizzle. I began down the steps towards him.

Hearing the crunch of my feet, he lifted his head out of the journal he was writing in, squinting in the bright light.

'You look as awful as I feel,' he remarked.

Charming.

I perched beside him.

'Manage to get *any* sleep?' he asked.

'Ghosts must have been having a night off. Didn't hear a peep from them.'

There was a crooked smile, then he slapped the journal shut and dropped it in the empty space between us. He stretched and yawned. Watching him I marked he had the pasty, puffy complexion people get when they've been up beyond the early hours, drinking until they collapse in an undignified heap. But he was still impossibly handsome. Nothing could change that. He lit a cigarette, folded his arms and glanced at the house.

'Just look at the place. Depressing as a ruptured haemorrhoid.'

I was beginning to think I preferred drunken Will. Either he wasn't a morning person, or something had happened in the few hours since our chat at the kitchen table to make him so crotchety. 'You don't like old buildings?' I asked cautiously.

'I don't mind 'em if the mood's right. But that place lost its charm a long time ago, when they decided to turn it into some third rate haunted house attraction. D'you know they're selling souvenirs? Teacups of all things.' He shook his head and drew in yet another laboured breath that seemed to carry the weight of the world with it. 'Still, I s'pose they need some selling point if they're gonna pull the punters all the way out here. And they get enough by the looks of it. Ghost hunting teams are popping up all over the country like weeds. God help us.'

I opened my mouth to reply but was interrupted by Will's phone ringing, the ringtone the theme to an '80s film I struggled to remember the name of. Will fished it out of his coat, scowled at the screen and jabbed a button.

'Hello?' He waited. 'No, he's not here ... Well, Mr Anderson is sharing with his personal number. I should know, I'm his massage therapist.' He threw me a glance, rolling his eyes. 'How the hell should I know? Bye.' He rang off before the caller could say anything else, shaking his head disbelievingly, as if mobile phones weren't supposed to ring and people weren't supposed to try and contact you via them. He acknowledged me again with a curt nod. 'Sorry, business matter. You were saying?'

'You confuse me,' I said. And I wasn't referring to those poor business skills.

He looked at me askance.

'You write books about the supernatural, yet it's as if you hold a disdain for anything associated with it. Like when you accused the ghost hunters of being frauds. Like how you're staying in one of the country's most haunted buildings but acting as if it's a nursing home you've been forced to visit to see a dying grandparent.'

'Supposedly haunted building,' he corrected me.

'Doesn't the not knowing thrill you? Shouldn't people like you be trying to convince people like me that this stuff is real, that ghosts really exist?'

'People like me? You know nothing about me.'

I know you could learn a thing or two about manners, I felt like saying, but held back.

'Fine, I'll admit it,' he said. 'I'm getting tired of this stuff. But is it any wonder? When most people's understanding of the supernatural comes from tacky fiction full of cheap scares and gimmicky misrepresentations — even people who work in the field itself. I'm not interested in folklore or magic tricks. I'm fascinated by what's really going on out there.'

'Such as?'

'I want to know what's happening when I have deja vu, when I predict what someone's about to say a second before it comes out of their mouth. I want to know why there are remote viewers who can picture a target in their mind they've never seen, that's in a country they've never even visited, then draw it to almost exact detail. Why there are people who couldn't tell you who Jack the Ripper is but can recall vivid past lives under hypnosis with historical accuracies that would leave your average historian stumped. That's the sort of stuff that fascinates me.'

'If ghosts are just folklore, why not write about those topics then?'

He shrugged. 'I have professional obligations, this nasty thing called a contract. And everyone needs money. Ghosts sell.'

I eyed him as he sat bordered by the old house, trying not to look too cynical. It mustn't have worked, though, as he said in a tone that sounded as if he was trying to explain himself, 'I got an idea and ran with it, mainly to block out how shitty life was at the time, to prove to myself that I really could finish my own book, not spend my life filling drawers with unfinished manuscripts. And, if I'm honest, to stick my finger up to all those people who said I couldn't do it. I never thought someone would want to publish the damn thing, or that it'd become a mild success. Plus, just because my book centres around hauntings it doesn't mean I don't explore other themes I'm interested in. And it doesn't automatically make me a believer.'

I stared at him, watching mist escape his mouth. I wasn't sure I believed him. He didn't seem the sort of guy to commit to a task as all-consuming as writing a book series unless there was something in it for him. Especially when the last I heard your average author makes a pittance from their work. Or maybe I just didn't want to believe him, didn't want someone whose judgement I felt I could trust telling me ghosts were for fantasists. If Will believed in them, enough to want to write about them, then it validated my own belief.

He spotted me ruminating. 'Look, I'm no sceptic. And I never said ghosts were folklore. I was fascinated with the topic for a while, even a little obsessed at one point. And I still am to some degree. It's just that if there's one thing I've learnt immersing myself in this world over the last few years, it's to believe something only when your own eyes are able to back it up. There's simply too much division between the scientific and metaphysical fields to believe anything else.'

A low breeze whistled and a bird squawked as I took a moment to digest this along with the huge breakfast sitting heavy in my stomach.

'You have seen something, though. Haven't you?' I said.

His eyes flicked in my direction. He might not have remembered what we talked about last night, but I did.

'Jesus, you never stop pecking,' he said, avoiding my question. 'Why are you so obsessed with finding out if ghosts are real, anyway?'

I averted my eyes to the gravel path. What was I trying to avoid by concealing my secret? Shame? Ridicule? Fear?

Will lit another cigarette. Quiet fell on the garden, just the patter of light rain hitting the dead leaves blown against the edges of the dew glistening stretches of lawn. I stared at the fountain, watching water trickle down each tier, the sound soothing. A robin redbreast alighted on its crest, surveying its surroundings before flying off again. Its brief appearance brought a flicker of a smile to my lips. I remembered Elliot telling me they were an omen of strength, the red breast representing the shield of a warrior. He loved searching for meaning in everything. And I loved that about him.

Could it have been a sign from Elliot himself, letting me know he was around? The notion wasn't new to me. A prayer I had read on a flyer at Grandma Ethel's funeral had put the thought in my mind, the way it talked of the dead returning to the earth and being born anew to nature. And there had been signs before. Like the robin that sat on my bedroom windowsill after Grandpa Seth's funeral, silent, watching, consoling, staring in at me as I lay on the bed in the foetal position, struggling to understand why people I cared about kept dying, wondering where they went when they did. Then the blue butterfly that landed on the frame of my specs when I was sitting in the garden one summer, returning to the same spot no matter how many times I brushed it away, as if determined to make sure I knew it was there. Blue because that was Elliot's favourite colour? Or was that just wishful thinking?

The memories drifted away and a fog descended in their place. The autumnal garden, as picturesque as a greetings card just moments ago, felt bleak and dull all of a sudden. A bite in the air made me regret not fetching my blazer. Especially looking at Will, buttoned to the chin in his trenchcoat, the pale light bringing out the cool blue in his eyes.

A cacophony of screeches and squawks came from somewhere behind us. I glanced over my shoulder and saw a flock of crows scrapping and pecking at the grass beneath a weeping cherry tree. The tree stood out against the deciduous species that surrounded it, its drooping leaves a brilliant array of yellow and bronze hues with touches of resplendent red. I knew its name from going on jobs with my uncle Max, a gardener, when I was a kid.

'Bugger off!' Will flicked the burning tip of his cigarette at the birds. They croaked angrily before taking off over the caretaker's cottage towards distant trees.

He sat back and folded his arms. 'Tell you what,' he said, a wry smile audible in his voice. 'After last night I'm thinking they don't need the dead to pull the punters to this place. They could just get old Lurch to wander about the corridors. Be enough to frighten the life out of anyone, that would.'

'You shouldn't make such flippant jokes about the dead,' I replied sharply. 'You'll regret it one day when you lose someone you love.'

I got up and stalked away from the bench, my feet hitting the ground hard enough to kick gravel into the air. As I stomped up the steps and back towards the entrance of the house, thunder rumbled. Grey clouds swirled overhead. There was going to be another storm tonight. Which felt very fitting for my current mood.

* * * * *

Heading back inside the house I collided into Mr Crouch. Literally. He stumbled backwards on creaky legs as I lunged forward to stop him toppling over like a bowling pin. The response I got wasn't one of gratitude.

'Gerroff me, dirty little sod!' he snarled, snatching his arm away, his rheumy eyes wild and intense, his cheeks veiny and empurpled.

I stood and stared, incredulous. I'd given the truculent senior enough of my patience up until now, but that was just plain rude.

88

'Is there a problem?' I countered.

'Your sort make me sick,' he growled.

My sort? My thoughts drifted back to the early hours. His shadowed face watching me and Will through the kitchen window, our hands touching. Had he thought there was something intimate between us? 'D'you mean —'

He lifted a gnarled, quivering finger and his whiskery jaw fell open to reveal a mouth with few teeth. 'You bunch of freaks have no business being here!' Spit showered me as he spoke.

'We have permission to be —'

'I don't give a rat's arse what you've got, boy.' His face turned threatening. 'Your kind are nothing but trouble. And if you bring it anywhere near this place I swear I'll —'

'You'll what?' Miraculously, an hitherto courage had overtaken me and I was challenging my aggressor. This was a miracle because, unlike a lot of men my age, the first hint of conflict would ordinarily have me shrinking away like a penis in cold weather. But not now. Even my chest had puffed out, albeit still as flat as a tortilla wrap because the only workout my chest muscles got were when I pushed myself out of bed in the morning. But I was standing up for myself. And it felt good. Really good.

Stan looked rattled at being challenged, his saggy eyes, roofed by wiry brows, flitting about in their sockets as they tried to figure out a way to counterstrike. Then, as if suddenly possessed by a cunning thought, he leaned in closer and said in an evil whisper, 'There's a darkness 'haunts this place. Mess with it and you'll never sleep sound again. It'll haunt you till you're so scared you'll wish you were dead yourself.' The leathery mouth, lips almost blue with age, became a canine snarl. 'If you had any sense you'd get out while you still can. D'you hear me? You'd get out while you still can!'

Anger finally boiling over, he jabbed me firmly in the midriff with his cane before jostling past me out of the front door.

Alarmed and insulted that I'd just been assaulted, I started after him. But a torrent of rain hit me the moment I stepped outside, so heavy it forced me to retreat back inside. I stayed sheltered beneath the entranceway, watching the elderly brute limp around the side of the building, one arm lifted above his head like an umbrella, the other stabbing the ground with the cane.

I went back inside and shook myself off like a dog, spraying the stone floor with rainwater. I headed upstairs, miffed by the old man's discourtesy, trying to make sense of his ominous warning. What had he meant by a darkness living inside the manor? Could it be the lady in black? The other phantoms Annie had told us about? And what about it was so threatening that he thought I should be fleeing out the front door not heading back inside it?

Maybe Mrs Brown had the answers. Reaching the top of the stairs I spotted her hurrying up the corridor, her feet barely able to catch up with her. She noticed the wetness on my clothes and her eyebrows came together like a pair of curtains. 'Oh, this awful weather. When will it finally let up, eh?'

Most likely never since we're in England, I thought but didn't say aloud. She reached me and began sweeping remnants of rain from the shoulders of my jumper.

'Do you have any idea why your handyman would tell me that I need to get out of this place?' I asked.

I didn't mention the homophobic slur. Or the assault. Even if I was itching to vent about it, complain to whoever was in charge. Ever since reading somewhere that defence is the first act of war I'd been trying to develop an automatic brake when it came to starting wars with people. And I had gained at least some social skills from those years of teen therapy. I aspired to be the guy who let it go even when it was obvious the other person was in the wrong. Life tends to go more smoothly that way, usually.

Mrs Brown became suddenly attentive. 'Stan been troubling you, has he?'

'His manner wasn't exactly what I'd call courteous just now,' I offered generously. 'He said there was a darkness living in the building and if I had any sense I'd get out while I still can. Do you know what he means by that?'

The little woman stared up at me with unblinking eyes. No sixth sense was necessary to know she felt troubled by this piece of information. Then, suspiciously, her face became its usual friendly countenance once again. She batted the air dismissively with a wedding ring adorned tiny hand. 'Ignore the old curmudgeon, dear. This house has been Stan's home for decades, practically a permanent fixture of the place he is. He's a wee overprotective of it, that's all. I'll have a word with him, make sure he doesn't bother you or your friends again over the weekend.'

She gave me a wink before turning and carrying on her way. I stayed at the summit of the staircase and watched her descend. Midway down she snatched a glance at me over her shoulder. And it was in that motion, for the very first time, that I sensed something dishonest about the kindly housekeeper. Mrs Brown knew more about Stan's warning than she was letting on.

When I got back to our room I found Kat there. She was standing in front of the dresser mirror, buttoning a fresh shirt, a look of annoyance creasing her ordinarily unwrinkled forehead. She paid no attention to me as I crossed the room to the wardrobe.

'I thought you were doing interviews?' I said, my voice curter than intended.

'I was. But I had to change because I spilled coffee all over my blouse.' She sighed loudly. 'It was that man's fault, the one with the bald head and silver beard, all those tattoos on his arms. He kept looking at me in this really inappropriate way, putting me off my questions. I know I'm an attractive woman, but he's old enough to be my father, if not my grandfather. And he burped. Burped! Right in front of me, like some sort of feral hog. It's a good job he didn't fart or I'd have had to get verbal.'

'Maybe he had indigestion after breakfast?'

'He was drinking beer. Beer! And barely past morning. How on earth that poor girl, Carrie, can share a room with him I'll never know.'

Kat was talking about the parapsychologist, Norman, who did have a slight slovenly manner about him now I thought about it. But still preoccupied over my encounter with Stan Crouch I was unable to muster much sympathy for her plight. I peeled off my rain-damp jumper and sifted through the clothes rack for a dry one. I was wrestling it onto my head when Kat noticed I hadn't responded.

'What's up with you? You look like you've seen a ghost.'

I refrained from rolling my eyes. The ghost gags were getting old fast. Or maybe I was too agitated to find them amusing after just being assailed for no good reason. 'Still hungover,' I replied, which wasn't exactly a lie; I still wasn't a hundred percent and felt the urge to get into bed and hide away from the rest of the day — and cane-wielding madmen.

Kat moved to her side of the bed and began rooting through her handbag. She pulled out a paperback, haphazardly tossing it onto the unmade covers. I closed the wardrobe, crossed to the dresser mirror and prodded my damp hair. In the mirror's reflection I watched my partner squirt perfume into the air, letting the invisible particles alight on her head and shoulders like minuscule snowflakes. Her eyes drifted craftily in my direction.

'Manage to find him, did you?'

'What?'

'The writer guy, Will Anderson. I know you went looking for him when you saw he wasn't in the dining hall earlier.'

'I needed fresh air,' I lied. 'And how do you know he's a writer? How do you know his last name?'

She lifted up the paperback she'd dropped on the bed so I could see the front cover. 'A gift from Carrie. She was excited about having an author on one of the hunts and brought a copy of his book for him to sign. She let me borrow it, said it was a good read.'

I stared at the book, interested. 'And is it?'

Kat made a 'tsk' sound, casting the book aside again. 'I haven't got time to be faffing about reading books!'

She whisked around the fourposter carrying a stick of lipstick and nudged me out of the way so she could touch up in the mirror. I shuffled out of her way and picked up the paperback.

The title on the cover read *Ethereal* by Will Anderson. A quote said it was, "A Supernatural Thriller that'll chill you to the bone." The cover art appeared to vouch for that: a misty figure hovering in front of the arched entrance of a decrepit looking church, a Gothic font spelling Will's name.

I flipped it over to find a photograph of him on the back. Black and white, a studio style shot you often see authors and professionals using. Will was pulling off the enigmatic writer pose like a pro, looking simultaneously pensive and laid back in a crew neck and blazer, his hair coiffed in a slick '50s quiff. The only concession from his current look was a shaven jawline, baby-smooth as it accentuated the Cupid's bow shape of his lips. Even in black and white you could see the Irish blue of his irises.

'You can stop leering now,' Kat taunted.

Feigning nonchalance, I dropped the book and walked around to my side of the bed. I fished around inside my rucksack until I found my own current read, *The Physics of Everyday Life*. But no luck. Kat wasn't giving up that easily.

'I'm not surprised you fancy him,' she said. 'He's very attractive, if a little … distant. And creativity in a man is always sexy, especially writers. You have to wonder what goes on inside their broody minds. A man who can elicit emotions out of you with his words must be a talent in the bedroom.'

Blushing like a macaw, I punched up my pillow and dropped down on the bed, lifting my legs and wriggling into a comfortable position. I opened my current read at the bookmark and tried to bury my embarrassment in the pages' paragraphs. Still no luck. Kat turned away from her reflection, placing a manicured hand on her hip and pressing her freshly painted lips together for even coverage as she frowned at me.

'What are you doing?' she asked.

I lowered the book and peeked over the pages. 'Reading this book on physics.'

She rolled her eyes. 'Of course you are.'

'What's wrong with studying the structure of the atom?'

'What can you do when you know it?'

It was a … reasonable question. One to which I had no answer. To deflect from this, I said, 'I think it's time we had a word about the disrespectful way you talk to me.'

Kat, predictably, was unfazed by this, striding back to where she'd left her handbag.

'I might be new to the job, but it doesn't give you the right to talk down to me,' I persevered. 'I'm a person and I deserve some respect.'

Handbag on her shoulder, Kat came to a halt before she was

about to exit the room. 'You want respect? Give me something to respect you for. Find and photograph something I can write about. And make it interesting.' She peered out the door, perhaps to check there weren't any ghosts lurking there, then vanished into the corridor trailing clouds of citrusy perfume in her wake.

I shook my head wearily, listening to the tread of her shoes taper away. When I was certain she wasn't coming back, I leaned over and picked up *Ethereal*. I flipped it open to the first pages and saw a quote:

*The scariest monsters are the ones that lurk within our souls -* Edgar Allan Poe

The quote made me shudder. I closed the book, placed it on the bedside table. Different emotions pulled at my gut. I felt guilty for getting short with Will in the garden. Maybe his lack of tact when it came to talking about the dead was because he had never lost someone whom he loved. He wouldn't be able to understand the way it made you a raw nerve when it came to flippant remarks, especially when you've lost someone in such a traumatic and unexpected way as I had. Because that's why I snapped. That's what this was really about. Elliot.

I sat there in the quiet room, thinking. Will might not have been able to relate to what I'd been going through in the last few months. But there was someone who perhaps could.

# - CHAPTER SIX -

# *A Gift of Amethyst*

ESTHER'S ROOM WASN'T traceable by the scent of burning incense. No dried herbs hung over the door to ward off negative energies. The only thing distinguishing it from the others was the way the door opened before I'd even knocked to announce my presence, as if its occupant had sensed exactly what was about to occur before it happened.

Esther stood on the other side of the threshold, one arm propping the door open, a twinkle in those green eyes of hers. Her appearance was significantly restrained this midday. The golden mane had been teased into a bushy mass on top of her head, she was devoid of any colour in a grey shawl, loose white trousers and comfortable sandals, and her face was bereft of makeup. Previously hidden flaws were now exposed and at least a decade had been added to her years, but she remained just as alluring.

'Hope I'm not disturbing anything?' I said.

'Oh, you absolutely are. But I always have time for handsome young men like yourself.'

Her lips broadened into a wide crescent of gleaming white teeth. She pushed the door wide for me to enter.

I was blushing as I stepped inside the room, but no one would have known since it was cloaked in an almost impenetrable blackness. The only light came from flickering candles dotted around a small table standing on what looked like a yoga mat spread across the middle of the floor. Moving deeper inside, I could discern the numerous items arranged on the table's surface. A brass bowl containing a stick that resembled a fat cigar — a singing bowl, I recognised, from the window display of a witchy shop in Cricklewood. A pestle and mortar was filled with an organic material of either crushed herbs or dried flowers, letting me know where that aromatic smell drifting up my nose was coming from. Crystals of varying colours and sizes twinkled in the candlelight. A large cushion bearing the imprint of a generous sized pair of buttocks was positioned in front of it all.

'My meditation space,' said Esther, closing the door and drifting up behind me. 'Ordinarily, I'd do at least an hour first thing. It helps to align my vibration to the present moment so that I'm focused throughout the rest of the day.'

She moved over to a winged armchair in the corner, sweeping her arm for me to find somewhere to sit. An ottoman storage box at the foot of the bed looked sturdy enough, so I settled there as Esther squeezed herself into the armchair. Once ensconced, she pulled a hand-rolled cigarette and lighter from the folds of her shawl. 'Do you mind?'

I shook my head, even though I absolutely minded. I only get one set of lungs in this life and a bout of asthma in my early teens had made me forever wary of anything that might induce another attack. As Esther lit the cigarette and inhaled, I imagined the look on poor Mrs Brown's face had she been here to witness the crime being committed before her.

'So,' said Esther, wisps of smoke rising up from her lips. 'How can I assist you on this fine noon?'

There was no point beating about the bush, especially talking to a woman who could intuit people's thoughts. 'It's about someone from my past. Someone who died,' I said. 'I think he's haunting me.'

There are few people to whom you can say such a sentence and not have them look at you like you just told them you were recently abducted by aliens. Esther Hill was one of them.

'Yes. They have a funny habit of doing that, don't they?' she chuckled. 'What is it? Poltergeist activity? Familiar smells? A feeling someone's in your presence when you're alone? I once had a particularly persistent soul who refused to let me use the bathroom in private. I'm happy that rather unpleasant ordeal is behind me.'

'One night, I was lying in bed. I was upset and couldn't sleep. When I was lying there crying, I could have sworn someone lied down behind me, placing their hand on my shoulder. I felt it. It was so real. And it was him. His touch. His smell. And I can't stop dreaming about him. Only, they're not like real dreams. They're memories of our time together.'

'Dreams … of your memories …' said Esther, squinting sagely through the gloom and taking a long, slow drag on the cigarette. 'Interesting. I've never heard of that before.'

I entwined my fingers and leaned forward, anticipating what she thought it could mean. I felt at ease in Esther's company. An openness, an acceptance, of which I had never witnessed in another person, emanated from her. I could have divulged my deepest, darkest thoughts and emotions and she would have listened without a trace of judgement. Either that or my senses were being affected by that cigarette she was puffing on; my nose detected something a little stronger than nicotine in the crackling tobacco.

'What is it you want to know?' she asked, after her moment of thought.

'How is it possible? I mean, where is he? Elliot? In this world or another one?'

'How to explain ...' Esther murmured. 'When someone passes away, their physical body disappears. But a part of their identity, what you might call their soul, can remain. It's usually a part of their soul that had a strong energy when they were alive, and was still present during the moment of death, like an intense desire or intention, or a goal they had yet to achieve. When this remnant of their soul takes on form and interacts with the physical dimension, that's what we call a ghost.'

I held my silence. Esther read my need for clarification and continued.

'Everything in this universe is made up of energy. The human ego, our identity, our beliefs, feelings, desires and memories are no different. They're energy known as thought forms. If a person has a strong identification with their emotional self, if they experience great mental distress or die in particularly violent circumstances when they have much desire to live, those are very strong forms of energy.

'But the residual energy that's left behind when the body dies usually only has enough power to project itself into the physical dimension, not interact with it completely. And it weakens over time. Think of it as a sort of looping echo, an imprint. That's why you often hear of ghosts walking along the same corridor or crying coming from one particular room in a house. If the haunting is more on a poltergeist level — apparitions, objects being thrown around, electrical equipment being tampered with — the energy is being fed by something else.'

I frowned. 'Fed by what?'

'Our own energy, usually. We keep ghosts alive by being aware of them, by fearing them, by wanting to know more about them.

And if their intention is to interact with this dimension, to communicate a message or finish their business, they will take advantage of those strong points of attraction. They will reveal themselves, they will come for our physical energy sources and they will communicate with people who are able to perceive them. People like me.'

A strong point of attraction? Is that what I had created over the last decade? By constantly thinking about Elliot? By longing for him? Refusing to let the memory of him go? But if that was the case, then why the sudden activity now? Why didn't he make his presence known years ago? I thought again about the robin redbreast sitting at my bedroom window. The butterfly that had landed on my specs. *Were* they authentic signs of Elliot's posthumous existence I had dismissed as irrelevant at the time?

'I still don't understand,' I said. 'I mean, why now?' I shook my head, averting my eyes to the candles, their flickering light mesmerising.

Esther considered me affectionately for a long moment, a blue haze of smoke issuing from the arm of the armchair where the cigarette was held between pudgy fingers. It felt like her eyes were penetrating deep into my soul, seeing things there even I couldn't see. Calmness suffused my body in spite of my eagerness to discover more.

'You don't have to understand everything at once. You just have to be open to the signs, to watch and learn. Recall what I told our writer friend, Mr Anderson, last night, about twin flames?' Esther asked. Ash fell from the tip of the cigarette, but she didn't even flinch. 'I believe this applies to you and your loved one. You share the same soul, therefore you share a bond like no other. In life and in death. I'd hazard a guess that if he's still around he has a message for you, something important to teach you.'

My heart began to race. A message?

'You, Quentin, unlike most others, possess deeply emotional and empathic traits,' Esther went on. 'You are affected by the world's challenges, retaining your own and other people's emotions like a sponge. Because of this you are gifted with exceptional extrasensory abilities. But I sense you are only just opening up to this gift. When you open completely, however, any spirit would find it hard not to be attracted to your energy. You have the power to create a special connection with them. You are the door they use to stay connected to our dimension.' Even in the poor light I could see Esther's face had become sorrowful. 'Until now you have feared that part of yourself, you have tried to push it away and suppress it. It's normal to fear it. I should know, I speak from experience. But you must trust it. It isn't a curse. It's your super power, there to be nurtured and used to your advantage.'

A shiver travelled the length of my spine. Was Esther saying that I ... that we ... were the same?

Her words hung in the smoke-filled air for a long moment before she pushed herself out of the armchair, heaving a sigh that carried years of wisdom. She walked over to her meditation space, unceremoniously crushed the cigarette in the singing bowl and seized from beneath the table a large patchwork handbag. She rummaged inside it, retrieving something before stowing the bag away again and sweeping over to me.

'This is an amethyst,' she said, unfurling her palm to show me a violet crystal attached to a cord of rope. 'A good choice for you, I think. It will help bring fortune in love and freedom from past heartache.'

I stared at the stone, the candlelight affording enough light to see the cracks and veins beneath its translucent surface. It was beautiful, almost magical. I glanced up at Esther questioningly. She smiled and nodded.

'A gift from me,' she said. And without asking, she looped the necklace over my head and straightened it at the chest with a stroke of her fingers. She stared intently at my eyes, reading something in them.

'You're an intuitive soul, Quentin. And strong. Your strength comes from a knowing deep inside that there's a higher calling. Having that knowing is half the battle, not all people are so fortunate. Trust your heart and watch for the signs. They will guide you. They're everywhere if you'll just take the time to notice them.'

I lowered my chin and touched the amethyst necklace, stroking its smooth surface with my thumb. I felt strangely emotional. And slightly intoxicated. I couldn't work out if it was being in Esther's presence, the aromatic herbs or those fumes from her dodgy cigarette. Her voice brightened suddenly.

'Now go and enjoy your afternoon. Tonight we will be delving deeper into the spirit world. I think you'll be surprised by what we'll discover. I had a walk around this morning, feeling the place out. Hilderley Manor has more surprises than I first thought. And not all of them benevolent.'

I stood, thanked her, turned and walked to the door. I was just about to open it when her voice came out of the gloomy darkness once again.

'Oh, and about the smoking ...' She was tapping one nostril with her index finger, grinning mischievously.

I winked and turned the door handle. Esther didn't have to worry. Her secret was safe with me.

* * * * *

I left Esther's room deep in thought. Half of me felt relieved, relieved that the uncertainty I'd been feeling for so long was beginning to clear. The other half was bringing up all sorts of new worries, emotions and questions. The naive part of me that had believed in the ghosts of fiction — the ones you could see and almost touch, that at least held some resemblance to a human being — felt disillusioned at this new understanding of what a ghost actually was. That part of me hoped Elliot still existed, at least as some sort of shadow of his former self. Remnants of his energy, like an intangible lock of hair or childhood tooth, just didn't feel the same. But the shadowy figure in my bedroom ... the smell of his skin ... his unmistakable touch. Those things had felt very real indeed. Do our minds, as Esther had said, have more to do with ghosts than we think? A sort of symbiosis between the living and the dead.

I remembered watching a video online where a woman was helping people  question their painful thoughts. In the video a father who had lost his daughter to cancer was plagued with thoughts of regret, of wanting his daughter to be alive when she was not. The questioning process allowed space for an alternative perspective: 'She shouldn't have died' would become 'She should have died,' because that was what had happened, and arguing with reality, according to the woman, was a sure-fire way to make yourself suffer. When we allow ourselves this different perspective, not holding on so adamantly to our original thought, it opens space to consider how the turnaround could be a good thing: Why is it a good thing she died? The father thought: 'Because she's no longer in pain.' 'Because the rift in the family wouldn't have been rebuilt had it not been for her death.' But the most intriguing part of the video, once the bereaved father had become untangled enough from his painful thoughts to think more widely, was that he began to see that his daughter wasn't as dead as he had originally thought. When our loved ones are in another room, if they're on the other side of the world, do they not only exist inside our heads and hearts at that moment? Who knows if their physical body isn't already gone? And if it has, does that have to take away our love for them, just because we'll never get to see them again? 'But I want to watch her grow into a woman, see her smile again,' sobbed the tearful father. 'And therefore you suffer,' replied the woman. A hard pill to swallow, and a very radical way of thinking, but it was the truth nonetheless.

Why was I letting my desire for Elliot to exist in some shape or form beyond his death dominate my memory of his existence? Why wasn't I content to just remember him how he was, remember how much he made me smile, remember that despite being taken so young he couldn't have died a happier person, loving nature, loving life. Because those happy memories were there, when the pain wasn't so strong, when the guilt and trauma didn't have me in its grip, and they could light up my heart, make me forget the pain, make me feel exactly as I had felt when I was with him all those years ago. We want love so much, yet when we have it we take it for granted. Is losing love the only way we learn to appreciate it in this twisted game called life?

I needed to take my mind off the thoughts. I went back to our room and picked up *Ethereal*. There was a couple of hours to go before the prearranged time we had to be back in the lounge for a regathering, and with Kat still busy doing her interviews it gave me time to read a few chapters. I polished my specs, tucked the amethyst inside the neck of my jumper and went looking for a quiet place to settle.

Downstairs, book in hand, I wended the corridors, peering through giant doors. The house was impressively large, so large in fact that it was hard not to get lost in its maze of staircases and passageways. And it really was stunning. Now I had chance to appreciate it without projecting my fears and judgements on the place. Much work had gone into crafting its impressive architecture and Mrs Brown was clearly the perfect woman for the role of housekeeper, given the way every surface gleamed, every room was meticulously presented.

Eventually I stumbled upon what looked like another of the house's central living rooms. But unlike the lounge's pictures and paintings, this room's walls were lined with rows of bookshelves. Two plush sofas were positioned in front of a striking fireplace, where kindling snapped and crackled enticingly in the hearth, keeping the autumn chill at bay. A cosier place to sit down and start a new book couldn't have existed.

I slipped inside and closed the door quietly behind me. I chose one of the sofas and switched on the floor lamp that stood beside it for better light. Dropping onto the velvety upholstery I wriggled my back into the plush cushions, trying to get comfy. One of the windows was ajar, allowing a cool breeze to snake into the room and take the edge off the heat from the fire. It carried the scent of the garden flora, the singsong of birds and the soothing trickle of the water fountain. The perfect background noise to complement the cosy setting. I flipped the book over.

*Ethereal's* blurb said the book's story was about a parapsychologist named Jack Reid, who ventures to a picturesque village in Yorkshire to investigate a series of disturbing events and reported hauntings. When he discovers Harrington House, an abandoned building with a shady history and infamous reputation, he experiences shocking things that leave him questioning his beliefs and even his sanity. An intriguing premise to say the least.

A couple of pages in I found myself enamoured with Will's

writing style, succinct sentences littered with strong verbs that conjured vivid images of the narrator's retelling of events. I liked the novel's protagonist, Jack Reid, a self-deprecating and intelligent Scotsman with a contagious fascination for paranormal claims. I once again wondered if Will had based the character on himself. Jack Reid, toughened and distrustful due to a troubled past, bore more than a small similarity to the northern writer. Both author and main character shared the same preoccupation with uncovering the truth. It made you want to know what was going on deep in their psyche, what was driving them.

I figured it was safe to assume that fiction writers put a little of themselves into all their characters, that regardless of the gender, and the genre, their DNA would be identifiable if you searched hard enough. It was a real talent, to be able to get into so many different heads, to embody someone else entirely, a person who wasn't even real. A gift you could see came with many benefits. The ability to see the intentions of others, and turn the tables on them should one wish. However Will did it, I liked having at least some insight into the mind of this enigmatic man.

A few chapters in I was already lost in the story. But the lack of sleep after last night's impromptu nightcap was fast catching up with me, making it hard to keep my eyes open. The soporific effect of the fire wasn't helping. I had reached what I recognised as the first major turning point of the plot when my eyelids fell shut ...

*I thought I'd missed the ceremony, that I was too late. But then I saw them, a sombre procession of grief-stricken faces coming out of the church to face the unforgiving daylight. In the time elapsed, I have been watching the proceedings from my discreet spot by the cemetery's lychgate. I don't want to get spotted, don't want to do anything that could disturb this most private service.*

*The final stage of Elliot's funeral, the burial, is now well underway. The coffin, embellished with wreaths of white lilies, has already been lowered into the freshly dug grave. Mourners stand around it, their garb as black as the carrion crow that sits and watches from its perch on top of a tilted gravestone. The vicar, an aged and handsome figure, peers up from time to time over his prayer book, keeping his eye on a tearful woman riven with heartbreak. I don't need to have seen her before to know this is Elliot's mother, Shelly.*

*The sombre setting of the church and its graveyard is brightened only by the unhindered sunlight of spring, the smell of flowers in bloom and the buzz of insects as they fly about stealing nectar. So much life and yet so much death in one scene, I can't help thinking.*

*A short figure appears beside me suddenly, making me start. I blink through my specs at a blond haired girl with anaemic looking skin and owlish grey eyes. She's a few years younger than me, maybe fourteen.*

*'I'm Amy, Elliot's sister,' she says.*

*I evaluate her nervously, wondering if she's come to tell me off for spying on the funeral. 'Quentin,' I reply.*

*'I know who you are,' she says with a weak smile. 'The glasses gave it away.'*

*This is a surprise. I have never met Elliot's family before, only heard of them. His mother Shelly, his father Gideon, and his only sibling, the girl standing before me.*

*'You do?'*

*'Elliot talked about you a lot,' says Amy.*

*'Oh.' I returned an equally faint smile. 'He talked about you, too.'*

*Amy's face becomes sad. Our eyes disconnect and drift to the proceedings taking place in the shadow of the ancient church.*

*'Shouldn't you …' I start.*

*Amy shakes her head absentmindedly. 'Dad gave me permission to leave. I don't want to see the part where he goes into the ground. It'll* only make me think about it constantly, him down there in that pit on his own, with the beetles and worms.'

I dwell on this mental picture and feel ill suddenly.

'He never told us,' says Amy. 'You know, that he was gay. But we knew.'

Anxiety flutters inside my chest as I wonder where this is going. She goes on.

'I could tell he loved you. In the way his eyes lit up when he talked about you. He worried about you, too. I never saw him be that way with anyone other than our spaniel, Monty. Elliot looked after him when he was dying. He hated seeing anyone in pain, even small insects and animals. His heart was really big.'

I feel my ears and cheeks burn as Amy no doubt watches them turn scarlet. But she doesn't have to tell me how big Elliot's heart was. You couldn't be around him and not feel it.

'He loved to write poems, did you know?' Amy's face brightens a little as she holds out a cream card for me to take. 'We had these printed, it's Mum's favourite. Uncle Rory read it out at the sermon.'

I take the card and stare at its contents, the ink crystal clear thanks to the new prescription in my specs. There's an illustration of a robin redbreast perched on a bench in the bottom corner, and in the middle, verses of Elliot's poem printed in a calligraphic font.

'You can keep it,' says Amy.

I look up at the owlish eyes.

'He would have wanted you to have something to remember him.' She smiles again, but it's tinged with more sadness.

'Thanks,' I say, swallowing the dryness in my throat.

We glance over at the mourners again. The vicar is reading a prayer now: 'earth to earth, ashes to ashes, dust to dust ...'

'Take care of yourself, Quentin. Bye.' Amy bows her head and slips through the lychgate, her black dress rippling around her ankles as she heads to where a row of awaiting black vehicles are parked.

*I look at the card again. 'I really mean it,' I say, my voice too quiet for her to hear it. But the gratitude sincere nonetheless …*

I opened my eyes, saw the decorative molding of the sitting room's ceiling. There was no confusion this time, no wondering where time had elapsed. The dream — memory — had been as vivid as the last. But there was no full moon shining beyond the window this time. There was something else. The sound of voices. Raised voices.

I couldn't discern the words being spoken, but instantly recognised the rhotic cadence of Mrs Brown's Scottish accent. She sounded flustered. Worse. Angry. Lured by curiosity I brushed Will's book aside, peeled myself off the sofa and crept over to the window to see what was going on. I concealed myself behind a floral curtain and peered out into the garden.

Stan Crouch and Mrs Brown were ascending the steps that led to the courtyard, Mrs Brown looking fraught with worry as she struggled to stay abreast with the belligerent caretaker.

'You can't go around scaring the guests, Stan,' she was saying. 'Someone might complain. Mr Blackford would find out.'

'Mind your own business, woman,' Stan spat back.

They stopped at the top of the steps and Stan bent down to rub his knee, supporting himself with the rake he was holding.

Mrs Brown looked staggered by the retort. 'Please, Stan. I'm thinking of you.'

'Codswallop, woman. You're thinking of yourself. More concerned with scoring points to impress old Blackford. I should have known you were the sort. A backstabber. Everyone's the same. That what you're going to do after you've finished bothering me? Report me? Well, go ahead. See if I care.'

'Of course not!' Mrs Brown shrieked, so startled by the

accusation her voice trembled. She began after Stan as he took off. 'Stan, please! I'm concerned about you. You've not been yourself lately.'

Stan spun around, almost causing his pursuer an injury with the sharp tines of his rake. 'Of course I'm not myself, you foolish hag. What with that lot in there, interfering where they're not wanted.'

'They're not doing anyone any harm.'

'Yes they are. They're messing in that dark stuff,' Stan growled. 'Conjuring up spirits. I saw that flame haired one carrying one of them spirit boards inside. Who knows what they're inviting into the place? Probably thinks she's a witch, the ginger rat. And I bet she's a dyke. I bet the whole lot of 'em are a bunch of perverts.'

'Keep your voice down!' screeched Mrs Brown, shooting a look at the house as if someone might have overheard.

Someone had. I inched behind the curtain, trying to dodge her gaze.

'What on earth's gotten into you?' Mrs Brown was losing her patience now. 'Is it because it's the anniversary tomorrow?'

'What are you bringing that up for again?' Mr Crouch looked near to suffering a burst aneurysm he was that red, the rake held out to one side like the Grim Reaper's scythe. 'Didn't I already make it clear I wasn't interested?'

'Yes, you did. But ... but it's the anniversary, Stan! I mean, it's everything to you.'

'Not anymore it's not. Anniversaries are for sad folk. Folk with nothing better to do than think about the past. I'm done with the past. Hear me? I'm done with it!'

Purpled-faced with anger, Stan did an about-turn and took off again. This time Mrs Brown didn't go after him. She stood there at the top of the steps, a pitiful figure in her tidy cardigan. After a moment she began a slow, forced walk in the same direction.

I peeled away from the window and pressed my back against the wall, almost knocking loose a framed picture with the crown of my head. I steadied it with my hand and remained pinned against the wall, my head swimming, anger swirling in my belly.

It's a grotesque thing to see such ignorance, such immaturity, in your elders. We expect age to refine us, to make us the learned teachers of grace and wisdom. But I guess for some it just means more time to get better at being dreadful.

Just what had got the old man so rattled? And what made him think it was all right to call me and my sort dykes and perverts? Mr Crouch might have been raised in less liberal years. But there was a fine line between ignorant and plain insulting. His prejudice almost made me want to get out a rainbow flag and start waving it around a bit. Almost.

# CHAPTER SEVEN

# *Stone, Bones and Forgotten Names*

WE RECONVENED IN the lounge at lunchtime for a rundown of the evening's schedule and more refreshments. Entering later than everyone else, I spotted Will reclining by the fire, brow creased in concentration, journal resting on his crossed legs. There was no show of greeting, no smile, not even a brief nod. I could only presume we were still on speaking terms. Regardless of the aloofness, I got the feeling Will wasn't the type to hold a grudge.

Kat, too, did not acknowledge my arrival. She was busy chatting with Annie near the upright piano, all professional smiles and feigned attentiveness once more since her unfortunate encounter with the parapsychologist. The act wasn't fooling me, however. I could see the tenacious reporter beneath the veneer, the one who would later twist and embellish every piece of information given to her. The masquerade dropped the second Norman walked into the room, carrying a camera and looking like he had something important to reveal.

The surveillance footage of the cursed bible was ready for inspection. Everyone — apart from Kat, who kept a guarded distance — gathered around the silver bearded giant, anticipating what he had to show us.

'Good news is we captured something,' said Norman. 'Bad news is it wasn't a ghost.'

He held out the hi-tech camcorder so we could see the video playing on its rotatable screen. Everyone leaned in for a closer look. In the night vision footage, the bible was sitting on the rocking chair undisturbed. After a few seconds a mass of fluff jumped into the frame. There was a lot of movement as what looked like a wagging tail remained on the screen for a few moments. When it turned around, the tiny Pomeranian it belonged to came into view. Cottonball, having already flipped open the bible's cover with his snout and began eating its pages, settled into a comfortable position on the rocking chair and proceeded to finish the job.

Ash's hand went to her mouth. 'Oh, Cottonball.'

Cottonball, perched in his usual spot on her arm, barked at the footage of himself tearing pieces out of the sacred pages, as if he was very proud of himself. A real 'good as gold' boy indeed.

'Babe, I told you to make sure the door was locked after you took him out for his last walk,' said Matt.

'I did!' said Ash. 'But he must have got out later, when I had to go to the bathroom. I was scared of the ghosts so I dashed in and out and then jumped straight back into bed.'

Matt was very apologetic, telling Norman he would compensate whatever financial debt the team wanted in return for the loss of the precious artifact. I just hoped the pooch didn't sprout fangs and develop red glowing eyes after consuming the supposedly jinxed thing. A cursed ball of fluff running around the place was all we needed.

I questioned once again if my stay here would yield the indisputable proof I craved so much. Then I reminded myself we'd been here less than twenty four hours and there was still plenty of time for it to show itself yet.

I peeled away from the subsequent chatter and walked over to the windows that faced out over the front grounds. The crows, which felt like a permanent fixture of the manor by this point, were fighting over something on the front lawn, wings flapping, feathers flying. I watched until a split in the chaos made them break apart and I could finally see what they were squabbling over. It was a baby mouse, limp and bloody. I grimaced and looked away, catching Will rising from the armchair. He cast me a sideways glance on his way to the door, journal clasped in hand, the stride slow and carefree. I debated going after him, but chickened out immediately. I'm as bad at apologies as I am at taking things too personally.

After we snacked, conversed small talk and sat down for a briefing of the evening's schedule with Carrie, Kat and I went for a walk along the tree canopied lanes with close beech hedgerows her Mini had sped along on the journey up here. It was the perfect setting for a moment of respite, to reflect on the happenings of the weekend thus far.

'Fresh air,' said Kat, inhaling deeply before taking a drag on her Marlboro Light.

She was taking advantage of being able to smoke as much as she liked away from the watchful eyes of Mrs Brown. We'd been outside minutes but she was already on her second one. I wafted away the poisonous cloud, edging closer to the hedgerow.

'You're quiet,' she remarked. 'What's the matter?'

I gazed at the winding road ahead, mentally replaying the conversation I'd overheard between Stan Crouch and Mrs Brown.

'Have you noticed anything odd about the caretaker?' I asked.

Kat frowned. 'There's a caretaker?'

'Ancient man lurking around the manor with his tools.'

'Haven't noticed him. Why?'

'Just concerned about a conversation I overheard earlier.'

She lifted a brow, her interest piqued. 'Anything juicy?'

'Juicy?'

Irritably, she replied, 'You know, captivating, contentious. Like a seedy affair.' Her eyes lit up with wicked glee. 'Or a murder confession.'

I shook my head. 'Just an argument. I couldn't work out what it was about, though.'

'Then snoop some more. It could be worth investigating.'

So much for confidentiality. I was beginning to understand why journalists had such a bad reputation. I worried for a moment I might have unintentionally revealed a few skeletons in my own closet over the last week, until remembering, ruefully, that I'd lived a life so boring no one would ever want to write about it. I didn't bother explaining to Kat that I hadn't been snooping, nor did I intend to, and that I was genuinely concerned about Mrs Brown after seeing the poor woman's plight, instead asking, 'Are you ever not in journalist mode?'

'Like I told you, this job is everything to me. And I can't afford to take my eye off the ball at the moment. We're up to our necks at the *Gazette* right now.'

'In what way?'

'The *Gazette's* been struggling for a while. Compared to its competitors, at least. And it's a small newspaper as it is. We're overworked and underpaid. Josh has major plans for a revamp, though. He wants us beating our main competitor's circulation by the middle of next year, doubling our online readership, all while extending our monthly print magazine. And he's counting on us to help him do all of it. That's why he's got us out here in the middle of nowhere looking for Casper and his elusive mates.' Her eyebrows knitted anxiously. 'It's also why it's important that I get this article right. It's a great opportunity for me, a chance to show Josh what I can do under pressure. It could even get me promoted to chief reporter, knocking Abigail off her perch.'

Abigail Cresswell. I had met her briefly during my initiation into the workings of the press team. An arresting looking, dark-haired woman with overly tanned skin, bleached teeth and an affected laugh.

'That doesn't sound very friendly,' I said.

'You don't know Abigail. She makes me look like Mary Poppins, and I can be a right bitch. She's a complete covert narcissist, got more faces than Michael Jackson. Pretends to be everyone's best friend, will do *anything* for them, but always has another agenda. Once she's charmed her way into a better position she isn't qualified for, her true colours begin to show. She's currently got everyone below her doing all the hard work while she sits there barking orders and taking all the credit. And half of the work is digging ourselves out of the mess she's got us in. She's reckless, and a terrible reporter. Josh is too blindsided to see it. Don't get me wrong, the man's a brilliant editor, but when it comes to spotting a bitch he hasn't got the first clue. The fact he's divorced while still under forty and lodging on company premises while his current girlfriend shacks up in his house with another bloke should tell you that.'

'Can see why business is booming,' I said sardonically, picturing my new career disappearing before it had begun.

'Then we better work our arses off and create something worth reading, hadn't we?'

We walked some more. Breath misted from my mouth against the crisp rural air. Birds tweeted in the trees. A car drove towards us, forcing us into the mulch that had built up near the road's edge. When its engine had faded from earshot, Kat asked, 'Where did you get to earlier, anyway?'

'I went to see Esther Hill.'

'Ah, the seer.' There was a caustic tone in Kat's voice as she lit her third Marlboro Light, her porcelain nose and cheeks now red with cold. 'I've yet to speak to her myself, but I want to. There are a few things I'd like to ask her. How much she makes off that popular platform she's created online for one.'

'You should listen to some of the things she has to say about the metaphysical,' I said, feeling annoyed at Kat for being more concerned with monetary matters than Esther's supernatural abilities. 'It's really interesting.'

'You believe that psychic hogwash?'

'I don't think it's smart to dismiss something just because others have ridiculed it, especially if you're not willing to hear what someone has to say about it.'

'That's what they all say, the gullible.' Kat shook her head. 'The bereaved are willing to give anyone the benefit of the doubt if it'll give them closure for their pain. We covered a story last year about a medium exposed as a complete fraud by a local documentary team. Half the people he duped had been booking him for personal readings for years. They never once questioned how he knew so much about them.'

'That doesn't mean everyone who claims to be psychic is a fraud.'

'No. But as long as people like that exist, I'm keeping my bullshit detector turned to high. You learn to do that when you're a journalist. I've had too many people try to outwit me in this game. When people are aware everything they say is going to be interpreted by a lot of people, it's amazing how articulate they suddenly become, how carefully they consider every word they say. It's easy for the truth to get lost. And, despite my flair for embellishment, I actually care about delivering honest journalism, believe it or not.'

'You weren't calling bullshit last night when you hightailed it out of the manor after hearing those knocks on the walls.'

'I don't know what I believe after last night. But I *know* this world is full of frauds and liars. And I'm easily spooked. I got pranked walking home from singing lessons by a gang of mean girls when I was younger, four of them jumped out of an alley, the ringleader wearing a Ghostface mask. My nerves have never been the same since. You know, the negative effect of fear isn't taken seriously enough. It can cause psychological damage for the rest of a person's life. It's why I've never been able to watch scary films, I'm a heart attack waiting to happen. I'm dreading what the Freaky Foursome have got planned for us tonight. Wouldn't be surprised if they took us out gravedigging or something equally ghoulish.' Kat shuddered, then considered me with a sideways glance. 'Maybe we will make a good team, me and you. Me and my bullshit detector, you and your trusting nature. Usually I have to play dumb to get people to reveal their true intentions. With you I won't have to bother.'

My request for courtesy had clearly gone unheeded. I ignored the jibe and carried on walking, feeling frustrated by Kat's obstinacy. I believed in Esther Hill. A feeling in my gut told me she was the real deal. But I also knew it wasn't my job to convince others that unexplainable things were genuine, especially when I took so much convincing they were real myself.

The hedgerow gave way to wide fields bordered by spiny trees reaching up into the dark, louring sky. A sky that wouldn't have looked out of place in a Hitchcock film. A familiar bird's squawk echoed in the distance. A church bell pealed. Kat lit her fourth Marlboro Light. We continued to walk.

'So, do you have a boyfriend?' Kat asked out of the blue.

I didn't need a mirror to know my cheeks had flushed like a red cardinal. 'I do not.'

'Didn't think so.'

My voice shot up a register. 'Why?'

'You're the most awkward person I've ever met. I can't even begin to imagine the sort of guy who would put up with that. It isn't the looks, though, if you'd sort out your dress sense. You're cute, in a virginal kind of way.'

Both flattered and offended, I replied, 'There was *someone*. But, well, he died.'

Kat's crimson lips wilted sympathetically. 'Oh, I'm sorry.'

'It was a long time ago.' And yet still so very present.

'That why you're single?' she asked.

I frowned.

'Because you're scared of losing someone again?'

Scared of losing someone again. I absorbed this thoughtfully. I wasn't only currently single, I had been single every year since Elliot's death. Instead of focusing on relationships, I devoted my time to books, studying, photography and various jobs. Virginal didn't come close to describing my love life: it *was* my love life. I didn't need a psychologist to tell me what I was running away from, that I spent so much time with my head in a book because if I stopped and thought for one second, I was right there again on that cold lake, in that never ending nightmare. But I hadn't expected the time to go so fast. It was as if I lifted my head out of a book one day and noticed a decade had passed. I wasn't a teenager anymore, I was a fully grown adult. And still very alone. Had the fear of losing someone again stolen those years away?

Noticing I hadn't answered, Kat said, 'Thought so. Nothing like the death of a loved one to keep you tied to the past. We put them on this posthumous pedestal we never would have done when they were alive, forgetting there's a world full of other people out there.'

I could have been wrong, but I detected a bitter edge in her tone, a flicker of resentment in those baby blue eyes. Had she lost someone she loved? Or was she talking about someone else who had?

'Perhaps it's time you give men another go,' she suggested. 'Life's short, and Prince Charming won't sit around waiting until you're ready. He's out there looking for his prince, too. Let's just hope he has bad eyesight, or an equally awful dress sense in your case.' With this she flashed me a wicked grin, nudging me playfully with her shoulder.

I allowed myself a smile. But as her words lingered in the autumn air, I could feel they had hit a hitherto unprovoked nerve inside me. Luckily, nature provided a welcome distraction from the discussion of my love life at that very moment. The trees opened up to reveal a churchyard standing beyond the low stone wall that had appeared at the side of the road.

'Wonderful,' said Kat. 'Even when we go for a walk we can't get away from the dead.'

Her phone's ringtone made us both jump, Destiny's Child *Independent Women*. She fished it from her coat and crossed to the other side of the road to answer the call in private. I walked over to the wall and gazed into the churchyard's sacred grounds. A small church with lancet windows and stonework worn by centuries of inclement weather stood watch over a sea of ancient gravestones. A crow swooped out of nowhere, landing on the crest of one that sported a tall cross. It cocked its head, the black, beady eyes appearing to look directly at me. I could have sworn it was one of the pesky crows from the manor. Could it be the same one that had tried to peck its way through our window? It was an ominous thought. What bird followed you around like a feathery stalker? I felt relief when it took flight again, vanishing over the church's spire.

There was a moment of quiet, punctuated by the howl of a growing wind, the scrape of leaves as they scudded along the road, the *bip bip bip* of Kat tapping the keys on her phone. She had finished her brief call and was sending a text message. I heard the click of her lighter, and a second later the crackle of burning tobacco as she took the first drag of her fifth Marlboro Light. I wished she'd stop smoking. I wished Will would, too. I had witnessed death, seen how it could take you at any moment, and struggled to understand why people were so willing to gamble with it.

And yet ... maybe it was me who was wrong, for trying to outrun it, resenting it for taking those I loved. I stared at the gravestones, their inscriptions illegible through age and deterioration. I wondered if anyone still  bothered to visit them. When everyone who ever knew us is also dead and gone, what meaning does a gravestone have? It's just stone, bones and forgotten names. I imagined my own grave, weathered and crumbled with time, my loved ones long gone, no one left to remember me. I pictured Elliot's, which I had visited time and again, the epitaph that talked about the young man who could pet bees, who had returned to the stars, and those birth to death years so close in time compared to the dates normally seen on memorials.

Kat was right. Life is short. She would join him one day. And

Will. And Mum and Dad. The only thing certain about life is that we're going to die, yet we never think about it, can't believe it when it takes someone we love. Yes. Life is short. And too precious to spend it fearing what could be, what shouldn't have been.

'I think you should stop smoking,' I said, wiping away the tear that had rolled down my cheek.

Kat made a snort. 'What? Why?'

'Because ...' I turned and looked at her. The raven curls billowed around the collar of her coat as she squinted at me distrustfully. 'Because I like you and I don't want you to die.'

Like I'd thrown her a grenade, she stood there expressionless, unsure how to respond. She glanced from side to side. 'You like me? But I'm horrible to you.'

I nodded. 'Yes, you are. But it brings out a part of me that I actually quite like.'

Still suspicious, but looking slightly flattered, she said, 'OK.'

I turned around and looked at the churchyard again. There was a pause before Kat resumed the *bip bip bip* on the keys of her phone. What she couldn't see was that I was smiling.

\* \* \* \* \*

When our walk had ended and Kat resumed interviewing the ghost hunters, I began to feel restless. So, naturally, the first thing I went looking for was food.

The dining hall was quiet when I entered, empty except for two elderly women gabbling like parakeets over scones and tea-filled china cups at the table in the bay window. They paid no attention to me as I walked to where a buffet of sandwiches, cakes and pastries had been laid out for us to graze on. My mouth watered as I lifted the plastic covers, loading my plate with an amount of sugary pastry that would make my dentist's toes curl. I'd just bitten into a cream cake when a figure drifted into my periphery.

Will had materialised beside me. Momentarily startled, I just stood and stared at him, eyes wide, cheeks full like a hamster's. He cleared his throat, pointing at his lip to tell me I had something on my face. I licked away the moustache of cream and the powdered sugar coating my lips. Will licked his lips, too. But not because he had food on them. He was looking nervous, like he had something to say.

'Look, I'm only good with all that head stuff when I'm writing my characters. Real people ... well, I'm still trying to figure those out. But if I offended you earlier then I'm sorry.'

I blinked, swallowing the cake.

'I only mean real offence when it comes to arseholes,' he said. 'Cross my heart.'

That was ... reassuring, I guess. But my face mustn't have shown it. Will flattened his shoulders.

'If you think I'm too abrupt, just say it,' he said, a defensive edge entering his voice.

'You could work on your delivery a little,' I offered.

His expression didn't alter. 'There's a lot of fakeness about. People need to hear it like it is. They might not like it at first, but if you hit a nerve in them maybe it's something they need to look at —' He stopped, catching himself. 'Fine. Point taken.'

'Sorry I snapped,' I said.

'It's cool. Just don't do it again or I'll have to punch you.'

I waited for the grin that told me he was joking. Disturbingly, none was forthcoming, his face remaining deadpan. Instead he snatched a strawberry tart off my plate, turned around, then headed for the door.

'Come on,' he said. 'Found some balls for us to play with.'

By 'play' he meant join him for a game of pool. After leading me into the recreational room, a richly decorated space given ambience through the many picture lights embellishing its dark wood walls, he began setting up balls in the middle of an antique billiards table that possessed a set of very elaborate ornate legs. I set my plate of pastries on a side table positioned next to a small Chesterfield as he handed me a cue.

The first time I learned how to play the game was on a sunny afternoon in a small bar in Southern France with Dad. It's the only sport I like. It's slow, intimate and requires little athletic agility. Which is good since I'm about as agile as a slug.

Will took the first break, cursing when he failed to pot a single ball. When, much to my own surprise as well as his, I managed to pot two stripes on my first shot, Will looked as if he was genuinely regretting choosing me as his opponent. The writer had a competitive streak, it seemed.

'Played a bit, have you?' he asked, more mindful as he took his next shot.

'It's my dad's favourite game.'

He returned a curt nod. 'Must run in the genes.'

'He's my adoptive father, actually.'

Will potted a solid and glanced up. 'Oh. That's cool.'

'Cool?'

'Cool that you have a dad.'

I bent to take my next shot. 'Don't you?'

Will straightened up and with a surprising dispassion said, 'Walked out when I was ten. Haven't seen him since.'

'I'm sorry.'

'Don't be. Greatest thing he ever did for me.'

We played some more. Will had soon caught up to my score,

which, unexpectedly, irked more than I thought it would. Perhaps it was the casual manner he had about him, the way you felt you had to work to penetrate that steely edge he exuded, but I was starting to feel that I needed to impress him at every turn. Or was it just because he was so handsome? Beautiful people have that about them, a way of making you feel inferior but wishing you knew more about them at the same time. I was feeling prickly around the collar when he decided to probe more.

'Have you ever met your biological parents?'

'No,' I said through a mouthful of Battenberg cake. 'My birth mother is dead and I don't know what happened to my biological father.'

Will glanced up from squinting at a ball on the billiards table, trying to predict his next shot. 'Sorry,' he said.

'Don't be,' I replied, echoing him. 'My parents gave me a good life. I've been lucky.'

The thought lingered. My parents, Belinda and Dominic Strange, certainly aren't perfect. Belinda and I clashed more than once during my teens. She couldn't give birth to children of her own, and failed treatments had led to much heartache and tragedy. She thought she was going to lose me like she'd lost those unborn babies, no matter how much I grew up. Her excessive worry made her question every choice I made, and the fear began to rub off on me, turning me into a persistent worrier and a hypochondriac, conditions even child psychologists and therapists failed to correct. When you spend your childhood around someone who thinks it's a miracle you're still alive at the end of another year, it's hard not to wonder what dangers are out there waiting to kill you. And the influences you have around you as a kid are like the programmers that write the software you run off when you're older. Dom is a kind, simple man, but that simple verges on being a little detached.

And I sometimes wonder if adopting me was more about assuaging his wife than fulfilling his own need for a son. But these are small shortcomings for the stability and security they provided, which are the things that really matter the most when you're growing up.

'How'd your biological mum die, if you don't mind me asking?' Will asked, chalking the tip of his cue.

'She perished in a house fire. I was eight months old at the time. She threw me to safety out of an upstairs window and a neighbour caught me.'

I relayed the story with little emotion, but I'd had plenty of time to come to terms with the grisly tale that surrounded my origin. Belinda and Dom told me when I was thirteen, not wanting me to grow up resenting them for withholding what they considered my birthright: to know exactly what had happened to the people who brought me into this world. They couldn't tell me who my biological father was, or what might have happened to him. My mother appeared to be single at the time she gave birth to me, as no father had been registered on my birth certificate. From what little was gleaned, she was a troubled young woman, a nomad who was treated for various mental health problems. And as shocking as the story was, I felt far removed from the situation. I was eight months old at the time. I can't even remember having another mother, let alone remember her voice, her face.

It's a strange thing, knowing you're connected so closely to someone you've never met. Even stranger when that person is dead. You expect to feel some heartache, but how do you mourn someone you never knew? I had wondered about them at times, though. Tried to picture their faces. Imagine what might have brought them together to create me, and where they were laid to rest — if my mother even had a memorial that marked her existence and my father had endured a similar fate. It had never

126

crossed my mind to go digging into my ancestry. When you've always had a family, especially one as large and close as mine, there isn't the incentive to desire much else. Still, it was there. The longing to know more. Maybe one day I would.

Will whistled. 'You really are lucky.'

'Yeah, I owe my life to her in more ways than one.'

'Wish I could share the same sentiment about my mother.'

Will had stopped playing the game and was leaning against a walnut panelled wall next to a window that looked out at wiry trees that failed to hide the field bordering one side of the house. One half of his handsome face was lit with pale light.

'Do you have a relationship with her?' I asked, sitting down on the Chesterfield.

'Barely. She made life hell after my old man left. Drinking, neglect, reckless relationships with various men. I buried my head in books to escape it all, became fascinated with the written word, the power it had to take you to other places, places that often made more sense than this world. Mum thought they were a waste of time. When I told her I wanted to write, she said I wasn't clever enough, said only kids who go to posh schools end up writing books. She pushed me into dead end jobs, because, according to her, money was more important than 'pansy art.'

Will stared at his feet, arms crossed, a pensive slant to his mouth. I hadn't imagined such dysfunctional beginnings. But then, what does one know about a person's past from first impression?

'Did you defy her?' I asked.

'Telling me I can't do something is the surest way to ensure I do it, and do it well. I read hundreds of books, studied the craft every day. I'd rewrite entire classics, longhand, to break down how they were made, experience how the words felt coming off the pens of masters.

'But it wasn't just the technical aspect of the craft I loved, it was knowing I could write about the things I was itching to say. I knew I would write my own books one day. Nothing was going to stop me. No education can teach you how to write from the soul, like your life depends on it, which for some writers it actually does. It can't teach you to dig out what's inside a character that makes them like the reader, the thing that makes the reader forget they're reading at all. The writer who wants it more than anything, who loves the struggle of it as much as the joy, becomes the master.'

Will was gazing at the balls scattered over the green felt of the billiards table in a way that looked like he was trying to confirm his words to himself as much as he was to me. I regarded him from my position on the sofa, feeling both empathy and respect for what I could see was a very resilient and determined man. His eyes found my face again, as if he'd forgotten I was in the room for a moment.

'That's why I'm grateful to my old man for walking out of my life,' he said. 'He freed me, let me decide my own fate. If he'd been around he would have made sure I never got to do what I love. Emotionally abusive people don't respect autonomy, when it comes to their kids or anyone else. I'm grateful to Mum, too, for not believing in me, because it spurred me on to prove her wrong. Writing's a hard craft. Sometimes you need a firework up your arse to keep you going when the days get long and the words aren't coming. Just the image of her smug "I told you you'd never do it" face would be enough to get me out of a slump on those days.' Rhetorically, he said, 'Life feels back to front, don't you think? Like it's inverted. The stuff we hate to go through is good for us in the end, and the stuff we love usually leads to our downfall.'

I pondered this. And, once again, the same nerve unearthed by Kat's comments about being scared to love again began to throb.

What good was to come from the things I'd been through? And had the things I loved been bad for me? The only outcome after years of escaping into books and photography was that I had ended up more awkward and scared than ever, not to mention, worst of all, completely alone. I felt a sudden urge to change the subject.

'At least you got a good name off them,' I said, trying to lighten the tone. 'Will Anderson. It looks good on the book.' Then I blushed when I realised how completely insensitive that sounded.

'You've seen my book?'

'One of the ghost hunters lent it to Kat. I read the first few chapters. I enjoyed it.'

Will acknowledged the compliment with a perfunctory nod. 'Anderson's a pen name, though. Took it from a distant relative. My real name's Will O'Donnell.'

'Oh.'

A silence fell across the billiards table and, too scared of putting my foot in it a second time, I decided not to break it. I didn't need to. It seemed Will's mind had got to thinking and he had more things to say.

'Just because I found a way to turn something negative into a positive, that doesn't mean I'm not stung by my past. If I don't sound bitter it's only because you can be grateful and a bit bitter at the same time. I have my scars. I just hide them well. It's not easy living a life where you feel like you always have to prove yourself. Sometimes you just want people to accept you exactly as you are, without all the frills, you know?'

I didn't know. Frills were elusive things in my world. I didn't have the talent, the looks and the magnetism Will had. Getting people to accept me with all the flaws was more my problem.

We listened to the gentle brush of trees and a crow cawing outside the window, the faraway tick of a grandfather clock out in the hallway. Mrs Brown's bell tinkled. Had more strangers just arrived?

Will lit his lighter, blew out the flame, lit it again. 'Who did you lose?'

Distracted, it took me a moment to figure out he was talking about the comment I'd made when I snapped and left him sitting on that bench. I hesitated before answering. 'My first love.'

He blew softly, the sound someone makes when they understand how significant something is, and, unintentionally, blew out the flame at the same time. 'That's rough.'

'I'm getting closer to finally coming to terms with it, though.' At least I hoped I was.

'Well, at least now you know that I did lose someone. Not to death, but when they're out of your life they're as good as dead.'

A cheerful laugh out in the hallway jarred with this sombre sentiment. Both Will and I glanced at the open door. The exit looked attractive suddenly. I'd pondered death enough for one afternoon.

I rose from the sofa and picked up the crumb laden plate off the side table. 'I should take this back to the dining hall.' Glancing the time on a wall clock, I added, 'I should probably take some photographs, too. Won't be long before the second ghost hunt starts.'

Will said nothing as I walked to the door. I paused when I reached it and turned.

'Thanks,' I said.

'What for?'

'For trusting me enough to share.'

I didn't tell him why I felt the need to thank him, that I sensed trust wasn't something he found easy. I didn't need to. There's a tacit feeling you get with certain people where those sorts of things don't have to be said. And that feeling was in the room at that moment.

# - CHAPTER EIGHT -

# *The Seance*

GHOSTS MIGHT HAVE attracted me to Hilderley Manor, but I'm not sure I'd have felt so brave coming here had I known we'd be calling them forth using the Ouija board. The name alone put my nerves on edge. I'd heard enough tales in my youth about the dangers of dabbling in the occult, about opening doorways for negative energies to escape and cause problems for those intrepid enough to venture. Then there was my own experiment, age eleven, with Melissa Dandridge in the derelict building behind the cinema. My memory of the event is mostly a blur — and perhaps for good reason — but I do remember that we saw a black shape hovering in a doorway that had us scarpering out of there like two startled ferrets. Poor Melissa was never quite the same again. In fact, last I heard she'd become an anxiety ridden recluse — and was it any wonder? Why then was I agreeing to take part in a seance using the blessed thing?

'It's completely safe as long as we follow the rules,' Carrie assured us as we filed into the dining hall like lambs being led to slaughter. 'For legal reasons, Giles and Annie will be the only ones touching the board. All we ask of you guys is that you focus on the questions being asked, try to visualise them while putting all other thoughts from your mind, and that you remain serious about the experience throughout, respecting the team and the board itself.'

Convincing as this sounded, it was obvious no one believed a word of it. Especially Kat. She looked like she was on her way to get a tooth pulled as she shuffled beside me, eyes flitting nervously, her notebook pressed against her chest like a protective crucifix. I offered what I hoped was a reassuring smile. 'Just think of the article. The journalist in the war zone, remember?' A flash of doubt from those baby blues was the only response I got in return.

The backdrop for the evening's event couldn't have been more appropriate for its subject matter. Lightning flashed through the bay window, heavy rain pelted the glass, and the building itself seemed to creak like a ship in unsteady waters. The dining hall's panelled walls and dark wood furniture created an abundance of shadows for ghostly entities to conceal themselves should they wish. Even the hunters themselves gave off a sense of foreboding, their solemn faces suggesting we were about to summon an entire graveyard back from the dead.

Giles and Annie awaited us at a colossal round table, sitting across from each other, the famous board sitting between them on the table's surface. Flickering tealights highlighted the contours of their faces. They weren't the only ones waiting in the darkness. Norman was perched atop a small, round table some feet behind Giles, stroking his beard and thumbing the screen on his camcorder; it looked like we were going to be documentary stars for the second night in a row. Esther was sitting in a tall-backed chair at the helm of the table. The makeup and accessories had returned, and her hair was a nimbus once more. But unlike the solemn bearing of her companions, she was displaying an airy unconcern for whatever lay ahead, humming and filing her nails casually, more like a woman settling down for an evening in front of the TV not overseeing a seance.

As we approached the table, her eyes crept upwards and landed on my neck. The amethyst necklace was tucked away, but you could still see the string peeking through the neck of my jumper. She winked, a mutual understanding. And suddenly the events ahead felt less daunting.

'Evening, folks,' said Giles, the candlelight flickering in his thick-rimmed glasses. 'Everybody gather round and grab yourself a seat.'

A chorus of squeaking wood followed as we spread around the table, pulling out chairs. Ash couldn't stop gaping at the Ouija board, clearly excited, but still clutching Matt's biceps for protection as the couple claimed the two chairs next to Annie. Cottonball looked enthusiastic too, dressed for the occasion in a miniature tuxedo, though in fairness that permanent smile would have made him look happy to be wherever his mummy decided to take him. Kat and Carrie chose the seats adjacent to Giles, leaving me and Will to naturally gravitate into a pair. We took the bottom of the table, facing Esther.

With everyone seated, Carrie began explaining the rules of the board. Giles and Annie demonstrated using the tips of their index fingers to push a thing called a planchette — a heart shaped piece of wood with a circular hole near the point — around the Ouija board. If a spirit wanted to communicate with us it would use the couple's energy to move the planchette, guiding their fingers to letters, numbers and the words *yes* and *no* which were printed on the board. We would be required to place our hands on the table, touching the hand of the person sitting next to us to form a chain of energy around the board.

'Esther's going to be raising her frequency through an intense meditation,' said Carrie. 'It should increase the chance for energy to find its way through to us. We're holding the seance in the dining hall because it has a reputation for being especially active. A staff member claims they've been touched numerous times while doing the cleaning in here. Apparitions that appear to be dancing in the spaces between the tables have also been reported. That would make sense since the room was a small ballroom at one point.'

'A ghost that likes to feel people up,' said Will, grinning immaturely as he pulled out his tape recorder and set it on the table. He pressed record. 'Make sure you cross your legs if you're wearing a skirt, ladies.'

Esther shot him an austere look from across the table that quickly wiped the juvenile smirk off his face.

I might have grinned, but my attention was on the board, running over Carrie's instructions in my head. *Focus on the questions being asked. Visualise them. Clear all other thoughts from your mind.* I touched the amethyst necklace beneath my jumper and thought of Elliot. Esther had said that if he was still around it meant he probably had a message for me. If I focused hard enough might it help him use the spirit board to come through and give it to me?

'OK, let's begin,' said Giles.

He and Annie placed their index fingers on the planchette and everyone else joined hands. Norman appeared from the shadows with his camcorder trained on the board from behind Giles' shoulder, the blinking red light indicating the next chapter of his documentary had begun. Everyone braced to see what would happen next.

'If there are any spirits here, please come towards my voice,' Giles said aloud.

In the quiet that ensued you could hear the wind and rain

howling beyond the window. More lightning flashed, casting trickling shadows on the panelled walls. A floorboard creaked above and everyone's eyes shot up to the ceiling.

'We're inviting you to come and speak to us, to move this planchette,' Annie intoned. 'Could you do that? Could you use our energy to move the planchette?'

Any doubts among the guests that anything was going to happen were abruptly disproved when the planchette suddenly shot across the board, taking Giles and Annie's fingers, and the last of my nerves, with it. Bodies recoiled from the table amid a chorus of gasps, yet the ghost hunters looked disturbingly thrilled.

'That's excellent, thank you,' said Annie calmly. 'Could you move the planchette to either *yes* or *no*, or any number and letter on the board in response to our questions?' She gave Giles an instructive nod.

'Are you a male?' said Giles.

*Are you a male?* I thought. And thought.

Another creak upstairs. The flames of the candles flickered as if a breeze had swept into the room. There was a crash of thunder in the distance. And the planchette moved again. Straight to the word *yes*.

Out of nowhere there came a loud gasp, similar to the sound of someone bursting through the surface of water for a life-saving intake of breath. Esther was clasping the chest of her pink and black zebra-print blouse, as if she'd just had a sudden fright. Everyone stared at her, faces etched with concern.

'He's here,' she whispered.

Ash's hand went to her mouth. '*Who's* here?'

Matt peered over his shoulder to see if anyone was lurking there. Kat, already on the paler side of the complexion scale to begin with, became so ashen she could have been mistaken for a ghost herself. Will, however, looked as unconcerned as if Esther had just announced she was off to visit the lavatory.

'Such a tormented soul, so angry,' Esther said in a pained voice. 'It's a strong energy, too. He has been trying to make contact for some time. There is momentum in the energy of his struggle.'

My heart began to race at an ungodly rate. It had to be him. Let it be Elliot, I thought. Please let it be Elliot.

'Quick, ask him something else while the connection is still strong,' Carrie urged Annie. She had a pen and paper at the ready to record the response.

'How did you die?' Annie called out, her voice echoey in the large room.

Everyone fixed their eyes on the board, awaiting the response. But movement came from somewhere else. Above us. The group looked up in unison at the same moment feet ran across the ceiling. And not the light footfall of a child. They were the footsteps of an adult, heavy and fast. The chandelier swayed on its hanging, the decorative crystals rattling like hailstones. For a nervous second I pictured the thing unscrewing itself from its fitting and landing on one of our heads. Then came another noise. One of the double doors to the room, left ajar up until that point, slammed shut.

Ash screamed, burying her head in her boyfriend's chest. Cottonball barked protectively, but the tiny yap wouldn't have scared off a kitten let alone whatever force had slammed the door. Esther was right. Whatever it was, it was angry. Kat, who had made no indication up until this point that she was a religious woman, blessed herself with the sign of the cross. I felt my pulse quicken as my heart began to race. The air in the room felt electric suddenly. Eager to exploit the poltergeist activity while it was at its strongest, the ghost hunters pressed on.

'How did you die!?' Annie shouted, more determination in her voice now.

It took a few seconds, but then the planchette began to move in response, spelling out a word:

M

The planchette shot to another letter.

U

Giles and Annie's arms were pulled with impressive force.

D

Thunder reverberated in the distance.

R

It was a miracle the planchette didn't give off sparks, it was moving so fast.

G

Carrie scribbled down the letters as fast as she could.

U

Ash gripped Matt's hand and squeezed it hard.

N

Kat looked like a statue, frozen with fear.

N

Giles and Annie's arms became still.

Carrie stopped scribbling and pushed the piece of paper into the middle of the table. In the candlelight, everyone leaned closer to read the word she had written on it.

'MUDRGUNN?' Matt read aloud. It sounded like he said *muddergun*. 'What's that?'

'Another language maybe?' Norman suggested from over Giles' shoulder.

Giles was shaking his head. 'No language is as indecipherable as that.'

'Shit,' said Annie. 'We mustn't have been focused enough. Or the connection was too weak.'

I couldn't care less what the odd word meant. I was too disappointed that whatever had just communicated with us wasn't Elliot. I glanced across the table for a sign of hope from Esther, but the psychic had her hand still pressed against her bosom, eyes closed, face creased like she was in anguished prayer.

'Maybe his spelling is a little rusty?' offered Ash sincerely. 'You know, with him being out of practise for so long.'

'Ask it it's name,' prompted Matt. His umber eyes, glinting in the candlelight, were intense now. A boldness had possessed the muscular Greek, but his chest, rising and falling anxiously beneath his shirt, betrayed the apparent bravery.

'What's your name?' Giles called out.

Once again, we stared at the board, waiting. And once again the planchette started to move:

M

It squeaked across the board.

O

A flash of lightning lit the alphabet electric blue.

U

You could hear Carrie scribbling as she wrote down the letters once again.

S

More thunder rumbled beyond the window, but farther away this time, weaker.

E

The planchette, along with Giles and Annie's hands, came to a stop.

Carrie slid the piece of paper into the middle of the table, frowning. 'MOUSE?'

Ash drew in an abrupt breath, making Cottonball yap and the rest of us jump. 'Oh my God, a mouse ghost. How cute!'

There was a violent clatter as the Ouija board suddenly flew off the table, taking the planchette and half a dozen tealights with it. Everyone jumped back from the table, letting out shrieks and gasps. The board had hit Giles in the chest, folded and then landed on his lap. But worse, he was now staring at his groin with a look of terror. One of the tealights, still alight with flame, was about to burn through his trousers and scorch his nethers. He swiped the tealight away, patting at the area to extinguish any remaining flames.

'There's nothing cute about that,' said Matt, his eyes darting around the darkness expecting further attack.

'I think we should bring this to an end,' said Giles, his face flushed, sweat breaking out near his temples. The ordinarily self-possessed leader of *Pluckley Ghost Hunters* was perturbed. Had we experienced activity even he had never witnessed?

'No!' cried Esther imploringly. 'We must make sure the spirit is at rest first. We can't leave it this angry!'

'No way,' said Giles. 'I'm running a responsible company here, Esther. The safety of the guests comes first. I won't put anyone at risk of getting hurt.'

'Flaming heck, Giles. After what we've just seen?' Norman had stepped out of the shadows, the camcorder lowered to his large belly. 'I don't fancy going to sleep tonight with that thing crashing about the place.'

'Nope,' said Giles firmly.

Norman shook his head. Esther didn't argue as Giles brushed off his knees and checked the Ouija board for signs of damage. However, I noticed worryingly, the look on her face said she believed Giles' decision would not bode well for all concerned.

The sound of chairs scraping the parquet flooring followed, everyone getting out of their seats. The guests departed the table while the ghost hunters remained to pack up their equipment. Kat dashed up behind me and Will. She grabbed my arm and I spun around, halting to a stop.

'Tell me I did *not* just see that,' she said.

'Oh, you saw it,' said Will.

'This place is cursed.'

Will gave her what could have, under the wrong circumstances, be perceived as a derisive snort. 'Sounding a bit gullible, aren't you, love?'

Kat's hand went to her hip faster than she'd legged it out of the first ghost hunt and her mouth became wider than a blow-up doll's. 'Excuse me, but I'll have you know that I was the victim of a very traumatising prank that has left me with a delicate disposition to this day.'

Will sniggered as he pulled a lighter and cigarettes out of his pocket. 'Delicate? Right.'

'What's that supposed to mean?'

Will returned a challenging but playful wink. 'I'm a writer. We're obnoxious bastards by nature. What's your excuse?'

Kat, not expecting this retort, looked at me for support. But, feeling very nauseous suddenly, I was too preoccupied with eyeing up the exit, considering a quick getaway to the nearest bathroom.

A hand went to Kat's other hip and she adopted a combative tone. 'So you're saying it was a stunt?'

Will gave a perfunctory shrug. 'I've seen more elaborate tricks pulled off by less skilled groups.'

'The ghost was running across the ceiling!'

'*Someone* was running across the ceiling. Never underestimate the power of illusion. There are other guests staying in this place. Who's to say they're not plants?'

Kat looked over her shoulder at the ghost hunters, thoughtful as she considered this.

'Think outside the box. And never take anything for granted in this game,' said Will sagely, before pinching a cigarette between his lips and sauntering away.

'Smart arse,' said Kat, watching him go. But I sensed more admiration than animosity behind her words.

'Do you think Esther's OK?' I said, spotting the psychic looking uncharacteristically troubled as she gathered her belongings. 'She didn't look well back there.'

'Serves her right for helping to bring the cursed thing through,' said Kat, her feathers ruffled. 'And I need a drink.'

I pinched her sleeve as she started for the exit. '*Now* do you believe Esther is the real deal?'

Kat looked conflicted, but just let out a frustrated sigh and walked away.

I snatched a glance at Esther again. I didn't care what Will thought about the seance. He was wrong about this one. Hadn't he seen Esther's disturbing reaction? Couldn't he at least give her, the woman he found so fascinating, a concession if not the ghost hunters? I knew what we'd just witnessed was no stunt. It had got not only the lead investigator of *Pluckley Ghost Hunters* worried, but a woman who spoke to the dead the way other people speak to their neighbours looking like she was about to run out of the place.

Esther was heading hastily towards the exit, the patchwork handbag swinging on her shoulder. I rushed over.

'Are you alright?'

She started at my hand touching her arm, but then became relieved when she saw it was me. If her face wasn't painted so colourfully I would have seen how white it was. 'Oh, Quentin. I'm afraid this evening feels like a terrible mistake'

'What happened back there?'

She shook her head gravely. 'He shouldn't have stopped the seance like that. A dark energy has been unleashed. This isn't just unfinished business. This is something looking for answers. And it won't rest until it's got them.' She glanced about the large room, gripping her handbag strap tightly. 'I knew there was something unsettled in this place. Oh, the things that must have taken place under this roof.'

'Can't you do something about it?'

'It will take more than little me to ward that thing off. The entire contents of an apothecary would have a job shifting it. I'm going back to my room to do what I can with the little I've brought with me.' Her green eyes were filled with worry as she warned, 'But be careful, Quentin. Things are about to get very turbulent around this place. And don't forget that you have the gift.'

The last words weren't a comfort, they were a warning. With an almost sympathetic wilt of her lips, she rushed off in the same direction as the others.

Later, on our way upstairs to bed, I was still mulling over what she had said. *A dark energy has been unleashed.* It sounded so ominous. *Things are about to get very turbulent around this place.* Like things weren't already unsettled enough. And that sympathetic stare, like she felt sorry for what was about to happen to me.

I shivered rounding the banister, as if I'd just walked through a spot of refrigerated air. I stopped and looked about me. A draught or the presence from an unseen dimension? Who knew. But what I did know was that for the first time since arriving at the manor I didn't just feel scared. I felt worried. Worried for my safety.

# - CHAPTER NINE -

# *The Nightmare*

IT'S ONLY A *faint tapping noise at first, so I ignore it and roll over. But then it gets louder, sharper, like hail hitting glass. I lift my head off the pillow and squint through sleepy eyes. Moonlight bathes the sheets of the bed in blue light. It's another second before the sound hits my ears again. And this time I see what causes it, see the stone as it hits the pane of the window.*

*I climb out of bed, cross the bare floorboards and pull back the curtain. Hilderley Manor's front grounds with its gravel driveway and manicured stretches of lawn is barely visible in the moonlight. But it's illuminated enough to see the shadowed figure standing a few feet away from the parking area, staring up at me.*

*I strain my eyes, trying to see anything identifiable, a face, gender, clothing. But the figure is a black silhouette as it remains ominously still, watching. Hair rises on my nape and arms when I hear a disembodied voice come from behind me. My name being whispered.*

*Quentin ...*

*Slowly, I turn around and peer through the darkness at the door. The male voice calls out again, the same shiver-inducing whisper.*

*Quentin ...*

*It's captivating, enticing, beckoning, a request for me to follow it.*

And despite the fear cementing my legs to the floorboards, I force them towards the door, answering its call.

I step out into the corridor. In the pale light flooding in from a far off window I can see the wet footprints trailing down the carpet runner. As I walk, I stare down at them. Are they the footprints of someone fresh out of a bath? I squint for a better look, noticing something isn't right. It isn't water that made them. It's a thicker substance I'm looking at, darker, shinier, with smears and splodges. It's blood.

They lead me to the staircase. I halt at the top, listening out for the voice. I start when it comes out of the darkness in the hallway, louder this time, enchanting, seducing.

Quentin ...

I begin down the stairs, avoiding the bloody footprints that continue down each step. Midway down I see the front door is wide open, casting blue light across the hallway's stone flooring. When I reach the bottom, I hesitate. Cold air from the open door blows in and nips at my exposed toes. I can't see much beyond the door, but I know the silhouetted figure is still out there, waiting.

Quentin ...

I carry on walking, my heart racing now, my shoulders tightening, breath bursting in and out. Why am I so afraid? What am I expecting to find?

I reach the door and step outside. The person stands in the same spot I saw from the window, twelve feet or so from my position at the doorstep. But this time they have their back to me.

'Hello?' I say.

I'm startled when a crack of thunder rips through the calm sky, followed by a lightning bolt that illuminates the figure for a split second. In this momentary flash I catch enough detail to discern I am looking at a young man, dressed in pyjamas, no socks covering his bare feet.

*'Excuse me?' I call again.*

*No answer.*

*But then his head slowly begins to turn …*

*I'm expecting a normal face, but a normal face is nowhere near what I'm about to see. Another flash of lightning illuminates the head and shoulders as he continues to turn. It's the odd colour at first, dark, almost black, where skin should be. Then, as he looks at me, there's another flash of light. And I see that he isn't looking at me because he doesn't have eyes to look at me with. He doesn't even have a face, just a gaping black hole where it should be, muscle, tissue and brain gone, the way you'd hack the flesh out of a Halloween pumpkin.*

*Every part of me is now frozen with fear. The only part that works is my mouth, which opens to let out a blood-curdling scream …*

I opened my eyes to find I was standing on the driveway of Hilderley Manor, my bare feet digging painfully into sharp gravel. But it wasn't just shoes I was missing. I wasn't wearing any trousers either. Or a shirt. I wasn't even wearing my specs. If it wasn't for the Super Mario boxer shorts I'd have been exposing my arse in all its pale-cheeked glory to anyone who might have been around to see it.

Nobody was. I was completely alone out here in the dead of night, the manor grounds looking like the exterior set on the shoot of a horror flick, moonlight gilding the spiked tips of the huge gate, fog swathing the building in a misty blanket.

With the night surrounding me, pitch black and horribly cold, I hugged my shivering torso and collected my wits. How long had I been out here? Some time, most likely, since the cold had seeped into my bones and frozen my jaw shut. How had I got here? The last thing I remembered was falling asleep. Had I sleepwalked? Was I dreaming? I pinched my arm to check, wincing when I felt very real pain there.

But then slowly, surely, the memory of the dream came back to me. A bad dream. A nightmare. I was woken by a tapping noise on the window, there were bloody footprints on the runner in the corridor, on the staircase. A young man in pyjamas stood in this very spot, he turned his head and ...

The trees shook suddenly, making me start. I peered up and saw clouds scudding through a chink in one of the canopies like grey smoke on a creeping wind, a couple of bats swooping in and out of the twisted branches. They weren't the only nocturnal creatures out tonight judging by other noises coming out of the darkness. A twig snapped. Tiny feet skittered through the undergrowth. An owl somewhere high up emitted its famous tu-whit tu-whoo call. The gate rattled briefly, followed by a deathly howl that rent the chill night air. Was it ... no, it couldn't be ... the demon dog from the stories Annie was telling us?

Now I was really worried. I cast the house a nervous glance over my shoulder. The front door was ajar, the dark hallway beckoning me back to safety. Upstairs, a light in one of the windows came on. A figure moved across the room unsteadily. They stopped, towel drying their hair, before approaching the window and looking down where I stood. It took a moment, but it looked like they spotted me. Then they were gone, vanishing out of sight.

I started back inside, treading carefully to avoid getting gravel stuck in my feet. Fear subsided the moment the door clicked shut, its cold, hard surface pressing against my back. I stayed there for a moment, listening to the steady tick of a grandfather clock hidden somewhere in the gloom. The quiet was interrupted by a light coming on, followed by hurried footfall on the staircase.

Will had appeared in bedclothes, worry etched on his face.

From the look of his wet hair and flushed cheeks, it was obvious he'd just got out of the shower, that it had been him towel drying his hair in the window. But his rescue attempt, if that had been his mission, wasn't going to be as graceful as he might have hoped. Coming off the last step of the staircase, he struck his foot on the hallway's stone floor, which made him buckle at the knees and release a cry that sounded similar to a baby elephant's trumpet.

'Jesus — effin — OW!'

The cry reverberated through the hallway, and probably all the way to the top floor corridor. Through blurry eyes I watched him limp towards me, hopping as he tried to nurse his big toe, the look of worry now a twisted grimace. I'd have had more sympathy if it hadn't become abundantly clear the second he came within inches what had caused the mishap. The alcohol on his breath was so strong it would have ignited had a match been held to it. Will was drunk for a second night in a row. He sounded in pain when he spoke.

'What are you doing outside in your undies, you muppet? You'll catch a death.'

'I ... don't know,' I faltered.

He'd fetched a thick blanket, which he was now swathing around my chilled shoulders. 'Let's get you upstairs before you freeze your balls off.' There was a slur in there somewhere, and a wince.

Will made a lot of fuss about his rapidly swelling toe — 'I think I chipped the nail.' 'It'll bruise for sure.' 'I might have broken a bone.' — as he escorted me up the staircase and along the first floor corridor. I didn't ask questions when we reached the open door of *his* room, not mine, and he shoved me inside. Getting out of the cold had warmed me up considerably, but I was still shivering like a hound that had been chained outdoors overnight as the door closed and Will hauled me over to the fourposter. He pushed me down onto the edge of the mattress, checking me over attentively. Well, as attentively as he could through the heavy eyes of his intoxication.

'I wish you'd stop creeping around in the middle of the night like a blimming hedgehog,' he said. 'That's the second time you've given me a fright.'

'I must have sleepwalked.' My voice was soft, distant.

'Do you do that often?'

'No, never.'

'First time for everything, I s'pose.'

As if he hadn't had enough to drink, he seized hold of a half-empty wine bottle on the bedside table and began swigging its contents. Then he started clearing debris off the bed. Socks, checkered boxer shorts and a damp towel flew into a pile of other clothes on the floor. More wine gurgled down his throat. 'I thought you were someone who'd escaped from the mental asylum up the road for a moment,' he said, chuckling drunkenly.

I blinked up at him, shivering, my jaw slowly thawing. 'There's a mental asylum up the road?'

'Whittingham Hospital. Victorian place abandoned years ago.' Spotting my bewilderment, he added, 'Well it doesn't have to be open for its patients to be wandering about in the middle of the night if this place is anything to go by, does it?'

I was still pondering that comforting thought as he hobbled over to a writing bureau in the corner and pulled out a chair. He dragged it over to the window, nudged open the latch with his elbow and dropped into the chair with a disgruntled sigh. He set the bottle on the floor and once again inspected his stubbed toe. 'Yup, definitely chipped the nail. Took me a year to grow that bugger back after my football accident, too.' Shaking his head, he reached for a packet of cigarettes, flipped the lid, pulled one out with his mouth and lit up. He flashed me a crooked smile. 'Tell on me and I'll have to kill you.'

Still in a daze from finding myself outside one moment, in a stranger's room the next, the last thing on my mind was snitching on him to Mrs Brown for smoking in his room. In fact, for the first time in my life I felt like having a cigarette myself.

I regarded Will in his t-shirt and boxer shorts as he tried to direct plumes of smoke out of the crack in the window, the contours of his face illuminated by the amber glow of the bedside lamp. Wet strands of hair were tucked behind his ears, with a few stray ones cascading over his forehead. The sweet, fresh scent of his showered skin carried on the breeze floating into the room, mixing with the smoke and alcohol. There was no denying in that moment I felt a strong attraction to this dangerously handsome man who had rescued me from the cold. It was hard not to imagine his arms wrapping around me, warming me further. Hard not to imagine sinking into the scent of him …

'Earth to Strange.' Will waved a hand in front of my eyes, snapping me out of the fantasy.

I blinked, swallowed, shivered.

'Still cold?' he asked.

I nodded.

He got to his feet. But the alcohol must have rushed to his head because he suddenly had the look of someone who was either about to pass out or topple over. He stumbled forward, and for a second it looked like he was going to fall on top of me. I was quick, jumping to my feet to steady him. The blanket slipped off my shoulders, landing near the ignited cigarette Will had clumsily let slip from his fingers as he struggled to stay upright. Tiptoeing around it, I managed to snatch it up in time, flicking it out the window before I had my own injury to worry about. It was a good job I did, too, because at that very moment Will gripped me by the arm and pulled me down onto the bed.

We landed on the mattress with a bounce, Will underneath, me splayed on top of him. Our faces were suddenly inches apart.

'How cosy,' he said with a wink.

Oh, blooming hell.

I attempted to push myself up, wriggle free, find my feet. But the writer had other ideas, keeping me locked in a tight embrace. 'Will, come on,' I pleaded. 'Let me up.'

'Aww, what's up? You don't like cuddles?'

His surprisingly strong arms squeezed me tighter. I tried to break free. But he was having none of it. Giggling mischievously, he rolled over, taking me with him, until we'd switched positions and it was him who was now on top of me. To make matters worse, I could feel his thighs, and perhaps more, pressing against my underwear. I froze as he scrutinised my face through heavy lids.

'Quite a handsome fella under the glasses, aren't ya?'

Heat flooded my cheeks. I persisted with a gulp, 'Will, you're kind of heavy.'

He released some of the weight. 'Better?'

'Yes, but what the hell are you doing?'

Sleepily, he thought about it. Then, with a shrug, said, 'Carpe diem.'

Oh good Lord.

'Will, you're drunk.'

'Yup.'

'You'll regret this tomorrow.'

'Probably.'

Pinned beneath him, I had no other option than to wait and see whatever was about to happen next. When he starting stroking

151

my hair, I wondered once again if I hadn't woken on that gravel driveway, that I was, in fact, very much still dreaming.

'I like you, Quentin. There's an innocence about you. I feel … safe around you, like I can trust you. I don't know why, I don't even know you. It's weird. You're weird.' Quickly, he added, 'In a good way, I mean.'

I blinked at the fuzzy outline of his face. Even without glasses he was ridiculously good looking. Too good looking to be attracted to me. I'm so unappealing I make the sexiest underwear look like a joke. I'm so plain I could be standing in a room entirely alone and I'd still blend in with the decor. If he even was attracted to me, that is. He was straight, wasn't he? I'd seen the way his eyes had roved suggestively over Kat when she wasn't looking.

But straight men didn't stroke another man's hair. They didn't stare lovingly into their eyes. They didn't — oh dear God — lean in to kiss me.

Will's lips met mine, warm and soft. When the bristles on his chin brushed my skin there wasn't a nerve ending in my body that didn't feel it. He tasted sweet, with a bitter hint of tobacco. And the kiss felt more than good, filling a hunger that had tormented me for years. Heat flooded my body, and other areas, melting the last remnants of cold. A voice in my head spoke to me. Yes, it said, life really is too short to resist this, to deny yourself the things your body craves the most. And with its permission I sank completely into the sensation.

A buzzing noise broke the spell. Will pulled away and glanced over his shoulder at the bedside table. The bulb inside the lamp was flickering on and off, struggling to stay alight. With a metallic *tink* is stopped blinking and became illuminated once more. 'Frigging ghosts,' he muttered.

The lamp was the last thing on my mind in that moment,

though. A feeling was overtaking me, an irresistible urge, a latent desire that had been reignited. With my palms I pushed Will up so he was in the straddling position. Then I gripped the hem of his t-shirt and began yanking it up his torso. Taken aback, he released a nervous giggle. 'Steady there, squire!'

But it was as if I had been possessed. Possessed by a horny devil. He'd had a taste, he wanted more, and he was intent on getting it. Will lifted his arms as the shirt reached his underarms, allowing me to pull it over his head and toss it with the other clothes piled beside the bed.

I ogled his naked torso in the atmospheric light, the sprinkling of wiry hairs growing in the middle of his chest, the nipples dark and erect. His olive skin was silky and flawless. With a sexual assertiveness I didn't know I had I pushed him onto the pillow, and, as he was reclining backwards, climbed on top of him, slipping between his legs. The tables had turned. Wide-eyed, looking up at me, Will gulped the words, 'Wasn't expecting that.'

I was about to go in for another kiss when the lamp began to flicker on and off again, distracting me. 'Why's it doing that?' I whispered.

'Faulty wiring?' Will offered.

The bulb started to flicker faster. It buzzed and flashed until there was a loud pop and an explosion of breaking glass. Will and I broke apart, scrambling to the other side of the bed to avoid flying glass. Then there was silence, punctuated only by the sound of our startled breaths. But not for long …

Another noise came from the shadows. Movement on the floorboards. Broken shards skittered across the floor, as if accidentally kicked by an unseen foot. One of the boards creaked. More silence. Was that breathing I could hear? The air became cold. Colder. Mist came out of my mouth. Then I could feel myself getting warmer. The thing, whatever the hell it was, was moving away. And then it was gone.

Other than moonlight glinting off shards of shattered bulb on the bedside table, the room was pitch dark. I glanced around, still wary of anything lurking in the shadows. Will was trying to see through the gloom too, squinting at the lamp in disbelief. But he was so drunk he'd probably forget about all of this come morning. I wouldn't, though.

Shame hit me. What was I thinking behaving like that? Sure, people get off with strangers all the time, do regrettable things while driven by irresistible impulses. But I'm not your average person. I'm Quentin Strange. I make celibacy an art form. Did I have to behave like such a ... man slut.

The whole thing, just like this sodding cursed room, felt wrong. I had to escape while I still had some dignity left. I clambered off the bed, cursing when I trod on one of Will's boots. I'd almost reached the door when a faraway *boom* and *crack* broke the silence.

I froze. Stopped there in front of a Georgian Chippendale Will's motorbike helmet was sitting on, my heart, already accelerating at a runaway rate, kicking into overdrive.

'Fireworks?' Will said stupidly.

I shook my head. 'A gunshot.'

In response to this Will scrambled over the covers, but misjudging the location of the edge of the bed in the darkness, he pitched forward and crashed to the floor with a bone-crunching thud.

'Fuck — OW!' he yelped, before I saw his silhouette rise from the floor. He limped to the window and peered out at the driveway where he must have thought the noise had sounded from.

'It came from the back of the building,' I said.

'Turn the light on.'

I flicked a switch and sconces dotted around the walls lit the room. Will rummaged through the pile of clothes until he found his t-shirt. He wrestled it on as he rushed around the bed, searching for his shoes. The wounded toe appeared to have miraculously healed, and even the drunkenness looked like it was dissipating, the gunshot shocking him into panic mode.

'I'll go and investigate,' he said, knotting the lace of his boot. He snatched his phone off a chest of drawers.

'Shouldn't we find someone instead? That bloke who stays in the house overnight to keep watch on the guests. What's his name? Rufus?'

'Of course I'm going to do that. Do you think I'm stupid enough to put myself at risk? And I'll call the police too if I have to. A lot of folks on rural land have guns, but robberies are common too.'

A robbery to add to a dark spirit being let loose on the place? God was having fun with us this evening.

Will eased the door open, checking the corridor for sounds before giving me a nod and slipping out. He looked comical in just boxer shorts wearing the boots, but modesty isn't high on your priorities when you're off to investigate a potential crime being committed.

Alone, I felt vulnerable. Useless. I needed to act. Through the window I could see land stretching far into the distance. For the first time I felt frightened not by Hilderley Manor's ghosts, but by the remoteness of our location. You're vulnerable in a remote place, where people can't hear your cries for help. No one knows that more than me. I had been here before. On a lake. And I hadn't acted then. Well, not this time.

I opened the door and followed Will out into the corridor. He was nowhere in sight. The corridor was empty, lit by sconces lining the walls. One of them flickered on and off. A cool breeze coming from the direction of the staircase told me Will had reached the front door. But I heard no voices. No commotion.

The door to the room across from me was open, the lights off inside, a window that overlooked the rear of the manor visible. I dashed inside, rushed over to the window and looked out at the garden. Without my specs I had to squint at first, but lights dotted on either side of the gravel path guided my eyes to the caretaker's cottage. Stan Crouch was standing at the entrance, his face illuminated by two lanterns hanging over the stable door. And in his hand he was holding a shotgun.

I watched him for a moment. Watched the shifty eyes redolent of a man with much to hide flit around the garden. Stunned by what I was looking at, I almost didn't see the other people descending the steps down to the courtyard. Will had found Rufus and it looked like they were on their way to ask Stan if he knew where the gunshot might have come from.

Stan, spotting them approaching, went back inside the cottage. A second later he was back, minus the weapon. He waved at the two men. Waved. A gesture that was noticeably out of character for a man who had been acting like the guests were pests he'd like to stamp out up until now. I'm no psychologist, but I understand enough about human behaviour to know when someone is putting on an act to hide their guilt.

Will was safe at least. But something else was now troubling my mind. I leaned closer to the window, the better to read the caretaker's face. My breath misted the cool glass. 'Just what are you up to?' I whispered.

# - CHAPTER TEN -

# *The Face in the Cellar*

*I'M JUST ABOUT to lose the towel and step in the shower when there's a knock on the bathroom door. I open it to find Will standing there in t-shirt and chequered boxer shorts, hair tousled like he's just rolled out of bed, eyes sober as they stare intently at mine. There's something else in that stare, I notice. A devilish glint. When he doesn't speak, I blink.*

*'Erm, hello?'*

*He just smirks. The cocky gesture makes me feel a little nervous. I swallow.*

*Then it's all so fast. He lunges forward and grabs me, kicking the door shut with his foot. One hand cups my face as I find myself walking backwards, my bare feet slipping on the moist floor tiles. My naked back meets the cold, perspiring tiles on the wall.*

*'Will, what the —'*

*My words are cut off by his mouth diving in to silence them. The kiss is firm, purposeful, intense. A release. My body relents to the madness of the situation, to Will's determination to get what he wants. That thing being me.*

*His hands move from my face to my chest, the tips of his fingers raking my skin. Before long they're near my navel, and deft fingers are untying the knot in the towel. The modesty covering piece of fabric slips away, pooling at my feet.*

*Will's hips press into mine as the kiss becomes firmer, his warm, wet tongue exploring my mouth. When his lips pull away I'm surprised to feel my mouth trying to find them again, begging for more. They work their way southward, short breaths heavy, oh so heavy, against my neck.*

*In the intoxication of my arousal, I see how much I have craved and yet resisted this for so long. But now that it's here, my body doesn't fight it, surrendering completely.*

*Will grips my shoulder and spins me around. My hands slap against the wall. I stand there with my cheek pressed against the cold tile, my fingers splayed, blood pumping through my veins, my breath heavy. I know Will is removing his underwear, and I'm ready ...*

'Quentin Strange!'

My eyes flipped open at the shrill voice exclaiming my name. Kat, draped in a bathrobe, her hair coiled in a towel like an ice cream whip, blurred into focus at the foot of the bed. But her eyes weren't fixed on me, they were fixed on my groin, and her mouth was wide in a look of horror. Following her gaze, it became clear why: my penis was currently standing to attention, creating a teepee in the bed covers.

My hand shot beneath the duvet and I scooted up to the headboard, pulling the covers with me, a vain attempt to preserve any modesty I had left. But it was too late. The sinking feeling in my gut told me I'd be struggling to live this moment down for a very long time to come.

My back against the headboard, the covers bunched to my chin, I waited, unblinking, for further reproach from my startled bedfellow. I knew my face was beetroot red from mortification. I'd also been called by my full name, a moniker I hadn't heard since I was waist height. And it had brought about the same fear it had struck in me then.

But no punishment was forthcoming. Instead Kat shuffled on the spot, her legs unsure which direction her brain wanted to take. Finally she made up her mind and hastened over to her side of the bed. She knelt down in front of her suitcase and began stowing away the toiletries clutched against her chest.

The awkwardness that followed was palpable. I wished a great hole would open in the floor and swallow me up. I trawled my brain for something, anything, that might break the tension. But how do you respond to your most intimate appendage being exposed in its most explicit state? Apologise? Make a joke about it? *That's surely the first time a gay guy has been that happy to see you. Has to be a compliment, right?* Kat broke the ice first.

'I'll pretend I didn't see that.'

In a pointless attempt to save face, I replied, 'We are staying in a shared room.'

'Yes, well, that won't be happening again.'

She rose from the floor, carried a selection of clothes over to the changing screen and slipped behind it. The bathrobe fell over the top a second later.

'I want you to take some exterior shots of the manor today,' she said. 'Explore the rest of the building, too. See if there's anything of interest you can find to shoot. I found out there's access to the roof terrace. Maybe there's something up there. There's probably a cellar, too. Look for things particularly unusual or creepy. Especially creepy. Shouldn't be hard in this godforsaken place.'

'Does Mr Mendy usually request this many photos for an article?' I asked the dark oak latticework of the changing screen, which was giving away Kat's movements but retaining her modesty.

'You collect a ton of images to get a handful you can use. It's just the nature of the editing process. Plus, the reference material will help me with my writeup.'

Kat reemerged in tight pants, a white shirt and a velvety maroon blazer, the towel still coiled atop her head. She eyed me heedfully as she grabbed her boots from where she'd left them at the foot of the bed and slipped them on. But there was no danger of her finding me in any more compromising positions. The bed covers remained clenched to my chest, covering my now very deflated privates.

'What will you be doing this morning?' I asked.

She unravelled the towel and her ordinarily silky locks fell to her shoulders like damp rat tails. 'I'm interviewing the location researcher, Annie, about the history of Hilderley Manor. I thought over what you said about scaring the crap out of the reader. Hopefully there's a dark legend surrounding the place I can elaborate on. Something grizzly to really put the shivers up the readers.' Kat clutched her chest and made a high-pitched noise of excitement. Her eyes twinkled dreamily. 'Who'd have thought sweet little me would have such a flair for this horror gig? I'm totally channelling Anne Rice and Shirley Jackson right now. Providing those creepy ghosts stay well away from me, that is.' She used the towel to squeeze out the remaining moisture from her hair, looking smitten with her mental fantasy.

I didn't quite remember having *that* conversation. Nor would I have used the adjective 'sweet' and Kat in the same sentence. Nor was I sure that writing an article for a magazine distributed by the local rag put you in the echelons of the literary horror genre. Nor was I willing to burst her self-aggrandising bubble.

I said nothing as I watched her carry a hairdryer and curling tongs over to the dresser. In half an hour she'd transformed her locks into something straight out of a hair product commercial. Next was makeup, which appeared to be more of an art than a routine, and one at which she was very skilled. Looking pleased with the final result, she grabbed her handbag and left to join the others for breakfast, leaving me alone in the same position on the bed. It was so much simpler being the male of the species, I thought vaguely, erection mishaps or not.

Autumn rays shone through the misted panes of the window. Hot water gurgled through the radiator pipes. The smell of fried food and freshly-brewed coffee drifted in through the door. Others were up and about in the building. But along with having no appetite, I felt reluctant to go downstairs and join them. Join *someone.*

Erotic dreams. It was so ... adolescent. And even worse after what had happened last night. Kissing a straight man I'd known barely forty eight hours. Will might have looked like an Adonis straight out of the pages of a fashion mag, but with behaviour like this I was on a fast track to becoming a brazen hussy, or whatever the male equivalent of one of those is.

At least, I assumed Will was straight. That was only because of his straightforward mien, the rugged edge he exuded, that slight kink in his nose that indicated he'd had a few punch ups in his youth (and with that candid tongue was it any wonder?) — and the best looking ones are usually straight. But I couldn't deny it: men just didn't kiss other men on the lips unless they were a little bit bent. Was my gaydar off-kilter after so many years of being out of use? Did he like women *and* men? I should have asked Kat what she thought, especially when she'd been so spot on guessing my 'preferences.'

On the plus side, depending how I looked at it, at least normal dream function had returned, telling me I didn't need to make an immediate appointment with a neurologist. There was last night's nightmare. Not the most pleasant of visions, but the first dream I'd had in weeks that wasn't a memory about Elliot. And the naughty dream I had just woken from. That certainly wasn't a memory from my past. Was it forgoing the pills that had caused it to return? Nah. Too soon. But it would explain the return of my libido. Come to think of it, I hadn't had as many of those crippling headaches. Or did it have something to do with the house itself?

A cold shower and brush-up banished these questions, and quarter of an hour later I was joining Kat in the dining hall, the DSLR around my neck, *Ethereal* tucked under my arm. The weather had taken a turn for the worse and in fear of getting the camera wet taking the exterior shots Kat had requested, I planned on reading some more in the sitting room until the rain passed. I started having cold showers not long after Elliot's death, remembering what he'd told me about cold water's benefits. The showers increased my emotional resilience and improved my immune response. And the one I'd just had had brought about a lift in my mood, evident by the increased spring in my step and renewed appetite. Unfortunately, all that was dampened the second I spotted Will sitting at the table over Kat's shoulder.

Affability, it seemed, was not on the breakfast menu this morning. Will, avoiding my gaze, got out of his chair and fled from the room like a man in a very deliberate hurry. He even abandoned his buttered crumpets.

I sat down across from Kat, staring over my shoulder as the hem of the grey trench-coat billowed out of sight.

'Do you think I'm getting smoker's lines?'

'What?' I said, distant, listening to Will's footsteps tapering through the hallway. I turned back to the table and saw Kat staring into a hand mirror, stroking the outer edges of her lips with a frown.

She rolled her eyes and dropped the mirror in her handbag. 'Never mind.'

Coffee was poured and the catering staff wheeled trolleys of food from table to table. But my appetite had vanished as fast as Will had left the room. I sipped black coffee, grabbed an apple and took off for the sitting room with *Ethereal*. But the cosy retreat I had stumbled upon yesterday wasn't to offer the solitude I hoped it would. Someone was in there. And there was a problem.

Mrs Brown was sitting on one of the plush sofas, sniffling into a handkerchief, her face red and blotchy. She jumped to her feet when she saw me and rushed to where a trolley full of cleaning products was standing in front of a handsome side table. With her head dipped low she began wheeling the trolley towards me, heading for the door. 'Heavens, this hay fever will be the death of me,' she said with a snuffly chuckle.

Hay fever in October? The tactic was fooling no one. I blocked the doorway before she had chance to make her escape. 'You've been crying. What's the matter?'

Her wide, bloodshot eyes wandered sheepishly to mine. For a moment it looked like she was going to say something, but then her eyes returned to the floor and whatever had been about to leave her mouth remained unspoken.

'Is it Mr Crouch?' I guessed. 'I heard you two arguing yesterday. The window was open.'

I didn't expect the reaction that followed. Mrs Brown's shoulders curled forward like an autumn leaf and strangled whimpers burst forth from her chest. Concerned, I took hold of her arm and guided her back to the sofa. She looked as vulnerable as a small child as she lowered herself onto the chintz upholstery. I sat down beside her, placing the apple and *Ethereal* near my feet.

'I'm so sorry,' Mrs Brown blubbered, pulling a handkerchief from her apron and blotting her tears. A sound like air being let out of a balloon followed as she blew her nose. 'It's just ... oh, it's awful.'

I touched her shoulder. 'What's awful?'

'Poor Stan. I was hoping it was just my worry. But I can't deny it anymore, not after these last few days.' She burst into anguished sobs once again.

I gave her a second to calm down before I asked, 'What is it, Mrs Brown? What's wrong with Stan?'

'It's Alzheimer's,' she sniffed. 'My late husband, Roy, suffered the same. Even if it was his bad heart that took him in the end. I know what it looks like when someone's mind is failing them. It's the worst fate. For those suffering from it and those who have to watch.' She stroked the wedding band on her finger mournfully.

Dementia? That's what had turned Mr Crouch into a cane-wielding grouch who crept around the manor in the middle of the night? 'Are you sure?' I asked.

Mrs Brown nodded vehemently. 'At first we noticed he was acting a bit odd — that's me and the lads and lasses that make up the cleaning and catering staff. He was keeping to himself more, refusing to join us for dinner, preferring to eat in his cottage alone. Then he started getting angry, snapping at people for no apparent reason. Like the day a couple of the lads from the kitchen wanted a game of football in the garden. They weren't out there five minutes before he came out shaking his fist and calling them names I could never repeat. He's never done anything like that before. And he knows they'd never do anything to ruin the garden, decent lads they are. They know that garden is his pride and joy. Way he hollered at them, though, you'd think they'd done it to be spiteful. When he started snapping at me I knew something was really wrong. We've always got on well Stan and me. We're friends. Well, we were …'

This time when Mrs Brown burst into tears, I sat and contemplated her theory. A mental disorder did make sense the more I thought about it. Stan looked almost as old as Hilderley Manor itself, and I was certain most people exhibited some form of memory loss, personality change and impaired reasoning beyond a certain age. Not to mention his odd behaviour was more than consistent with someone losing control of their faculties. But there is always an exception to the rule. And there are many other things that make people antisocial and angry. Stress. Financial trouble. A bad case of the haemorrhoids …

'Couldn't Mr Crouch, in his own kind of way, be asking to be left alone in his final years?' I offered.

'No.' Mrs Brown was adamant. 'I cared for the elderly before coming to work for Mr Blackford at the manor. Even the most obnoxious, the ones with sore, creaky bones, who've had enough of life and take out the fact nature won't take its course sooner on everyone else want someone to be there for them in the end. Loneliness does more damage to people than any illness, Mr Strange. Believe me, I've seen it take the best of them.'

Yeah, wasn't I fast starting to realise that, I thought but didn't say.

'And I've been close to Stan for years now,' Mrs Brown went on. 'He might not be the friendliest of blokes, he has had a lonely life without a wife and children after all, but he's always been happy enough looking after the garden, joining in good-natured banter with the rest of the staff. Nothing like the man he's become.'

Mrs Brown dabbed at her face and wiped her nose. I stared with sympathy at a woman who was compassionate enough to be concerned over a fellow worker, a man whom she clearly considered a valued friend.

'Oh, just look at me. I'm a wreck,' she said, as if noticing for the first time that she'd been crying. 'But it keeps bringing up memories of Roy. It killed me watching him lose himself, lose every memory we'd ever shared. It comes on fast, and as it progresses they don't remember anything, not even the important things. That's how I knew for certain it was the Alzheimer's. Stan forgot about the anniversary. He never forgets that, talks about it for weeks beforehand.'

'The anniversary?'

Less tearful now, the little Scotswoman was stroking the loose strands of hair escaping her bun and adjusting the strings of her apron. 'The day the young lad left and never came back.'

'What young lad?'

'Joe, his name was. Joe Maguire. He was a young man Stan looked after decades ago, a sort of apprentice. Used to help him out with odd jobs around the garden. Stan's never said exactly how they met. He wasn't all there, this lad. What people used to call backward years ago. You know, retarded. Had a funny walk that people used to pick on him for. I think Stan took pity on him, took him under his wing as if he was his own son. From what he's told me, the lad didn't have any family. A family that cared enough to look after him, anyway.

'But one day he just left, never said where he was going or why. It broke Stan's heart it did. It was on the lad's birthday, too. Stan wondered if he'd got into the wrong crowd, what with him being easily led. There was a rotten character who lived here back then, young man named Billy. Actually related to the Blackfords, he was.

166

Distantly, though, I think. Had a different surname. The Blackfords are the family who have owned Hilderley Manor for the last few decades. One of the richest lot in the country they are. Billy felt he had special privileges, used to use it to his advantage to intimidate some of the other workers. There was a spot of trouble between him and Joe before the disappearance. But Stan never told me what it was about.

'Joe did return about a year after the disappearance, so nothing awful happened to him. A young lass saw him in the garden looking for Stan one day, but Stan was visiting a friend down south that weekend. If you ask me, I think the family had something to do with it. Wouldn't be the first time rich folk have paid someone to vanish when there's a spot of bother involving one of their own that could make them look bad. I think Stan knows that deep down. There's a bitterness in him that runs bone deep, and it's mainly directed at that lot, no matter how generous they've been keeping him on as caretaker all these decades. He's the sentimental sort underneath is Stan. He's celebrated the anniversary Joe left every year since. See the weeping cherry out there?'

Mrs Brown nodded at the window. I looked out and saw, midway down the garden, the tree I had seen yesterday morning. The one that stood where those pugnacious crows Will scared away had been causing a ruckus.

'Stan planted it as a shrine to the lad,' said Mrs Brown. 'Some have said it's a little over-sentimental, especially the name of it, but I suppose to Stan losing Joe was like losing a son. He's out there every autumn leading up to the anniversary, tending to it, sitting by it, loving the thing as if it were the lad himself. That's why I know Stan's not right upstairs. It's the anniversary today and he hasn't been near that tree in weeks.'

I stared thoughtfully at the drooping tree moving in the wind.

The hazy mental image of Mr Crouch sitting by it, longing for his friend to return, dissolved almost as quickly as it had formed. Mrs Brown's voice started me out of my reverie when she spoke again.

'Oh, how awful of me. Stan's not the sort to go around talking about his personal life. He confided in me because he trusts me. And I've just gone and broken that trust.' Her brow wrinkled ruefully. 'Then again, I suppose it won't matter soon, not when he … when he loses his mind for—'

And Mrs Brown was off again. I placed my palm over her tiny wedding ring adorned hand to comfort her. But my eyes were still directed at the window, looking at the caretaker's cottage now. And my mind was ticking away just like it had done last night when I was staring down at the garden from the upstairs window. Shouting at the caterers for playing football in the garden. Trying to scare me away from the house. Firing a shotgun in the middle of the night. You'd have thought there was something Stan was trying to protect.

'Mrs Brown, did you know Stan owns a shotgun?'

Mrs Brown stopped crying at once. She glanced up at me, the pale brow furrowed with worry lines. 'A shotgun? No, I didn't.' The concerned expression on her face relaxed a little. 'I suppose it's not that surprising. Landowners around here have shotguns to protect their land or shoot game. Why shouldn't Stan? And it's like a junk shop in that cottage of his, easy to guess he'd have something like that in there.' She caught the thoughtful look in my eye. 'Wh — you're not saying you think Stan could hurt someone, are you?'

I remembered Stan's threat. Remembered him hitting me with the cane. 'If it's true he isn't capable of reason anymore—'

'No.' Mrs Brown shook her head. 'Stan's cantankerous, he's a bit antisocial, but he'd never hurt someone. He took a vulnerable lad under his wing at a time when few others would. The rodents around the manor and the odd fowl are the only things he'd harm.' But as she said it the Scotswoman didn't look so certain anymore.

'Mrs Brown, if you ever feel Stan poses a danger to *anyone* at *any* time while I'm still here, promise you'll come and let me know?'

She looked conflicted as she tried to read my thoughts, but then accepted my request with a nod. I wish I could have told her that she could trust me, that I knew exactly how to relieve her anguish. But inside I felt as futile as the Scotswoman herself. I did the next best thing instead. I gave her hand a gentle squeeze of reassurance. At the same time that I was looking out of the window and feeling very suspicious.

* * * * *

I was still agonising over the conversation after leaving the sitting room and coming out into the hallway, which was carrying a draught as a handful of incoming guests hauled luggage out of the cold. I heard Mrs Brown's friendly Scottish trill as she rushed out of the corridor, still wiping her face to appear more presentable after the crying fit, jumping back into housekeeper mode. The sky now dry, I squeezed past the cluster of people blocking the door and made my way around the building to take those exterior shots Kat had requested.

But as I weaved through the rows of trimmed hedges, gravel crunching underfoot, the smell of decaying leaves drifting up my nose, my mind just wouldn't focus. The things Mrs Brown had told me about Stan Crouch niggled at my brain like a rodent trying to gnaw its way out of a cavity wall. Was the curmudgeon really suffering from a memory stealing illness as the tormented

Scotswoman feared? Did it explain his odd behaviour?

Pausing near the fountain, I peered at the bottom of the garden where the caretaker's cottage stood half hidden by thick foliage that seemed intent on swallowing it up. Perhaps Stan was in there now, spying on me from the shadows. The thought gave me a chill as I recalled his face at the kitchen window, and later, outside the cottage holding the shotgun. Surely not the behaviour of a sane human being ...

The weeping cherry swelled in the breeze. I thought about what the tree meant for the old man. *'Some have said it's a little over-sentimental,'* Mrs Brown had said. I imagined once again Stan sitting by it, mourning, perhaps waiting for Joe Maguire's return. There was nothing insane about that. I knew the pain of losing someone I cared about, had spent years longing for their return. It isn't the pain that's abnormal. It's the way people expect you not to feel it, as if you have the choice. And some of us need to be sad. It's the only way we can get others to see just how much pain we're in.

Refocusing on the job in hand, I turned around to appraise Hilderley Manor, debating how the huge building would best fit into a wide angled shot. The old house had a sanatorium feel to it in the bleak midmorning light. Its frontage displayed signs of neglect — creeping mildew, uncleaned windows, the decorative plants in the pots beneath them dry and lifeless — a far cry from how it's presented in the marketing leaflet, an exterior shot of it lit up at night through a blue filter to give it that haunted look. And the neglect was a stark contrast to the tended hedges and clean pathways of the garden. It was clear where Mr Crouch's priorities had lain in recent weeks.

I peered through the camera's viewfinder, switched to the wide angle setting to frame the perfect shot, lowered it again and was wiping a speck of rain off the lens ... when I spotted something that made my heart skip a beat. I continued to stare ahead, squinting at it through my specs. It was a mist, rising up from the leaf scattered ground at the top of the steps. And not an amorphous mist. It had a clearly defined shape. The shape of a human figure, standing there as if it were about to descend the steps. If it had done that my heart wouldn't have just skipped a beat, it would have jumped right out of my chest. But the misty figure didn't descend the steps. It stayed there, unmoving, shining with a soft, slightly wavering light. I blinked. It didn't disappear.

Still as a statue, I lifted the camera to my face, expecting the mist to still be there in the camera's viewfinder. But to my astonishment it had vanished, nowhere to be seen in the field of view behind the crosshair. I lowered the camera and discovered, to my surprise, that the misty figure was very much there again, standing, watching, wavering.

I lifted my specs, a crazy thought that they might be the cause of this unnerving manifestation. But the apparition remained as visible to my naked eye as it had done through my prescription lenses, albeit more blurred. A very unsettling feeling crept through my flesh and bones. My skin prickled as the hairs stood on end. For an indefinite time the space around me became intensely quiet and still, just the light patter of straggling drops of rain hitting the leaves, the rustle of surrounding trees.

Take a photo. The thought leapt into my head unbidden. So I did. With shaky hands, I took repeated snaps of the spot where the misty figure was visible one moment, invisible the next. And when I'd taken the final shot I looked up again to discover it had vanished. Unseen to my eyes as it had been to the camera.

Spooked, I glanced over my shoulder at the garden, expecting to find it lurking there. But only the trickling fountain stood there in the damp midday air. Steeling myself, I walked up the steps. I stopped at the top and waved my hand in the exact spot where the mist had stood, snatching it back when I felt the temperature was icy cold.

A frisson ran through me. As unnerving as this strange phenomena was, I was gripped by a hunger to know more about it. I began back towards the entrance of the house, intent on finding Kat, who I knew would be more than keen to hear about what I'd just seen, see what the camera might have captured. But I'd stepped only a few metres when a movement to my side made me halt. I looked down. There was a semicircular window near the ground, iron bars visible on the other side. I was looking at a cellar window. And as I continued to stare, another flash of movement came from behind the grimy glass.

Adrenaline coursed through me, both from excitement and fear. And there was another sensation. As if a magnet was pulling me, enticing me to investigate further. I had to go down there.

Back inside the manor, I crossed the hallway, now deserted, the DSLR swinging across my chest with each purposeful step, *Ethereal* tucked inside my blazer, the uneaten apple in my pocket. My stomach grumbled in protest, but I was too driven by the magnetic pull to stop and eat. The new arrivals must have been upstairs settling into their room; the only sound other than the tread of my feet was the steady tick of the grandfather clock and kindling crackling in the lounge's hearth.

I had no idea where the entrance to the cellar was, but as if I was being guided by a sixth sense I quickly spotted the barely visible outline of a door built into the side of the bifurcated staircase. I reached for the knocker-style handle, then hesitated, glancing back at the hallway ambivalently. Only people who had a death wish did such crazy things as venturing alone into the cellar of a haunted house. But the pull was stronger now than the urge to back out. I opened the door, stooped to avoid hitting my head on the low lintel and entered.

The space was dank and dark with a strong earthy smell rising up from the gloomy depths below. The stone steps that led to the bottom were a deathtrap, almost invisible in the poor light and slippery with damp. It's a miracle I didn't slip and crack my skull descending them as my eyes roved around failing to find a light switch. When I reached the bottom my eyes had adjusted just enough for me to make out the large, cluttered space before me. Beams of light from the semicircular window offered more visibility to see the grimness of it: the floor a carpet of dust, the brick walls glistening with damp, mummified insects hanging from cobwebs in the corners of the ceiling. My eyes scanned the clutter: dust-sheet draped picture frames, stacked wooden boxes, a furnace rusted from years of disuse standing against one wall.

I took a tentative step forward and whispered into the shadows. 'Hello?'

Silence. Or maybe there was some sign of life: a skittering noise was coming from the wall. Was it mice? Rats?

My eyes drifted back up the stairway. The door had blown almost closed from the hallway's draught, leaving a thin strip of light spilling through the crack. I felt alone and vulnerable down here in the dank and dark, no sound coming from the floor above. But a resolve to find out what had drawn me down here held firm against the urge to leave. An idea appeared.

I lifted my camera, the way a police officer retrieves his gun in uncertain territory. My camera wasn't a weapon, but it offered some security between me and whatever might be lurking in the shadows waiting to jump out. I switched it on and scrolled through the options on the screen until I found the night vision mode. I peered through the viewfinder and saw the cellar tinted by night vision's famous eerie green glow. And, to my amazement, there was something else.

Lambent orbs moved through the air in varying directions. And they didn't just move in straight lines; they paused, changed direction and sped up as if they possessed an intelligence all of their own. Some shot up and skimmed the ceiling, then swooped down to mingle with the others, all the while twinkling in the beams of window light like dancing fireflies. One floated up to the camera lens, appeared to take interest in what it was observing before shooting off again. This was energy. And it was everywhere.

My heart pumping with excitement, I waved my hand in front of the lens. The orbs didn't flee, instead flying around it, curious and playful. I watched in awe at the spectacle before me, which was as beautiful as it was unnerving. Hilderley Manor really was a hotspot of paranormal activity and I was seeing it with my own eyes, not hearing about it from haunted tales. Where the orbs of energy had come from, why there were so many, especially down here in this dank place, I could only wonder. My aim was getting evidence of their existence. I began to snap away, the camera's flash making the orbs scatter away. But they flew back immediately, resuming their dance in front of the camera, a swarm of luminescent-green fireflies.

I lowered the camera, smiling with the thrill of what I was witnessing. To my naked eye the orbs appeared like glittery dust motes dancing in the window light. But something else was now in the room that wasn't there a moment earlier. My smile faded fast as I stared at it. There was a person standing in the corner.

They stood there, hunched, their naked back, the brown mop of hair at the back of their head, facing me. The slim shoulders were shaking, as if they were freezing cold. No, not cold. Crying. I could hear the sobs. Strangled, male, sobs of terrible anguish. The fear running through me was so strong it paralysed my body. I wanted to scream out, but my vocal cords had abandoned me. The person stopped crying suddenly, as if they had sensed I was behind them. The head turned. My eyes widened with surprise. Because the face, half shadowed, half lit by the window light, was my face.

I didn't waste another second. I spun and bolted up the stairwell, taking each step two at a time. But with a misjudged leap my shoe caught the hard, slippery edge of one of the steps and I fell forward, concrete rising up and hitting me in the face. The sound of the impact on my skull, the pain and the shock — it was like I was in some awful nightmare. As if I was outside my body, I watched myself roll onto my back, the DSLR still around my neck, my glasses askew, my hand touching the bleeding gash on my forehead. I saw myself glancing up at the chink of light coming from the hallway, hoping Mrs Brown or Kat would spot the open door and find me, pull me to safety. And then my eyelids closed, blackness cloaked over me and my senses faded to nothing ...

*Hearing the turn of the door handle, my eyelashes flutter open. My head is pressed against the pillow, one ear muffled, the other listening so intently I can hear a pin drop.*

*A floorboard creaks.*

*My heart picks up a pace.*

*I feel strange. Not like myself.*

*The floor creaks again. I blink and more of the dark room blurs into focus. There's old furniture around me. A clock by the bed. It tells me it is past midnight. I recognise this room. It's the room I am staying in for the weekend.*

*But there's someone else in it now.*

*A tall hooded figure is walking up to the bed.*

*I glimpse the face beneath for a brief moment. It is vaguely familiar.*

*He stares down at me and I feel sad all of a sudden. I can't understand why. Is it because his face, partly lit by moonlight, glistens with tears? Or is it rain?*

*I lift my head off the pillow. I'm about to speak. But I see something in the man's arms that stops me. He raises it until it's pointing at my face. I freeze. It's a shotgun. And I feel even sadder now. Because I know he's about to pull the trigger.*

# CHAPTER ELEVEN

# *Revelations*

I KNOCKED ON Will's room then waited for a response, my nerves jingling, my chest rising and falling from the run up the stairs. The door opened after a beat and I was surprised to find myself momentarily speechless at the sight of him standing there. In jumper, black jeans and thick socks he looked straight out of the pages of a good living magazine. A pen was tucked behind his ear and two blemishes on the bridge of his nose indicated he'd just removed a pair of glasses. It was as if the wine guzzling, tobacco puffing man who slunk about the manor past midnight had been kidnapped and replaced with someone new, this stranger who looked, dare I say it, refined. Even lamp light was gilding his combed hair and the aroma of brewed coffee wafted enticingly over his shoulder — the opposite of the straggly haired man who stank of alcohol as he stubbed his toe running down the stairs to rescue me from the cold. Were the recent full moons bringing out the Jekyll and Hyde in him, like a sort of alcoholic werewolf?

'Can we talk?' I asked, still breathless.

He sighed and raked his fingers through his hair, glancing over his shoulder as if something more pressing awaited his return. 'If it's about last night …'

'It isn't,' I said, feeling a stab of rejection at the look on his face, the one that said last night was an event he'd rather forget, even if it meant he had, at least, remembered it. I knew now why he'd fled out of the dining hall, and I was getting the clear message again that broaching the subject would be unwelcome. 'There's something you need to see.'

Distracted, his eyes drifted to my forehead. 'Is that blood?'

The sound of approaching footsteps interrupted us. Kat was coming down the corridor, her head buried in her phone, but her stride brisk and purposeful. The second she caught sight of me it became clear why she was in such a hurry.

'There you are. I've been searching all over.' She got close and her expression faded from relieved to concerned. 'God, what happened to you? Looks like someone dug you out of a grave.'

Her observation wasn't far off the truth. I felt as near to death as I think I'd ever felt. But I was in no mood for standing around in the corridor having my appearance nitpicked for the umpteenth time since arriving at the manor. Not now I had evidence, something tangible to show my companions. I grabbed Kat by the arm and, jostling past Will, dragged her into the writer's bedchamber.

I got as far as the middle of the room, which looked markedly tidier than it did last night (even the bulb in the lamp had been replaced), before Kat stopped me, snatching her hand back. 'Easy, that's a seven hundred pound Gucci watch!'

I faced her, unapologetic. She scowled indignantly, rubbing her wrist. If this was the 'dragon' part of her personality she'd warned me about upon our arrival, it was not having the desired effect. Nothing was going to deter me from revealing what I'd just witnessed.

Will, too, wasn't looking best pleased at the abrupt intrusion.

He closed the door and swept over with a look that threatened to bring me aggressively under control if I didn't explain myself in the next five seconds.

'You said I should only believe something when my eyes are able to back it up,' I said in a conciliatory tone, unhooking the DSLR from around my neck. I gestured to the corner where a laptop, e-reader and thermos flask were sitting on the surface of the writing bureau. 'Well, you need to see what's on this.'

Still wary but with his curiosity pricked a little, Will plucked the camera from my hand and carried it over to the desk. Kat and I watched him as he disconnected the e-reader from the laptop and plugged its USB cable into the camera. While we waited for the laptop to recognise the device, Kat threw me a murderous scowl.

'Just wait until you see,' I said.

The laptop pinged an alert sound. Will clicked up a folder filled with hundreds of thumbnails of the photographs stored inside the DSLR's memory. I rushed over to the desk and tapped the computer's screen.

'Look at the last few photos I took. Those, there, on the top row.'

Will double clicked one of the thumbnails and it expanded to fit the whole of the laptop's screen. Both of us stared at the photo. It was the last shot I'd taken in the cellar before I fell and hit my head trying to get out of there. You could see the spherical, transparent orbs floating in midair. A mixture of excitement and panic was coursing my veins. There was some evidence, at least, of the supernatural things I had witnessed. But I wasn't sure my companions would believe what else I had to share with them.

Kat sidled into my periphery, peering nervously at the laptop from behind Will's shoulder. Will opened his mouth to speak.

'It isn't dust,' I said, sensing his thoughts before he had chance to speak them. 'The camera has night vision. I was watching them. They were moving in unpredictable patterns, as if they had intelligence. Go back a few more.'

Will shrank the photo and clicked on another thumbnail. The next photo that appeared was one of the shots I'd taken at the exterior of the estate, the house standing tall and formidable against a slate overcast sky.

'There, at the top of the steps,' I said. 'There's an apparition.'

Will leaned closer, scrutinising the misty figure I'd just pointed out. My body tensed uneasily as I remembered standing before it, remembered walking up the steps and feeling the icy cold temperature where it had stood.

'Hmm. Doesn't look like a lens refraction,' said Will. 'Could be flash photography. When the light reflects off particles in the air. It's been raining all morning. It's not uncommon for mist to rise from the ground if the conditions are right. The flash would have reflected off the water particles giving the appearance of —'

'No,' I interjected. 'When I looked through the camera lens it wasn't there. When I looked with my eyes it was. But it's there, captured in the photograph. It had nothing to do with the weather. And you can clearly see the shape of a person's body — the legs, the shoulders, the arms, the face.'

'He's right.'

Kat had spoken, even if it was barely a whisper, reminding me there was a third party in the room. Her long lashed eyes looked like a child's as she stared at the screen.

'It does look like a person,' she said. But a reluctance in her voice gave away that she was struggling to believe it as much as she could see it.

Will squinted at the photo, stroking his chin. 'You're sure there wasn't any foreign material on the lens?'

I resisted the temptation to clout him around the ears. Hadn't he heard what I had just said? He really had drawn the inspiration for his protagonist Jack Reid from himself. As much as he denied otherwise, he was blinded by the same scepticism that afflicted the burly Scotsman depicted in his books.

'I told you, I saw it with my own eyes. And if it was a mark on the lens it would have shown up on the subsequent photos, wouldn't it?' I shrank the photo myself and expanded another. It was an almost identical shot, except zoomed in a little closer. 'See, a fraction of a second later and it's disappeared.'

Will contemplated this for a moment, chewing his lip in deep thought before rising to his feet. 'They're interesting shots,' he conceded, retrieving cigarettes from his pocket and skirting around me to the window. He used his palm to push open the stiff latch and the crisp midday air flooded into the room. He popped a cigarette in his mouth and lit it. 'It's a digital camera, so there's no issue with a scratched film, double exposure or a developing issue —'

'You're saying that thing is actually real?' said Kat.

'Spirit photography has been around for hundreds of years. There are fakes and there are some images that are more difficult to explain. Images like that one.' Will blew out smoke, then gazed at the glowing tip of his cigarette. 'Wasn't there some early photographs of the manor on the walls in the lounge?'

'Yes,' I said, remembering the framed paintings and photographs on the walls. The misty figure — or was it a smudge? — standing in the window before it had vanished.

'Investigators describe residual energies from spirits like a film loop, repeating the same action over and over,' Will replied. 'In the same way the energy imprints itself on a specific location, cameras capture the energy as a photograph. If older photographs taken at the back of the manor show something similar it'll help to corroborate the authenticity of your photos.'

'You've studied this?' I said, feeling simultaneously relieved and impressed.

Will frowned. 'Why do people always assume authors don't research the subject of their books?'

'This is too much,' said Kat, shutting her eyes and inclining her head as if in silent prayer.

She hadn't even heard what else I had to tell them. Noticing the trepidation in my face, Will narrowed his eyes at me shrewdly. 'What is it? What are you not telling us?'

I swallowed. My companions wanted answers. Yet despite being so keen to divulge my secrets on the way up here, with their expectant eyes trained intently on me I didn't feel so forthcoming in giving them. Once the words were out of my mouth there was no taking them back.

'There's more,' I said quietly. 'When I was in the cellar I saw someone. I'm convinced it was a ghost. I legged it out of there and fell on the stairs. That's how I got this graze. Then I blacked out.'

I didn't tell them what had unsettled me the most, that the face in the cellar looked so much like my own. My mind was busy trying to reason this. It had been dark down there, dark enough to make me think I had seen something I hadn't ... and yet ... the face appeared in my mind's eye once again ...

'I knew it,' said Kat. 'That fall has broken his head.'

'I'm perfectly lucid,' I said defensively. 'But when I blacked out I had a vision. I've been having similar visions for weeks. They're like dreams, but they're not. They're memories, events from my past, exactly as they happened all those years ago. Except, the vision I had in the cellar wasn't from my past. It was from the future.'

The cigarette froze a few inches in front of Will's mouth. He didn't blink as smoke snaked upwards from the burning tip. Kat went to speak, but he held out his hand to silence her. He continued to stare at me for a long moment. I could almost hear that logical mind of his working — ticking, whirring, spinning. He must have read my reluctance, because an uncharacteristic note of worry entered his voice when he next spoke.

'What happened in this 'vision' you had in the cellar?'

I hesitated before answering. 'I dreamt that I woke up in bed to find Stan Crouch standing over me with a shotgun. Just before he pulled the trigger.'

* * * * *

'It's crackers. Insane!' Kat, striding back and forth in front of me, making me dizzy, complained moments later. I couldn't recall if the threadbare patch on the rug under her feet was there before or after we'd entered Will's room.

Watching her from my position at the foot of the fourposter, I said, tentatively, 'I know how it looks. Believe me, no one has questioned my sanity over the last few months more than I have. I even went to the doctor. I was given pills. But I stopped taking them because I had a feeling the visions had something important to tell me. And they did. This proves it.'

'You stopped taking prescribed medication?'

The question came from Will, who was sitting astride a ladderback chair in front of the bureau, forearms stacked against the backrest, chin resting on them. There was a studious look in his eyes.

'The conversation we had the other night made me question their efficacy,' I replied.

He straighted up, shaking his head disapprovingly. 'Not wise, squire.'

'I feel fine. I was only taking them for a few weeks and I haven't had any withdrawal symptoms.'

'Oh, this just gets better,' said Kat. She had halted her pacing and was staring reproachfully at Will. 'See what you've done? Those pills were probably the only things keeping us safe from a raving madman. He'll be out of control without them. You've unleashed a monster.'

'Hello! Still in the room!' I protested. 'And I am not a madman.'

'There's no way you're sleeping in the same bed as me tonight,' she said, crossing her arms vehemently.

'Katrina, hear the man out,' Will interjected.

'My name's Kat!'

Kat stalked to the desk, seized Will's packet of cigarettes and his lighter, then, giving me a wide berth as if I was Jack the Ripper, retreated to the open window to get a much needed hit of her poison.

Will remained unruffled by her theatrics. But I did detect a grin playing at the corner of his mouth as he continued to stare at me from across the room. 'So let me get this straight,' he said. 'You've been having dreams from the past. But they're not dreams, they're memories. And you reckon the one you had about old Lurch, which obviously isn't from your past seeing as you've never visited the manor before, must be from the future?'

Hearing it spoken aloud by another person made it sound all the more unbelievable. But unbelievable was a word that was fast losing its meaning in my vocabulary. 'It sounds ridiculous, I know,' I said. 'But it's no more weird than everything else that's been happening.'

Will raised an inquisitive brow.

I drew in a weary breath before shambling over to the Chippendale. I moved Will's motorbike helmet to the chest of drawers, sat down and started raking my fingers up and down my temples to ease my burgeoning headache. Depressed is a word I would use to explain how I felt. The opposite of how I expected to feel after releasing my burden. Even one of the lenses in my specs was scratched from that fall on the stairs. And these were my best pair.

'Quentin?' Will prompted.

'I've been experiencing weird things for months,' I said, too tired to hold back any longer. 'Hearing, seeing, sensing stuff. Ghostly stuff. At first I imagined events happening in the future, and then they happened for real. I thought it was a coincidence. But then anomalies started appearing in my photographs, when they never have before. It's happening here in the manor, too. I've seen other apparitions, not just the one in the cellar.' I glanced from Kat to Will, my faith not mirrored in their faces. I added, 'Esther Hill told me that spirits can have unfinished business, such as needing to help a loved one they left behind or give them a message. The dreams from my past are always about the same person, someone I lost, someone who would have done anything to protect me. I think he's communicating with me through my dreams. If he is, and the vision I had in the cellar is really from the future, then I think it's a message. A warning.'

I thought coming out was hard. But coming out of the metaphysical closet was even harder. In the silence that followed you could have cut the tension in that coffee-smelling air with a knife. My secret might have been off my chest, but the two people staring at me with doubt in their eyes were now free to judge and ridicule me. Would they do that?

Kat, standing in front of the open window with a freshly lit cigarette just shook her head wearily. The strain on Will's face showed the patience he'd afforded me up until now was waning. Resignedly, he said, 'And why would old Lurch want to kill you?'

'I bumped into him yesterday and he threatened me, hit me with his cane even. I think he thought you and I were being intimate the night he saw us through the kitchen window. He's homophobic. He said 'my sort' in a derisive way. And later, when he was arguing with the housekeeper, he explicitly shouted out an homophobic slur.'

Will looked unconvinced. 'So the old man was born when they were still stoning your sort. But I'm pretty sure even homophobic dinosaurs like him need a stronger motive for murder than disagreeing with a person's sexuality.'

'He has a shotgun,' I said, trying to strengthen my argument. 'I saw him holding it last night from the window, when you and Rufus went down to investigate the loud bang.'

'You saw someone holding a weapon and didn't tell me about it?' Kat, having discarded her cigarette, had rounded the fourposter, her brow furrowed above wide eyes like an accusatory owl.

I glanced up guiltily. I hadn't told her for good reason. Her current reaction was one. Being too traumatised to mention it when I woke up because she'd startled me awake while sporting a very embarrassing erection was another.

I said, 'Listen, it isn't just that Mr Crouch is homophobic.' I got up and moved to the rug in the middle of the room, perhaps to shrug off the intimidating feeling of Kat's eyes bearing down on me. 'Mrs Brown is upset because she thinks Stan is losing his mind. The way he's been acting — the creeping around, throwing accusations, the threats, firing the shotgun — she could be right. His behaviour looks delusional, paranoid. It isn't completely unreasonable to think his condition could be distorting his

186

rationality, that he plans to take his prejudices, this anger he has, out on me. He's had his eyes on me from the second I arrived at the manor, staring at me like I'm vermin that should be put down. He's already assaulted and threatened me. He clearly doesn't want me here. I think I'm right about this. I think the vision was a premonition, shown to me to warn me —'

'I've heard enough!' Kat, pale and shaking, looked imploringly at Will, who was still sitting in the chair. 'Can't you make him stop? Hit him or something?'

My eyes widened and I instinctively braced, expecting attack.

'You have to admit it sounds compelling,' said Will, his lip curling in wry amusement. He was finding Kat's hysteria quite entertaining, even if I was not. I was genuinely concerned for my personal safety.

'I don't care if it's the story of the century and I'm the first journalist in the world to get the scoop on it,' Kat snapped.

'You're not even happy that I managed to get those interesting photographs you were after?' I said in a vain attempt to allay her distress.

She made a sound similar to a horse snorting through its mouth, then, much like a toddler being forced to surrender defeat during a temper tantrum, swept dramatically to the door. She twirled when she reached it. 'You two can talk about this stuff if you want, but I'm having no part of it. This place is cursed. Messing with its ghosts and its crazy old people is a death wish.' She opened the door and stalked off into the corridor, slamming the door behind her.

Will whistled. 'And Hurricane Katrina has left the room.'

In the ringing sound that followed from the door slamming shut, he rose to his feet, strode past me and unhooked his coat from the back of the door. He pulled it on as he slipped his feet into boots. 'Come on, let's go,' he said.

'Where?'

'Outside.'

He opened the door and crossed the threshold.

'Will?' I called out.

He turned, adjusting the collar of his coat. 'What?'

'Do you believe me?'

He hesitated. Then said, 'You're the real deal, Strange. I know that.' A softness flickered in his eyes. Was he remembering last night, remembering the words he'd spoken while stroking my hair: *'I like you, Quentin. There's an innocence about you. I feel safe around you, like I can trust you.'* 'Yeah. I believe you.'

# - CHAPTER TWELVE -

# *Extrasensory Perception*

'I'M SORRY ABOUT Kat,' I said. 'I know she can be a bit ... volatile.'

'Don't be. The harshness isn't personal, it's coming from fear. And at least you know where you stand with her. It's the ones who conceal their true feelings you have to worry about.'

Will led the way through a rusty door and up a cobweb-ridden stairwell tucked discreetly away from the house's main staircases and draughty corridors. The grey coat swished behind him and the tread of his boots echoed as they trotted purposefully up the stone steps. Exiting another door, we came out onto the puddle dotted asphalt of the house's open roof terrace. I paused in my tracks, stunned by the unrelenting panorama before me.

A diurnal bird of prey soared across the slate-coloured sky, which stretched impressively for miles above the desaturated countryside. Winter was approaching early this year and it showed; all the usual colours of autumn — the reds, yellows, golds — were nowhere to be seen, just faded greens merging to white-grey as the rural land met the sky. I could see just how far we were from the bustling towns and cities in which I spent most of my days. Tolling church bells, the rustle of trees and that haunting quietness made up the sound of these remote lands, not the babble of people and rush of motorway traffic my ears were used to.

Will, however, was in no mood for sky gazing. He glided over to the parapet, a cigarette already lit and trailing smoke in his wake. I scurried after him, wrapping my blazer tighter as a soft breeze whipped at my hair and face.

'Why up here?' I asked, drawing up beside him. No fan of heights, I stayed a safe distance from the rail, trying to ignore the mental picture my mind had just conjured of a fatal fall to the gravel driveway below.

'The fresh air helps me think,' he replied.

Pity he couldn't think in the comfort of the dining hall, I thought, imagining the hot cross buns and pots of warm tea on offer there. The sky was getting darker, the day drawing on — just how long had I been blacked out in that cellar? I still hadn't eaten a thing since breakfast and the grumble in my stomach had become a permanent ache.

Will continued to gaze over the grounds, puffing on the cigarette, one knee protruding through the rail's balusters. I debated taking more of the photographs Kat had requested as I waited for him to finish whatever it was he was doing, especially with the impressive view up here, and vistas being one of my favourite things to photograph, but it would have felt odd under the circumstances.

'ESP,' he said, finally. 'That's what you're experiencing.'

'ES what?' I said, wondering if he'd just mentioned the acronym of a disorder I had hitherto heard about.

'Extrasensory perception. It's a widely reported phenomena. Ever heard of the four Clairs? It's the French word for 'clear.' Clairaudience (clear sound); that's the ability to hear what's inaudible to most people. Clairvoyance (clear seeing); the ability to

190

see into the future. Clairsentience (clear feeling); feeling and experiencing intuitively, including other people's emotions. And Claircognizance (clear knowing); that's knowing things without any doubt, and with no prior knowledge of the thing or subject. It's been happening how long now?'

'A few months,' I said, my mind lagging as I tried to remember everything he'd just said.

'Unusual. Most people exhibit signs from early age. You're sure you've never experienced anything like it before?'

I combed my mind, looking out at the distant fields, the wind ruffling my fringe. Vague memories rose to the surface. That time, when I was twelve years old, at the fairground that came to Cricklewood every year. My friend, Evan Bradshaw, wanted to ride the Dodgems. But a feeling in my gut told me that if we did, something really bad would happen. I persuaded Evan not to go on the ride, and the next time the Dodgem cars set off there was a devastating crash that left a dozen youngsters with minor injuries and a nine year old with a collapsed lung.

And there was that dilapidated house that stands on the corner of the road where I grew up. I knew when the old lady who lived there, Mrs Morton, had passed away. There was no reason for me to know it, no prior evidence; it was really odd, like I just knew she was dead. I told no one, brushing it off as a random thought, even when people showed up soon after to cart the body away.

Then, more ominously, there was the sighting. On the way home from school I used to cross a small bridge that overlooked a stream. One day I had a strange feeling I was being watched from the trees that flanked the gushing water. I stopped and stared, squinting through my specs. There, between the spindly tree trunks, stood a boy about my own age. He had pale, bluish skin, the colour of a corpse, and his clothes were sodden, dripping at the wrists and streaked with claw marks of mud. Paralysed with terror, I watched as he just turned, unblinking, and disappeared into the trees. I couldn't walk on that side of the road when I had to cross the bridge after that, and whenever I did I felt my entire body shiver as I imagined him still standing there.

I was beginning to see that I wasn't such a newbie to these experiences than originally thought. Esther's words echoed in my head: '*Until now you have feared that part of yourself, you have tried to push it away and suppress it.*' Might other occurrences have happened had I paid more attention to my unusual senses?

'There have been times,' I said. 'Now that I really think about it.'

Will nodded, blowing smoke through the corner of his mouth. 'Thought so. The photograph part is odd, though.'

'In what way?'

'Well, your photographs are the same as any other example of spirit photography, from what I've seen and read on the subject. But from what you've described there's one main difference.'

'What's that?'

'You,' said Will.

'Me?'

'Most spirit photography is taken by people who say they didn't see anything at the time the photo was taken, but the camera still picked up the apparition. You, however, actually saw the apparition with your naked eye.'

I pondered this. It had been the strangest thing about seeing the apparition. The way it was there one moment, then gone when I looked at it through the camera's lens. A bite in the breezy air caused a head to toe shiver as I waited for Will to elaborate.

'You're not the first person to see something that looks like a ghost. But things seen with our eyes are subject to modification by our fears and beliefs. That makes sightings unreliable. You explained seeing the apparition exactly how it was captured by the camera. This tells me that what you saw was genuine. Images taken by the camera are captured exactly as they are, frozen, not distorted by our emotions or beliefs, making spirit photographs the most reliable evidence of ghosts we have.'

'But I could only see the apparition with my own eyes. I couldn't see it when I was looking through the camera's viewfinder,' I said.

'Exactly. Isn't that interesting?' Will's eyes glinted with fascination in the harsh light. 'You saw what everyone else sees when they look through a camera's viewfinder while taking a spirit photograph: nothing. And yet you still saw what was captured in the photograph with your naked eye.'

'Well, what the hell does that mean?'

'How should I know? I'm a writer, not an optician.'

A pathetic sound issued from my throat.

'What I'm saying,' said Will, curbing an urge to laugh, 'is that it's a sign you have extrasensory abilities far above what's normal. Especially with everything else you've described, like these 'dreams' you tell me about.'

He lapsed into pensive thought again. I gazed worryingly at the grey clouds drifting across the sky, processing this deluge of information. Incongruously (because it didn't seem like the appropriate time to be thinking about films), an image of the boy from *The Sixth Sense* came to mind. I refrained from quoting the famous line, 'I see dead people' and adding a question mark on the end, instead asking, 'There hasn't been anyone else who sees this way before?'

'Oh, you can bet there has been. Extrasensory abilities are common, with new kinds of experiences being reported all the time. Seeing auras, remembering past lives, telekinesis to name a few. There's a condition, Hyperthymesia, where people remember large amounts of their life experiences in vivid detail. Our retinas receive images and imprint them on our consciousness the way images are captured on the camera's film. Who knows what the brain, that complex thing that continues to baffle us, is capable of recreating with a lifetime's worth of imprinted memory?'

'Do you think it could explain the dreams?'

'It could,' said Will. He lapsed into thought again.

'What are you thinking?'

'I was reading about fibromyalgia recently, a chronic pain condition that creates head to toe pain in the sufferer, even when medical tests reveal no underlying physiological cause. Experts believe it's psychosomatic, that their brains are responding to stressors on the nervous system to a much higher degree than most people, and there does appear to be a link to past trauma. It's sort of like a physical PTSD.' Will's eyes, even bluer up here in the harsh daylight, studied me intently for a moment. 'This is conjecture, but if the brain is capable of making people experience heightened sensations through emotional trauma, who's to say it isn't capable of making people experience heightened senses?'

'You mean the way I'm seeing, hearing and feeling things that aren't there?'

'Maybe your brain responds to stressors by heightening your intuitive senses. Whether what you're seeing and feeling is really there or not is another matter.'

'But you said yourself that what I described seeing was the same as in the photograph, and photographs are the most reliable evidence there is.'

'I know that, squire. But I'm not the one seeing ghosts.'

Did I see that sceptical look return in his eye? I felt alone again.

Then I thought about what Esther had said that first night in the torch-lit nursery room. If it really was the way our universe worked then it didn't seem too crazy to assume that what I was seeing and feeling was real. If dimensions other than the one we could see existed, dimensions where energy went after death, yet everything was ultimately connected — Source, as Esther had described it — all it would take is for there to be a connection between the two, a way for them to become aware of each other. Was I that connection to another dimension? A spirit dimension?

Will finished his cigarette, crushing the burning tip on the weathered parapet and flicking it into a puddle on the asphalt. As it fizzled out with a hiss, I recalled books I had read by some of the world's most original thinkers in the study of altered states of consciousness. I'd read about material reductionism, dark matter, dark energy and theories on the links between matter and consciousness. The topic is vast and complex, and much of it was too difficult to comprehend at the time. But it had always stuck with me that there was much about our universe that science was unable to explain or understand. Perhaps my extrasensory perception wasn't so unbelievable after all, not when you consider the miracle of the universe itself.

Will broke my musing by proffering a packet of mints. I shook my head and he tossed one in his mouth. His perfect hair rippled in the wind. The lapels on his coat fluttered like a boat's sail. Those blue eyes were narrowed towards the other side of the roof terrace now, at the rear of the manor. Saying nothing, he took off across the asphalt.

Like a faithful dog I followed him, once again coming up beside him as he stopped and leaned against the rail. From here you could see the woodland that abutted the manor grounds, a small forest of dark canopies that appeared both oddly placed in relation to the location of the building and very uninviting.

Remembering Annie's tales I realised I was looking at the woods where crows had been found nailed to trees. What kind of person would do such a thing, all the way out here? And why? It was cruel and senseless, and deeply unnerving. I pushed the gory mental image away and looked at Will. The woods weren't where his eyes were directed. They were fixed on the caretaker's cottage at the bottom of the garden.

'There's one way to test if the vision you had about Old Lurch was real or not,' he said.

'How?'

'We've got one evening left in this place. If he's planning on bumping you off, it'll be tonight. That's our opportunity.'

'Opportunity for what?'

'To set a trap.'

Stirrings of dread grew in my belly. I did not like the sound of where this was going.

# - CHAPTER THIRTEEN -

# *The Drawing*

I COULD FEEL my body slowly thawing from the chill of the roof terrace as I walked back down the corridor, the radiators giving off a much welcome wave of heat. Will had gone back to his room to get ready for the evening and to think over how our plan was going to play out. My new mission was to find Kat, although considering how irrational she'd been before abandoning us, I wouldn't have been surprised if she'd hopped inside Petunia and sped as far away from Hilderley Manor as she could get.

Before that, however, nature called. Reaching the bathroom, I went to open the door, but it swung open before my hand had a chance to touch the handle. Esther, looking like she'd just stepped out of a beauty salon, and startled to find me standing there, let out a sharp gasp.

'Quentin, dear,' she said, clutching her chest. 'Do forgive me. But this place has put me right on edge since last night.'

'You won't believe it,' I said, eager to tell her about the afternoon's events.

'Can't talk now, sweetheart.' Smelling like a perfumery, she brushed me out of the way. 'The team want me ready in the next hour and there's a lot of preparation to be done before tonight's escapades.'

'But I wanted to tell you that you were right. Elliot did have a message to give me. It's why I've been dreaming about him. He's trying to help me.'

Esther halted near a gilded picture frame homing a landscape oil painting. She turned around. But the enthusiasm I expected to see mirrored on her beautified face was not there. Instead her lips were pressed together in a look of pity. 'Messages from the other side aren't something you can guess, dear. They are given in due time, usually when we stop longing so hard to hear them.'

'But you don't understand. I saw a vision. It was a message because —'

Esther was shaking her head. 'You're not listening for the message, Quentin. You're hoping it's the thing you want to hear. What is it that you are really seeking? You never needed me or this place to prove to you that ghosts existed, you already know they do. You will get the answers you're looking for when the time is right, but sometimes the answers aren't always what we hoped they would be.'

With a ghost of a smile, Esther turned and carried on her way. Confused, I stood at the threshold of the bathroom and watched her go.

I was still pondering the ambiguous words after I finished in the bathroom and returned to the room to continue my search for Kat. I peeked my head inside, seeing she wasn't there. Her belongings, however, were, letting me know she was around somewhere.

Hearing footsteps in the corridor, I stepped backwards, peering around the door frame. The person walking down the corridor with their back to me was not my partner. It was a young man wearing a flat cap and a tan-coloured shirt, y-shaped braces clipped to his brown trousers.

An ajar door midway down the corridor showed me where he had just appeared from. I continued to watch him as he walked. The gait was unusual, a sort of lame shuffle, as if he didn't have complete feeling in his right leg and had to drag it along the ground. It was a slight impairment, but noticeable nonetheless. I might not have thought more about him if I hadn't spotted the piece of paper that floated like a feather before alighting on the carpet runner. Had he dropped it?

'Excuse me!' I called out, but he didn't turn around, continuing to walk. 'Hello? I think you've dropped something!'

I rushed over to the piece of paper and bent down to pick it up. It was folded in half, concealing what was on the other side. I opened it and saw what looked like a child's drawing: stick figures, green grass, a yellow sun. 'Excuse me!'

He reached one of the doors at the end of the corridor, opened it and vanished from sight. I scowled, annoyed at being ignored. Until it crossed my mind that he could be deaf. I glanced at the door to my side where he'd appeared from. I walked over and pulled it wider, spying a staircase that led to another door at the top. The door was open. I was looking at the entrance to the house's attic.

A creak on the boards made me freeze. Then a face peeked around the door frame. A middle-aged bearded guy wearing a tool belt and a flannel shirt with the sleeves rolled to the elbows stuck up his thumb. 'Window repair,' he said in a cheery Lancashire accent. 'Just mending a couple of cracked panes.'

My body relaxed. I considered asking him if the young man was with him or not, but not wanting to disturb a working man going about his duties decided against it. Instead I began towards the room at the end of the corridor, the piece of paper pinched between my fingers.

I reached the door and rapped three times. I waited a second. No answer. I knocked again, glanced back down the corridor. Other than the gurgle of the hot water in the radiators, the banging of a hammer up in the attic, all was quiet.

'Hello?' I called out, making sure my voice was loud enough to be heard from the other side. When there was no response this time, I opened the door and peered inside.

I was looking at another guest room. This one didn't have a fourposter, but a king size half-poster that dominated one wall. There was other furniture, too. A chest of drawers, a chaise longue, a Queen Anne tea table — and absolutely no sign of the young man.

I blinked, an instinctive reaction to make sure my eyes weren't deceiving me. A very uneasy feeling crept over me. I glanced down the corridor. Looked at the empty room again. But no matter how many times I tried to conjure him back into existence, the young man had vanished like a ghost.

My heart picked up a pace, the same fear I felt in that dank cellar returning. I reimagined that face, the one that looked so much like mine. Did it also belong to the young man who had just vanished into thin air? I glanced down at my clothes. The clothes he was wearing were not my own. But they were similar. Clothes that Kat would have banished to a bygone era. The next thought that occurred was too chilling to comprehend. Was I ... no I couldn't be ... looking at my own ghost?

I recoiled from the room and shut the door, hard. Fear became anger. This blimming place was messing with my head. My own ghost. What a ridiculous thought.

But then my thoughts took me back to last night's nightmare. The young man in that dream had looked very much like me from behind. Whether his face looked like mine before it had been destroyed, however, I would never know. But it was easy to see what could have caused such destruction. A weapon being fired at close range. A weapon such as a shotgun.

Keen to get the hell away from this corridor, I stuffed the piece of paper with the drawing on it in my pocket and took off, throwing the room a very nervous parting glance as I descended the staircase.

Spooked by yet another encounter with one of Hilderley Manor's incorporeal residents, I was relieved when I found Kat in the lounge moments later. But what I hadn't expected to find was … was she … yes, she was … having a conversation with the stag's head that was surmounted above the fireplace.

Hearing me enter, she stopped talking and turned around. A glass flute of something clear and sparkling waved precariously in her hand. 'Quentin! Oh, I've missed you.'

*Missed* me? Was this some kind of joke? What had she missed? Berating me? I eyed her suspiciously. Could I, perhaps, not be looking at Katrina Brannigan, journalist for the *Cricklewood Gazette*, but at her doppelgänger? Whatever it was, I think I was about to find out, because she was heading towards me, glass flute held high between thumb and forefinger, her legs bending as they struggled to stay upright on the heels of her boots.

I'd barely had chance to brace when her arm wrapped around my neck. She squeezed me so tightly I could have sworn I heard my vertebrae crunch. After what felt like an eternity, because she was strangling my windpipe, she released me and her face swam into view amid a hundred tiny stars.

'There he is, my handsome photographer,' she cooed.

OK, something was definitely wrong.

She cupped my face with one hand. Her eyes were glassy, with heavy lids and dilated pupils. They were staring not at my eyes, but at the bridge of my nose. They finally found my eyes and her mouth widened into a smile. The fumes on her breath would have made me tipsy if I'd breathed them in long enough.

'You're ...'

'A little tipsy, that's all,' she slurred.

She giggled, turned around and staggered towards the refreshments table, bumping into one of the chairs and causing the glasses and bowls to rattle. 'Oops. Now, what was I after ...' She seized an already opened bottle of champagne and started refilling her glass, the stream of bubbly stuff missing the rim and splashing the tablecloth.

'I, erm, came to see how you are,' I said, rubbing my neck. 'You seemed scared earlier.'

Kat swerved as she carried her refilled glass over to the antique furniture, the drink sloshing against the sides of the glass as it threatened to drench the rug on the hardwood flooring. When she reached the sofa, she turned, lagging for a second as her eyes tried to find me. 'Scared? Me? I'm not scared. I'm fearless!'

She dropped onto the sofa, giggling over her rear hitting the cushion harder than she'd expected. More champagne sloshed over the chest of her silken blouse, but she just wiped at the stains sloppily. She patted the empty space beside her. 'Come and sit with me.'

I debated. I didn't know if I felt safer down here or upstairs with my own doppelgänger. I ventured over and sat gingerly on the aged upholstery. I began to wonder where the ghost hunters were, praying they'd interrupt us and rescue me from whatever was about to take place.

'Don't look so confused, pumpkin,' slurred Kat.

'Well, it's just that you were so alarmed by the photographs, by what I was telling you about the vision. And now—'

'Pfft.' She waved the air, almost taking my eye out with one of her manicured talons. 'I'm fine! As a matter of fact, I feel quite the lionheart. Watch ...' Struggling to keep her eyelids fully open, she sat forward and looked around the room as if she was about to address a small audience. 'Ghosts! Come out, come out, wherever you are.' She exploded into a fit of giggles. 'No?' she called. 'Suit yourselves, then!' She sat back and sipped more champagne, chuckling some more.

'Kat, maybe you've had enough —'

'No, Quentin, I haven't. And do you know why?'

I blinked, inching back at the sudden fire in her voice.

'I've been working my pretty arse off solidly for the last twelve months and haven't had a single day off, let alone a night out, a chance to let my hair down, god forbid have some of that elusive bloody thing called fun! Do you know what that does to a young, beautiful woman like me?'

I stared at her, wide-eyed and unblinking.

'It turns her into an irritable, bad-tempered bitch. That's what.'

She lunged at me and seized the lapel of my blazer. My jaw clamped shut and I'm sure I peed a little.

'Tell me I'm a bitch!' she demanded.

When I said nothing, she shook me vigorously until I came to a stop with my glasses askew. 'Tell me!'

'You're ... not that bad.'

'Pfft.' She let me go, shaking her head glumly. 'You're too kind to say it. But the truth is I'm awful, Quentin. And we both know it.'

I brushed the creases out of my blazer, watching her heedfully. She sipped more champagne, her lips pouty against the rim of the glass.

Staring at Kat in that moment, I was reminded of one of the many reasons I was afraid to drink. The stuff had made her as unpredictable as the British weather. And then came another sudden change of character. The glum pout turned into a contemplative slant of the lips as a thought appeared to occur to her.

'I wasn't always this way. I used to be shy, really respectful. I was head prefect at secondary two years in a row, you know. Always was a natural leader.' Gazing into midair, her glassy eyes and the Gucci watch catching the light from the crackling fire, she smiled proudly. But then the smile faded. 'When you're a person who follows rules, though, when you're willing to do hard work when everyone else isn't, people think you're a pushover. They take advantage of you. It's human nature, the predator and the prey. A perfect match.'

Sipping from the glass this time, there was a bitterness in the way she slugged it back. Against the crackle of the hearth fire, I chose to listen and stay mute, hoping it would save me from getting shaken again.

'And ambition isn't a bad thing,' she went on. 'It's just that everyone wants to be noticed today. They want to be great at something, but for the sake of being great not what they get out of it. And do you know, Quentin, not everyone can be great. Greatness wouldn't exist if we all were, it's dependent on someone else being inferior.' She released a weary sigh followed by a small burp.

I wondered where this was going. Fearing it turning into drunken rambling I was about to brave it and interrupt her, but she started speaking again.

'Do you know what happened to me when my first ever article

was published? A girl I'd had a feud with at college, Amber Simpson, spread it around social media that I'd plagiarised her college assignment when I hadn't. Do you know how painful that was, Quentin? To love something so much you spend years devoting every spare minute you have to becoming great at it. And when you finally achieve your dream, someone pisses all over it.'

The corner of Kat's long-lashed eyes glistened with the beginning of tears. For the first time I felt sympathy for my partner. There was vulnerability behind the sharp tongue, wounds beneath the tough exterior.

'I could prove it was original, thanks to my diligence in taking notes, in crediting all my sources. But mud sticks, and she knew it. Do you know what's the most screwed up thing about it, though?'

Still wary, I shook my head.

'The only reason she did it was because I stood up for myself. I exposed her for the bitch she was. Amber was a bully, a cheat, a manipulator and a liar. And when she'd destroyed every friendship I had, diminished every achievement I was praised for, I finally snapped and told people what she was like.' The glass flute almost slipping through her fingers, Kat turned a disenchanted expression on me. 'For some people it's the worst thing you can do, expose them for who they really are. They work so hard at creating a false self. Because if people knew who they really were they'd never be able to get the things they want. She waited all those years to get her revenge. And she finally got her wish, to have the world see me as a fraud, the very thing she is and always will be.'

A tear rolled down Kat's cheek. She wiped it away, causing her mascara to smudge. Her eyelids were still heavy. The glass of champagne listed precariously in her hand. But despite her intoxication, this had been no drunken ramble. Kat was recalling an event from her past that had deeply affected and shaped her.

'That's why I insist everyone calls me Kat,' she said. 'Katrina died years ago. She was too innocent for this world. Kat knows everyone plays a game. She knows people aren't who they say they are. She stays one step ahead so people can't manipulate, use and double-cross her. With people like Amber Simpson in the world, Quentin, I know which girl I'd rather be.'

I felt my body tensing, my upper lip flattening and my jaw tightening. Kat's story was filling me with anger. I had a new respect for my partner. My heart went out to her. She was beautiful, young, smart, shrewd, driven and confident. All the traits you need to be successful. All the traits I am not. But all that was tainted by a distrust of other people and an ugly outlook of the world because of the acts of this one person. 'Fuck Amber Simpson!' I said.

Kat spun her head, stunned by the uncharacteristic expletive. But then her face melted into a look of appreciation. 'That's the sweetest thing anyone's ever said to me.'

'Come on,' I said, spotting her tired red eyes, her mascara streaked cheeks. 'Let's get you upstairs to bed.'

Getting Kat up the stairs was a bigger challenge than anticipated. She stumbled and wobbled a lot, almost toppling back down them at one point. By the time we'd reached the first floor I'd worked up a small sweat.

Dusk was falling rapidly outside the window at the end of the corridor. The ghost hunters would soon be calling for us to join them on the final night's hunt. But Kat was in no state for such happenings. And, according to the plan Will had given me a brief rundown of on the roof terrace — "you get into bed, I hide in the shadows, we wait for the old man to show up with the shotgun, and before he has chance to kill you, bam, I leap out and floor the fucker" — Kat would only be getting in the way of things if I were to take her back to our room on the second floor. There was only one other option.

We had just reached Will's room when the sconces on the walls began to flicker on and off. I halted, causing Kat to loll in my arms like a stringless puppet. A bad power connection? Pretty unlikely since the lights weren't even switched on. They flickered again. My eyes darted up and down the corridor, expecting to see some phantom in the shadows. I had been here before. The incident with the exploding bulb was fresh on my mind and would be for a long time. And I was right to be worried. It was here again.

The air felt cold suddenly. Then colder. Breath misted from my mouth. I could sense the thing moving towards me. Then, as if it was passing right through me, my whole body became ice. I let go of Kat and she fell to the floor with a heavy thump. The cold moved through my body, shocking me into a statue. Then I felt myself getting warmer. Warmer. The thing was moving away. And then it was gone.

I stood stock still, my chest rising and falling from my panicked breath. I thought I registered the sound of tiny feet trotting up behind me, but still in shock I remained too frozen to turn around and see what it was. The lights flickered a couple more times and I finally felt safe to move again.

A groan issued from the floor. I looked down and saw Kat lying there, her hair curtaining half her face. She blinked up at me through her heavy lids. 'Did I fall?'

But whether she had fallen or not was about to be the least of her worries. Cottonball trotted out from behind my legs, stopped when he reached Kat's face, then cocked his leg and proceeded to urinate all over her fancy hair and makeup.

'Jesus!' I bent down to stop the pooch, but was startled by a loud shriek that reverberated through the corridor.

Ash had appeared from one of the rooms in her bra and knickers, wearing a look of alarm on her face. 'Cottonball! No!'

She ran towards us, her painted feet padding down the runner, her jewel-adorned hands covering her underwear. She reached Cottonball just as he was finishing his business and shaking off. She snatched the fluff ball off the floor. 'Naughty boy, Cottonball! You know you have to wait for mummy to take you outside before you go pee pee.'

Kat made another groan. We looked down at her. Half of her face was soaked and a small puddle of urine had formed a halo around her skull.

'I'm so sorry,' said Ash.

Matt, shirtless, poked his head out of the room. 'Babe, what's going on?'

I said, 'It's OK. I'll get her cleaned up.'

Ash scurried away with the guilty Pomeranian. I reached down and helped Kat to her feet. I hauled her over to Will's door and knocked. It opened after a beat and Will was standing there, halfway through buttoning up a clean shirt. I blushed at the sight of his partially exposed chest, the smattering of dark chest hair, remembering him straddled on top of me last night.

Kat had wilted against my shoulder and was drifting into sleep, her damp cheek making a wet stain on my blazer. I offered Will an apologetic stare.

He appraised Kat before the realisation of what I was asking dawned on his face. He inhaled a patient breath and blew it out slowly, then stepped aside for us to enter.

# - CHAPTER FOURTEEN -

# *The Man With A Hole In His Face*

WHEN IT CAME to spooky, the echoey hallway and shadowy corridors of Hilderley Manor were nothing compared to the woodland that abutted its rear. So much so I kept snatching glances over my shoulder as we trudged through its hazardous undergrowth, dark trees and the hum of insects surrounding us, with just enough moonlight filtering through the twisted branches to light our way.

Thoughts of being led by a dubious cult to a secluded clearing where torture and ritual was about to take place flashed through my mind. But the members of *Pluckley Ghost Hunters* looked as nervous as the guests as we continued to follow Esther, the person who had taken lead on this final evening of our ghost hunting journey. She, at least, whacking branches out of the way with her torch, looked confident enough to suggest we weren't heading into lands from which we would never return.

Where exactly she was leading us, or what she had in store for us when we got there, was still unknown. But whatever we were going to be getting up to on our final evening, it was certain to be interesting if last night's seance was anything to go by.

I eyed my fellow guests nervously as we continued to trek. To my right Will was humming blithely and smoking, his coat swishing about his knees as he walked. On my left Matt and Ash were walking arm in arm, grave looks on their faces, as if they were heading for the gallows. Cottonball's eyes reflected the moonlight every time it bled through the canopy and dappled his fluffy face.

Annie, walking ahead with the other ghost hunters, glanced over her shoulder. 'Miss Brannigan didn't feel like joining us tonight, did she not?'

'That's right,' I lied. 'She wasn't feeling well. Migraine.'

Unable to conceal his amusement, Will leaned close to my ear and whispered, 'She'll have one tomorrow.'

I tried not to laugh as I pictured Kat where we'd left her, in Will's bed, the safest place for her to sleep off the drink. Which conveniently left our room free for me and Will to carry out the plan.

Eventually we reached a clearing large enough to fit all nine of us without being so cramped you could detect if the other had washed or not. The canopy above had opened to allow a clear view of the full moon, which looked like an illuminated tarnished coin in the velvety sky as it bathed the ground in pale, otherworldly light. I looked down. The gnarly vegetation wasn't the only hazard underfoot you had to watch out for in these woods. Dark square shapes had appeared all around us, protruding out of the ground.

Squinting through my specs, the realisation of what I was looking at slowly dawned on me. I stopped cold in my tracks. 'Gravestones?'

'That's right,' said Annie. Her breath hung white in the chill night air. 'We're standing on the edges of an abandoned graveyard. Dates back to the 1700s. There are graves for acres.'

You could tell the stones were that old, too. Centuries of neglect made them look more like a part of the woodland's terrain than man-made creations, reclaimed as they were by nature, dotted between tree trunks, most of them listing and sunken into the ground, with moss and creeping plants hiding their inscriptions.

The crunch of feet on dried leaves and the smell of burning tobacco alerted me that Will had sidled up beside me. He whistled, looking down at the stones. 'Now that is frigging creepy.'

Matt and Ash looked like they shared the same opinion. Ash, her face barely visible tucked inside her scarf, was snuggled in Matt's arms, squeezing Cottonball protectively and staring at the gravestones as if she expected the dead to come crawling out of them at any moment. Matt, too, his olive skin giving off a slight shimmer in the bluish light, was giving them a wide berth and wearing the expression of a man who had agreed to something he was now seriously regretting.

Esther, draped in a woolly shawl, her gold hair luminescent as it caught the moonlight, was looking around herself like she'd just stumbled upon the perfect picnic spot. 'This is it,' she said, her large teeth gleaming through her beaming face. 'It's practically electric with energy.'

The ghost hunters, taking this as their cue, began setting down and unpacking the bags of equipment they had hauled into the woods on their shoulders. I glanced warily at the dark trees surrounding us. I didn't like how they concealed the depths of the woods. Or how they appeared to whisper as an intermittent breeze rustled their almost leafless canopies. Who knew what was out there watching us?

'What's on the menu tonight, then?' Will asked Giles, as the team's leader opened a laptop he'd just placed on top of a foldable stand and started tapping one-fingered at the keyboard.

'We're going to try and capture some EVP.' Catching my baffled expression, Giles added, 'That's Electronic Voice Phenomena, the spoken voices of the dead.'

Norman, who had half erected a tripod and was looking around for a place he might position it, shouted, 'Cameras or not, boss?'

'No cameras. But set up the EMF detector,' replied Giles. He spotted Will watching what Norman was doing with interest. 'Ordinarily we train cameras on the experiment so we can check the footage to see if anything else is responsible for the voice phenomena when we analyse the recordings. But with time constrictions and poor visibility out here we're going to skip that.'

'It's a great spot for it, though. And the weather's nice and calm.' Carrie had materialised beside us in a duffel coat, most of her mahogany and orange streaked hair tucked inside its fur-trimmed hood. Moonlight glinted off her face piercings. She was holding the Ghostbusters type device she'd carried around the nursery room the night of the first hunt. 'Some say this graveyard is the main reason Hilderley Manor is so haunted. But if there hasn't been enough death under its own roof over the centuries to disprove that theory my name's Britney Fox.' Suddenly, as if not expecting herself to have spoken so confidently, she averted her eyes to the floor and shuffled off to join Annie and Esther, who were standing over one of the headstones, discussing what was written on its epitaph.

Giles, sitting on a box in front of the foldable table, had brought up software on the laptop. Large wavy lines like soundwaves ran across the screen in different windows, surrounded by hundreds of options and buttons.

'That waveform software?' Will asked, bending down to get a closer look.

'That's right,' said Norman, appearing like a giant over their shoulders. The glare from the laptop's screen made the logo on his shirt look as if it was glowing in the dark. He sipped from a can of lager then gave a loud belch.

'Do the recordings have to be analysed on the laptop later?'

'Nope,' said Norman, 'thanks to that beauty released just this year.' A gappy grin formed a crescent in the jungle of his beard. 'This baby gives us *instant* playback, and the ability to edit out unnecessary interference on the fly so we don't have to wait to hear what the recorder captured.'

'Yeah, it's a life saver,' Giles agreed. 'And most older software altered the audio so much, half of the original sound got completely lost.'

'So we'll get to hear whatever you capture during the experiment?' asked Will.

'Yup,' said Giles.

Will nodded, impressed.

After further preparations, the third night's hunt had begun. Annie had made handwritten notes of the weather and the artificial and natural sounds of the selected area: the screech of a nocturnal animal, the croak of a frog, the gentle gush of a distant dell, Cottonball's permanent pant, even the squeak of Ash's leather boots. She stood watch over the group with the look of a stern headmistress, checking our arms and legs for unnecessary movements. The recorder, manned by Norman, was silently recording the sound around us, ready to be transfered into the laptop for instant playback; documentary duties had been passed to Giles, who was standing on the fringe of the group, the blinking red light giving away his location in the darkness.

Will, yawning, dipped his hand inside his coat and pulled out his cigarettes. But instantly Annie waved her hand, pointing at the recorder to indicate it would create too much noise. Reluctantly, Will stowed the cigarettes away with a roll of his eyes.

'We know you're here,' Esther called out in an almost stentorian voice. 'We know you haunt this ground and we want you to talk with us.'

We had been instructed to stay quiet, to not fidget, jostle or move around too much. But so engrossed by Esther's words and trying to see if I could hear any ghostly responses with my own ears, I took the instruction a little too literally and stopped breathing altogether. I gasped in a lungful of air, and Will, spotting me, resisted the urge to laugh.

'I feel a presence,' whispered Esther. Her face brightened into a smile. 'It's a child.'

Everyone stayed quiet as the psychic, standing like the Virgin Mary at the helm of the group, hands held out, her hair looking like a halo it was so illuminated by the moonlight, glanced about herself, as if she was seeing invisible things moving there.

Squinting through my specs at the gravestone upon which her eyes were currently transfixed, I saw a handful of dead leaves scud across the ground. And a wispy light appeared above it, as if something invisible had briefly caught the moonlight.

'That's the thirty second span for replies, Norman,' Giles shouted, looking at his watch. 'Quick check, yeah?'

Norman tapped at the laptop's keyboard as the rest of us waited to see what his equipment was about to reveal. Eventually audio came out of the laptop's speakers. There was amplifier hiss and static at comfortable levels. Then a couple of garbled fragments of speech. Norman stopped the playback and clicked more buttons. The audio came back on, clearer this time. You could hear the sounds of the woods, the whisper of the trees, the hum of insects, more static, then a voice. Esther's.

*I feel a presence. It's a child.*

The sound of the woods continued to play, and then there was another noise.

*Shieeseeeeezus*

Everyone heard it at the same time, exchanging shocked glances.

Giles' voice came out of the recording. *That's the thirty second span—* Norman stopped the playback and did something on the screen that looked like he was rewinding the recording. He clicked more buttons and the audio played once more, this time slower, less distorted.

*Sheeeeseeeeeesusss*

'"She sees us,"' said Norman.

And he was right. When he played the recording a third time, you could hear the words, when you broke the distorted sound into syllables, spoken in a high-pitched girl's voice: She. Sees. Us.

The ghost hunters shared enthusiastic glances. This was clearly a very special piece of paranormal evidence they had captured. I found the phenomena incredible myself. And genuinely creepy, that slightly robotic voice hissing on the tape, all the way out here in the blackness of the woods. Even Will looked intrigued by the sound, his eyes trained attentively on the parapsychologist's every movement.

'Let's continue,' Giles instructed.

Norman reset the software and once again we stayed quiet as it began to record us. I saw Will checked his watch. He cast me a glance, reminding me that we would soon have to make our excuses and head back to the house to carry out our plan. I registered the reminder with a nod and then looked at Esther, who was speaking to the ghosts again.

'That's right,' she said, in the gentle, high-pitched voice you'd use with a child. 'I see you. And you see me, don't you? Is there anyone else there with you? What else do you see? Can you tell us?'

Again we allowed the spirits time to answer Esther's questions, for the recording software to pick up whatever they had to say. When enough time had elapsed for them to give a response, Giles instructed Norman to let us hear if the recording had picked up any more EVP.

Norman played the tape. Again we heard the static, the background sounds of the woods. He fixed the quality once. A second time. A third time. And we listened. At first we heard Esther's voice:

*That's right. I see you. And you see me, don't you? Is there anyone else there with you? What else do you see? Can you tell us?*

We waited. More static. More hissing. Then …

*He's there!* said another voice on the tape. It was still young, the voice of a child, but less high-pitched than the first. A boy perhaps.

*Where?* said another voice. It was the voice from the first recording. The girl.

*There! Behind the man with the round glasses.*

I felt my body freeze, a sensation like icy nails raking my back. I spun round expecting to see someone standing behind me, but there was nothing there other than the blackness of the woods.

*I don't see him!*

*There! The man with a hole in his face.*

Ash gasped. Will, looking worried suddenly, glanced behind me. A wave of terror choked me. I spun around again, expecting to see some hole-faced abomination standing there. But again there was nothing. I scanned the darkness, my senses so heightened I could hear the blood pumping through the veins in my neck. *Tu-*

*tum. Tu-tum. Tu-tum.*

Seeing my terror, Will did a throat slash gesture to Giles, instructing him to pause proceedings. Giles lifted his hand, a gesture for Norman to stop what he was doing.

'I think Quentin's had enough. Haven't you, mate?' said Will. He checked his watch again. 'We're gonna head back inside if it's alright with you folks. Carry on, though. Great job.'

He gripped my arm and began leading me away from the worried looking faces dotted around the moonlit circle. My eyes were flitting around, trying to find a man with a hole in his face as we walked. When we were out of earshot, I found my voice.

'What the hell just happened?'

'I don't know.' There was a very uncharacteristic note of worry in the northern accent.

'That wasn't fake, Will. It couldn't be.'

He threw me a shifty glance under his eyebrows. 'People will try anything if they're desperate enough.'

But he couldn't hide the doubt in his voice, that hint of dishonesty. He was just saying it to try and alleviate my anxiety.

'Look,' he said, his hand coming to rest on my back, 'You're fine. Just stay cool until we're out of these woods.'

It would have been nice if I could have stayed calm. If I'd been able to believe him. But as we trekked back through the unruly undergrowth, towards the lights of the manor blinking at us through the trees, the only thing I believed was that something very terrifying was stalking me.

# CHAPTER FIFTEEN

# The Elephant in the Room

'KAT'S RIGHT, THIS place is cursed,' I said, a creeping doubt infiltrating my mind as we reached the second floor corridor. 'Aren't we asking for trouble messing with it?'

'Relax, squire,' Will, marching ahead, reassured me. 'Don't forget that we're dealing with the unexplained here. Everything is speculation.'

Easy for him to say. He wasn't the one about to offer himself up as bait to try and snare a murderous madman. He wasn't the one seeing ghosts around every corner. I felt like one of Stan's rodent traps. Only, lying in that bed, I was likely to end up as dead as a rodent myself. Perhaps I would get definitive proof the afterlife existed during my stay here after all, by ending up being sent there myself.

When we got to the room, Will ordered me to wait at the threshold. He peered behind the door, got on his hands and knees to check under the bed, then double checked the corridor before allowing me inside. It was like having my own personal bodyguard. One comforting part to this blimming madness at least.

He closed the door and switched on the lights. When he turned he saw me standing at the foot of the bed, hugging my torso. I must have looked like a man picturing his own funeral because his features slackened with sympathy. 'Nothing bad will happen to you while I'm around.'

The comforting words made me feel a little better. 'Promise?'

'Well, of course I can't prom—'

'Will!'

'Cross my heart.'

Feeling even more pessimistic about what lay ahead, I went and sat down on my side of the bed, removing my specs to rub the tiredness out of my eyes. Will surprised me when he came over and started removing my blazer. He folded it neatly and draped it over the coffer. Then he got down on one knee. For a mad second I thought he was about to propose, until he started unlacing my shoes. I frowned.

'What are you doing?'

'Helping you into bed.'

'Will, I'm twenty seven. Not five.'

Ignoring me, he removed the shoes and placed them neatly together in front of the bedside table, then lifted my legs onto the mattress. To my relief, he stopped short of tucking me in, instead walking over to the door to shed himself of his own coat. Hooking it on the back of the door, he turned and said, quite casually, 'Want some tea?'

I crossed my arms and adopted a sullen pout. 'Why not? If I'm going to be dead soon, I might as well enjoy a bit of comfort.'

He disregarded my petulance, kicking off his boots and rolling up his shirt sleeves. He had prepared for our interval by prearranging drinks and snacks. Chocolate digestives, a thermos flask and china cups stolen from the dining hall were set out on a tray on the dresser. Very romantic. He whistled to himself as he unscrewed the flask and poured tea into the cups.

I glanced around the room dejectedly. I could see Will's reflection in the paned window. 'Shouldn't we be staying vigilant, not getting comfortable?'

'In your vision Stan didn't appear until past midnight, remember?'

I sighed glumly. 'Oh yeah. Forgot.'

I had forgotten about a lot of things on the way up here. That happens when your mind is swamped with things to worry about. Seeing a naked man in a cellar that looks just like you. Seeing another that was impervious to walls vanish out of sight. Hearing the voices of spirit children telling you there's a man with a hole in his face standing behind you. Knowing a gay-hating loon who can't stand the sight of you is probably in his cottage at this very moment, polishing his shotgun, ready to enter the room and blow your brains out.

Will interrupted my daymare by appearing at the side of the bed with two steaming cups, a biscuit pinched between his teeth. I pulled my knees to my chest to allow him room to sit down. He positioned himself against the bed frame and tucked his feet beneath him, mirroring my position against the headboard. He dunked the biscuit and chucked the whole thing into his mouth in one.

I took a sip from my own cup, welcoming the warmth after being out in the cold, the tea's calming effect instantly easing my nerves. There's something comforting about thermos tea. Sipping it carried my mind to memories of camping trips with Elliot. Nights when we'd lie under the stars, the back of our heads cushioned by our coats, our crowns touching one another's shoulder, so if anyone was to look down at us from above we'd look like one very long person with a pair of feet at both ends. Not many people bother to look up at the night sky, too busy with their heads in their phones. But when you do it's surprising just how much is actually going on up there.

Will rolled his head back, massaging his neck. He looked gorgeous in the soft light. It was pleasing to see him sober on our final evening at the manor. Though I wouldn't have said no to having his arms wrapped around me tonight. Anything to distract me from the ghastly thoughts of what lay ahead, from mentally pencilling my last will and testament.

'About the elephant in the room,' he said. 'It deserves some explanation.'

The elephant in the room. So he was finally going to broach it. Was that what the tea making, the undressing me was all about? Softening me up before he gave me the typical excuses and feigned apologies?

I shook my head. 'Don't bother. I'm not in the mood.'

'Let me explain.'

'You don't have to. I know you're probably not even gay and you regret the entire thing. I'm not mad at you. I just don't want excuses, or pity. Not now.' I sipped my tea, very aware of how sullen I looked and sounded. But, quite frankly, I felt justified considering the circumstances.

'You're right. I'm not gay. I'm not anything. I'm just me. I like what I like. Sometimes that's a girl. Sometimes it's a guy. It's the person I see, not the gender.'

I was going to ask him why he'd ran a mile after seeing me enter the dining hall at breakfast if that was the case, but knowing the answer was probably that he felt so ashamed about last night he had to run to the bathroom and throw up, I didn't bother. 'Don't waste what time I've got left with excuses, Will. I know I'm as fanciable as roadkill. And I don't need James Dean's younger brother kicking me while I'm down by patronising me.' I set down the cup next to my physics book on the beside table and moved my legs to get off the bed.

Will reached out and gripped my wrist, struggling to hold back a grin. 'Stop talking like you're about to die, you muppet. I told you, nothing is going to happen to you. And it isn't an excuse. Would you just let me explain?'

My eyes moved distrustfully from the hand on my wrist to the earnest blue eyes looking at me. Downcast, I sat back against the pillow and folded my arms across my chest.

'I was in a three year relationship that ended eight months ago,' Will said. 'Olivia. I met her when she was temping as a secretary for the accountancy firm that manages my finances. She was stunning: auburn hair, porcelain skin, gorgeous body. And well aware of how she could use it to get me to notice her. The way she looked at me, it made me feel like a teenager again, excited. I knew life with her would be an adventure. And it was. I had the time of my life, socially and sexually. Especially sexually. That was where we connected like ink and paper. It was out of this world. Not just sex, we were reaching a higher place, transcending. She was like a drug.' Will's eyes were intent as he spoke. He swallowed the dryness out of his throat, plucked at the fabric of his socks. 'That was just the love bombing stage. The crucial part of her game. She knew what I wanted, what I needed, the love I never got growing up. And she gave it to me in spades: validation, making me feel seen and heard for the first time. I was an 'impeccable writer.' The most 'handsome man she'd ever laid eyes on.' A man worthy of giving her, the auburn haired goddess men would throw punches over, the perfect family she longed for.'

I watched him from the other side of the bed. Saw anguish crease his forehead as he remembered the things he was telling me. Ordinarily he was laid back, if a little hard to decipher. He seemed sardonically amused by life and all its tumultuations. Which I secretly suspected was a way of coping with his neglectful past. But he didn't look like that now. A sombreness had possessed his blue eyes as he recalled this auburn-haired vixen named Olivia. What had she done to make him look so grave?

'We were engaged, living with each other and venturing into business together within months,' he said. 'All her idea. I can't believe how stupid I was in hindsight, allowing someone I barely knew into every part of my life. But I was blinded by the whirlwind. And I guess I was good supply. A decent writer with some significant interest in my work. Good looking. Nature gave me the tools to please — if you know what I mean.' At this I blushed and tried not to let my eyes drift southward to his groin. 'I'm a bloody good mate if I think you're alright, too. And don't think I'm bragging, by the way. It's no compliment to be hunted and chosen for your most appealing qualities when you're dealing with someone like Olivia.'

'What, it wasn't genuine?' I asked.

'The mind games began about a year into the relationship, once I was ensnarled in the commitments, the joint accounts, the contracts. She managed to hide her true personality that long. It was the odd comment at first, criticising my looks or the amount of time I spent at the gym. Jealousy over other women, my friends even. When I got the publishing deal, I expected her to be thrilled — after all, she'd always said I'd write something worth putting on the shelves. But she questioned every part of it until I began to doubt it myself. When I got suspicious or annoyed, the old Olivia would come out and I'd feel things were fine again. She'd remind me of everything she'd done for me. She knew how to press my emotional buttons, the ones she'd worked so hard at figuring out, the puppet master she is. It's disorienting, getting the mixed messages, never knowing which character you'll get that day.'

Will sipped from the cup in his hand. But it seemed an action more out of nerves than thirst. I remained absorbed by his story, watching him silently from across the bed covers.

'She feared losing me more than anything,' he said softly. 'And yet, at the same time I was just a play thing to her, an accessory to make her look good. She tried to make me feel worthless, be worthless. She didn't need me to love her, because I think Olivia doesn't believe that real love exists. She needed me to need her. But the more I did, the more she saw me as pathetic. And I think she wanted to believe that I was pathetic, so that it validated how much better than everyone else she thinks she is. That's why she couldn't believe it when I finished it.'

'*You* ended it?'

'I finally grew some balls, yeah.'

'And it was as easy as that?'

He gave a bitter laugh. 'Ending it was the worst part. It was the ultimate insult to her, to her inflated sense of self. How dare I think I was worthy enough to leave the goddess Olivia, that I'd find anyone even close to matching her. She was the one who left again and again, throwing herself into the arms of other men, her exes included. I was expected to remain there, no matter how many times she left and returned, just taking the abuse hurled at me for whatever transgression I was supposed to have committed.' Will's lip curled in a semblance of a smile. 'Well, that last time I didn't. Her response? The way she always responds to pain: to try and hurt someone as deeply as possible. She'd been screwing my best mate behind my back, keeping him there as some sort of weapon she would pull out when the time was right, when she knew the game was up. Some best mate he was. Within a fortnight they'd moved in together and were engaged, announced all over social media to make sure I heard every last carefully orchestrated detail.'

Rain had started up outside, tapping against the window. Car headlights strobed through the curtains. I heard the sound of tires crunching over gravel on the front drive. Will's story had left an unsettling feeling in the room. And inside my heart. According to him and Kat, relationships were ordeals to survive not the perfect companionships depicted in a million romance books. Had I really missed out over my celibate years?

'So you see, squire, it's not just men that I'm not interested in. After Olivia, I'm not interested in people. I call her my beautiful nightmare. She made me aware of my weak spots. She showed me who my true friends really were. She taught me beauty means nothing if it doesn't come from the heart. She's one of the most beautiful women I've ever laid eyes on, and yet today I see her as the ugliest. But some nightmares are hard to shake off. Eight months and I'm still healing, still learning to trust again.'

I didn't know what to say. I couldn't imagine what it would be like to go through something as nightmarish as what Will had just described. I couldn't imagine that a person could be so vindictive. But watching him as he gazed into the corner of the room, that distant look in his eyes as he reflected on his story, I could relate to what it felt like to be haunted by the ghosts of your past.

'Let's hope we can both learn to leave the past behind us soon, eh?' I said.

Will's eyes drifted away from the corner and landed on me. He watched me for a moment before bending over the side of the bed and setting down his cup. He clambered over the covers until he was sitting next to me, his back pressed against the headboard on Kat's side of the bed. His hand came up to my face. He ran the back of his knuckles lightly down my cheek.

I felt the familiar nerves return. The shyness from being unused to another person's touch. The lack of confidence from being so close to someone as good looking as Will. The fear that hit me when I thought this was something I could get used to, because then it could be taken away from me again.

Will blinked softly as he looked into my eyes. 'You really are handsome, Strange. Glasses or not. And I'm not drunk tonight.'

My heart was beating so hard I was afraid he might hear it. A maelstrom of emotion felt like it was going to burst right out of my chest. Maybe there was some excitement in there, as well as the nerves. And it suddenly grew stronger when I sensed Will was about to kiss me a second time.

He leaned in, bringing his lips close to mine. I closed my eyes, anticipating their touch. But when I didn't feel anything I opened them again. Will had pulled away, his eyes no longer looking into mine but staring at the door.

'Wh—' I started.

'Shh. Do you hear that?'

I listened, but heard nothing. 'What is it?'

'Someone's coming.'

# - CHAPTER SIXTEEN -

# *The Trap*

WE'RE ALL USED to waiting for our death to occur, from the moment we wake up to the moment we go to sleep. Waiting for your own murder, though — now that is a place I didn't think I would ever be.

Lying under the covers, my cheek pressed against the pillow, I thought my heart might pack in all together it pounded so hard against my breastbone. And it didn't help that the lights were out, just a strip of gold light under the door to break the uncertain blackness. Helpless as I lay there, all I could do was stare at it, waiting.

The footsteps coming down the corridor grew louder with the sound of my heartbeat as they approached. Two foot-shaped shadows appeared in the strip of light. They stayed there for a moment, unmoving. Was someone listening?

I stole a glance at the changing screen where Will was hiding. Was that a flicker of movement I saw through the latticework? I remembered his reassuring words, *'Nothing bad will happen to you while I'm around.'* I just hoped he wouldn't be regretting them in the next few minutes.

A soft knock on the door made me start. Then the handle

turned and the door opened with a squeaky creak. I squeezed my eyes shut. At least I wasn't worried about my heart giving up on me anymore. Time seems to stand still when you meet your killer, when you know your final moments have arrived. All other worries disappear and you're focused on one thing and one thing only: this person who is about to end your life. Forget the fight or flight response. I couldn't do either. I had to lie there, a sitting duck, hoping my Superman behind the changing screen would save me. This was the moment I would find out if Will was true to his word. If I had made the right decision trusting him with the thing I treasured the most: my life.

A floorboard creaked. I braced for a gunshot. But I didn't hear one. I heard a high-pitched gasp. Confusion hit me. I stopped breathing to hear better. There was another creak on the boards. This time from the other side of the room, where Will was hiding. Was he bracing to jump into action?

Unable to bear the suspense any longer, I prised one eye open. It wasn't Stan Crouch who had entered the room. There was a diminutive person silhouetted in the light of the doorway. A person I recognised.

'Do forgive me, Mr Strange. Only, I saw the light on from downstairs ...' Mrs Brown's voice trailed off and a hand went to her mouth in embarrassment.

I sat up and switched on the bedside lamp. Hilderley Manor's housekeeper, donned in a rain spotted bucket hat and camel coat, blinked at me like a startled fawn. I blinked back, speechless and confused as my heart rate decelerated. What was the Scotswoman doing here? Especially since she left the manor at the same time each evening  and should have been tucked in bed at home. I glanced at the changing screen. Will remained hidden, perhaps worried he might give her a heart attack if he were to suddenly step out from behind it. I finally found my voice. 'What are you doing here?'

'It's so unprofessional of me to intrude like this, I know, but … well …' Mrs Brown hesitated, still taken unawares from stumbling upon one of her houseguests mid-sleep.

'Sit down,' I said.

She shuffled over and sat in the spot where Will had been sitting just moments before. 'I debated coming, what with it being so late,' she said. 'And my Fergus was howling up a storm for me not to leave him. He only got home at tea time after three days at the vets for his thyroid op. But I felt it was urgent and I knew you'd be busy getting ready to leave in the morning.'

I felt worried suddenly. 'What is it?'

'Do you remember telling me to come and see you if I suspected Stan was a danger to someone?'

'What's he done?'

'Oh don't worry, he hasn't hurt anyone. Well, not yet he hasn't. It's just that I remembered something he said to me about a week ago. I thought it was strange at the time. But it was only after you told me about the shotgun that it got me worried.'

I sat up straighter. I felt awkward half-covered by the bedsheets, even if I was fully dressed underneath. Rain was hitting the window harder now. I thought I heard another creak behind the changing screen. Mrs Brown elaborated.

'We were having another heated chat,' she said. 'Stan had been sequestered in his cottage for days and I was more than worried about him. I went to see him, suggested he might want to come to the market, look at some plants, if only just to get out of the cottage for a few hours, give him a change of scenery. But he got all irate, said he didn't have time to be wandering about looking at plants with the things he had to worry about. He wouldn't tell me what those things were. But he said he'd be "better off dead like mouse" if the "calibre of the only friend he had left in the world was a daft hag who wanted to faff about looking at sodding plants."' Mrs Brown became crimson, from either embarrassment or annoyance I couldn't work out which. 'Those were his exact words. Not 'dead *like* a mouse.' He said "dead like mouse." As if Mouse was a name.'

'Mouse ...' I whispered, recalling the word from somewhere.

'Well, with his mind going he was obviously confused. My Roy was the same near the end, getting his grammar and his words all wrong. He once called me Edith and I swear I felt my heart break in two. But 'dead like a mouse' is the sort of thing Stan would say; he's sent a fair few mice to their graves over the years with his traps.' Mrs Brown shook her head in despair. 'There was no need for such rudeness, not when you're only trying to help someone! And if he won't open up to me then what am I supposed to suggest? I'm not Mystic Margarita, or whatever it is that daft bat who does the horoscopes in the paper is called.' She blew out her frustration with a weary sigh. 'Regardless, Stan's message was that he'd be better off dead. I don't like him talking like that, Mr Strange. Not when he's got a weapon in that cottage. The serious harm he could do if he got any funny ideas!'

Mrs Brown's words percolated in my mind. The gravity of what she was telling me, that Stan Crouch could seriously harm himself, was sinking in. Yet despite requesting that she come to me with this very information, I felt completely clueless about what I was going to do about it. Not to mention something was making me very suspicious.

'What I was wondering, Mr Strange, was ... well, can't you talk to him? Get him to give up the shotgun somehow? It might work better coming from you, a man, than little old me. There's still time before you leave. I popped round the back just now and saw the lights on in the cottage. Or you could have a word with him first thing before you leave.' Her tired eyes blinked at me beseechingly. 'It's just a temporary measure. I'm going to talk to a doctor friend this week, ask her if there's anything she recommends, you know, to get Stan some proper help. But you'd be putting my mind at rest like you couldn't imagine.'

I hesitated before saying, 'Sure, I'll speak to Mr Crouch.'

The anguish in Mrs Brown's face rearranged into a look of mild surprise, as if she hadn't expected such willingness. 'Oh. Well, thanks.'

I forced a smile. 'It's no problem.'

The little Scotswoman got up to leave, straightening her coat. 'I might as well sort a couple of things in the kitchen before I leave, make things a bit easier for the cook. We've got a busy week ahead, what with Halloween coming up.' She checked the gloves and handbag were still in her hand, gave me a small bow and scurried to the door.

But when she reached it, she stopped and paused, turning her head as if bothered by a thought. I smiled at her again and she let the thought go, stepping into the corridor and closing the door behind her.

The second she was out of sight my smile instantly faded. I had no intention of going to see Stan Crouch to ask him to hand over the shotgun. My mind was busy coming up with another theory for why the caretaker had made such a strange comment. And, if I was right, the threat of Stan killing himself was going to be the least of Mrs Brown's worries.

* * * * *

'Reminds me of being a teenager, all those bedrooms I used to sneak into,' said Will, slipping out from behind the changing screen with a smirk on his face. But I wasn't paying attention as I sat on the bed, my mind racing.

Mouse … I had heard the word before. At the seance. It was the name of the spirit that made contact with us. A coincidence to say the least. Had Stan, contrary to what Mrs Brown thought, meant to say he wished he was dead like Mouse? Mouse being the name of someone he knew? Someone who was now haunting Hilderley Manor?

I recalled the vision I had in the cellar, Stan standing over me with the shotgun. It felt erroneous. Something about the room wasn't right. What was it? I glanced around me. The bed was different. There had been no fourposter in the vision. And the clock that told me it was past midnight was nowhere to be seen here. Stan, too, even if his face had been half hidden beneath the hood and difficult to see, looked different from the wizened creature who currently stalked the house. He was younger, more robust. He was the man he would have been years ago …

The realisation hit me with disorienting force. 'Oh my God.'

'What?' Will had opened the door to check the corridor. There mustn't have been any shotgun-wielding madmen coming down it because he closed it and came over to sit down beside me.

'Remind me what it's called when you can see and feel other people's emotions?' I said.

'Clairsentience.'

'Do you think it's possible that a clairsentient person could see another person's memories?'

'Quentin, with you I'm starting to think anything is possible.'

I shook my head. 'I've got it all wrong. The vision wasn't from my future. It was a memory from the past. Someone else's past.'

Will watched me blankly as my mind sifted through the events of the last couple of days. Arriving at the manor and seeing a figure standing in the window of the very room I was staying in. Mrs Brown, showing us the room, had said, *"It used to accommodate lowly staff many moons ago."* Had the figure been the ghost of someone who worked at Hilderley Manor, a worker who had stayed in this room?

Memories continued to flood my mind. I thought about the apparitions I had seen. The young man in the cellar who looked so much like me. The young man walking down the corridor before he vanished out of sight. I recollected that distinctive walk he had, the way he dragged it along the ground. And that's when the conversation with Mrs Brown in the sitting room came back to me. *'He wasn't all there, this lad. What people used to call backward years ago. You know, retarded. Had a funny walk that people used to pick on him for.'*

I leapt up from the bed and rushed to where my blazer was folded on the coffer. I reached inside the pocket and pulled out the piece of paper that I'd picked up off the carpet runner. I looked at the child's drawing again. There were two stick figures; one was wearing a flat cap, just like the one the young man was wearing when I saw him, and the other was holding a rake. Behind them stood a water fountain, identical to the one in Hilderley Manor's garden. It was the young man himself and Stan Crouch. And there, in the bottom right hand corner, was the signature of the picture's artist in capital letters: MOUSE.

'He's dead,' I whispered. And, like a stage cue, a thunderclap followed by a lightning flash returned a menacing reply.

Will gazed up at me. 'Who's dead?'

'Joe Maguire.'

'Joe who?'

'The young man Mr Crouch took under his wing, the one who worked as an apprentice at the manor.' I glanced around the room. 'This was his room. He found a way to show me how he died. It was him who Stan killed with the shotgun.'

Will blinked up at me, suspending disbelief.

'We have to stop Mr Crouch before he harms himself.'

Will got to his feet and gripped my arm. 'Quentin —'

'We haven't got time, Will! It all makes sense. Stan killed Joe. He's a murderer. And if he kills himself we'll never find out why he did it.'

Seconds later we were dashing out of the front door, on our way to the caretaker's cottage. A relentless torrent of rain was lashing the gravel driveway and battering the roofs of the visitors' cars as we ran.

'Can see where the surname comes in now,' said Will, as we rounded the side of the estate and the garden came into view. 'Life with you is certainly frigging strange!'

We rushed down the steps, past the bench and the fountain, up the gravel path, past the weeping cherry, until we had reached Stan's cottage. Will banged the stable door three times with his fist. 'Open the door, Lurch. We need to talk.'

The rain sounded more like hailstone as it continued to pour down, soaking my hair and blazer, running in rivulets down my cheeks as I kept a wary distance. There was a dim light on inside the abode. I thought I glimpsed a shadow move in one of the grimy windows. I nodded for Will to check. He went over and cupped his hands against the glass. He rapped one of the panes with his knuckles. 'We know you're in there. Open up, old man, or I'm breaking that weak as shite door into splinters and dragging you out of there.'

'He has a shotgun,' I reminded him.

'Shit. Forgot about that.'

There was an unlocking sound. The stable door opened. Through a slim crack, Stan's face appeared, concealed inside the hood of his raincoat. At first I thought he was frightened, intimidated by Will's threats. But then the door swung wide and he stepped out, holding the shotgun. He lifted it and pointed it directly at my face.

'Step away, boy,' he growled. 'Or I blow a hole through your head.'

I stood there, blinking through my rain-speckled glasses down the barrel of the weapon. I didn't move. I couldn't.

Stan took a step closer. 'I said step away!'

A voice came from behind me. 'What in the blazes is going on?'

It belonged to Mrs Brown. I didn't turn, too petrified to make a move in fear it would get my head blown off. Stan, distracted, let his eyes flit from mine to where she must have been standing over my shoulder.

My life flashing before my eyes, I had momentarily forgotten that Will was feet away. But then, just like Superman, he flew in from the side, bringing Stan crashing to the floor. The shotgun exploded with a flash. I ducked, dodging the bullet by inches. Mrs Brown let out a scream.

Will and Stan struggled on the ground, Will trying to remove the weapon from Stan's grip. For such an arthritic looking person, Stan could certainly put up a fight. Will finally managed to prise the gun from his hands, hurling it into a nearby flowerbed. He pushed himself to his feet, hauling the wriggling senior up with him. Then he stood there, his prey restrained against his chest in a headlock, looking dishevelled but proud of his catch.

It had been a close call. But he had kept to his word and just saved my life.

# - CHAPTER SEVENTEEN -

# *Stan's Story*

'JUST STOP RESISTING and it'll be less painful for both of us.'

Will had finally got Stan inside the kitchen after much difficulty getting through the hallway. But even he had misjudged the elderly man's determination to resist capture, evident from his wheeze and the disarranged quiff cascading over his forehead. Stan edged towards the table as I ushered Mrs Brown through the door and shut it behind us. Will flicked a switch and the candelabra light fitting came on, bathing our soaked faces in its amber glow.

With nowhere to run and realising any further attempts at escape would be futile, Stan finally relented and dropped into a chair at the table. He unburdened himself from the hood of his raincoat. Underneath, he was red and clammy. He looked even older under the artificial light, his knobbly chin frosted with white stubble beneath his purple-veined nose. And he sounded as battered as an old tractor, his chest rasping and wheezing from exertion.

There was a beat of quiet as everyone calmed down from the struggle that had brought us into the room. Mrs Brown, still dressed in her drenched coat and hat, her handbag dangling from the crease of her arm, was staring heedfully at her friend, hoping he would offer an explanation for his impromptu capture. But Stan was purposely avoiding eye contact with the captors standing around him, averting his rheumy eyes to the grainy surface of the table.

Mrs Brown looked at me, her eyes imploring. 'What is it? What's this about?'

'It's Joe Maguire,' I said. 'He didn't leave. He's still in the manor. Isn't he, Mr Crouch?'

Stan's edgy eyes drifted sheepishly from the table. They twinkled for a second in the light. Was it rheum or the first sign of tears? He didn't answer, but he didn't have to: the guilt was written all over his face.

'Joe's here? Wha — how?' faltered Mrs Brown.

'He's dead, Elspeth,' said Stan. 'Joe's dead.' There was a lightness in his voice. A man unburdening himself of a secret that had haunted him for many years.

'Dead? But —?'

'I killed him, didn't I?'

The starkness of Stan's words smarted as they lingered in the quietness of the kitchen. And as they released from the old man, so too did a single tear, running in a rivulet down his flushed cheek and vanishing into the whiskers on his chin.

Mrs Brown had turned a deathly white. So much so that she looked as if she was about to pass out. Seeing this, I reached out and guided her over to the table, pulling out a chair for her to take the weight off her feet. She lowered herself into the seat, which was directly across from Stan's. I removed her hat and set it on the table.

Mrs Brown placed her handbag near the hat with a shaky hand. 'You killed Joe?' she whispered.

'It was Billy Crowley's fault, the evil bastard,' Stan blurted. 'He caused this, not me!'

'Billy?' Mrs Brown recollected the name. 'The relative of the Blackfords?'

'He were a bully, a rotten snake. Not just bad, he was bleeding evil. He got off on hurting others, enjoyed it. He set his eyes on Joe and like a wolf with a baby lamb the poor lad didn't stand a chance.'

Stan hunted a wallet out of his raincoat. He pulled out a dogeared black and white photograph and dropped it on the surface of the table. I stared at it. It showed a younger Stan Crouch, the same age he was in the vision, standing in what looked like Hilderley Manor's garden with his arm around the shoulder of a young man in his early twenties. A young man who bore more than a striking resemblance to myself. The same young man I saw naked and sobbing in the cellar before falling and blacking out. But he wasn't sobbing here. He was beaming with a joy that was radiating off him like light. It was Joe Maguire.

'Just look at the lad,' Stan implored Mrs Brown. 'I told you what he was like, how he didn't see the world the same way others did, how he was slow in that way, childlike. And sensitive. He'd smile at flowers, at a summer sky, be in his glory watching a ladybird crawl across his hand. If my traps killed rats and mice around the manor he'd get upset and ask if we could bring them back to life. The lad wouldn't have hurt a fly. Billy Crowley sniffed out that vulnerability like a shark sniffs out fresh blood.' Stan's face turned mottled purple with a seasoned bitterness. 'When Crowley befriended him he was flattered. Of course he was, he'd never had that sort of attention before. Folk weren't so keen on being associated with what they called a 'freak' back then. But it was all a ruse. Crowley was just taking advantage of Joe's naivety, grooming him. He wanted to use him for his disgusting urges. Crowley was a pervert, just like them two.'

Stan had jabbed his gnarly finger at me and Will. Instinctively, Will stepped forward, eyes narrowing threateningly. 'Watch your filthy gob, old man.'

I held my arm out in a conciliatory gesture. Reluctantly, Will flattened his shoulders. 'You mean Billy was gay?' I said.

Stan bared the few teeth left in his mouth. 'A filthy queer is what he was! And the reason I hate the perverts as much I hate the arthritis that rots the bones in my legs. If Billy Crowley's anything to go by, it's proof being queer is the curse of the Devil.'

I could feel Will's urge to retaliate as he stood beside me, but he managed to restrain himself despite Stan's derogatory insults. Mrs Brown was staring at Stan with a look of dread on her face.

'What did Billy do to Joe, Stan?' she said, her voice so frail she sounded childlike.

'I caught them down in the cellar. Doing that filthy stuff queers do. Poor Joe, with no clothes on. Billy forcing himself on him. I know he did because Joe was terrified, wouldn't stop crying.'

I recalled the sight of Joe Maguire down in the cellar, naked and crying. So that's what I was seeing. But what was it? A sort of visual echo of his memory?

'Joe was never the same after Billy started messing with him.' Stan looked pained as he spoke. 'If the bastard hadn't done that, if I hadn't caught them, then none of this would have happened.'

Mrs Brown blinked at her wizened friend. 'You killed Joe because Billy Crowley abused him?'

Stan shook his head. 'It got complicated. After I caught them, Billy got angry with me. He knew what the consequences were of a secret like that getting out. Back then you were in serious trouble if you were caught buggering another man. And I only went and made it worse. I threatened to tell on him if I caught him anywhere near Joe again. I should never have said that. Because it was a lie. I never would have put Joe at risk of getting locked up. I was just angry.'

Stan's face twisted with regret. I saw Mrs Brown brace as he raised his hand, about to hammer it on the table. But then he let the hand relax, shaking his head despairingly.

'That threat was what made Billy do what he did. The conniving rat came to see me with his cronies. Told me he was going to blame it all on Joe, play the victim, get 'the freak' as he put it sent away to be abused where all the other queers were locked up. And he'd have done it, too, wicked gremlin he was. He knew people would believe him over anything Joe said. Joe was a laughing stock, summat to be jeered at like a circus freak. And how would he stand up for himself in court? He'd cry and beg for forgiveness if he did summat as innocent as break a glass. He didn't have the brains to defend himself against an accusation like that. And Crowley was clever enough to lie, twist and manipulate himself out of the truth. He had the entire house wrapped around his finger, cowards they were, intimidated by the grandiose facade that was nothing but an act. The flying monkeys would have backed him up and poor Joe wouldn't have stood a chance.'

Stan lifted his bloodshot eyes, looking at the faces watching him. He looked boyish for a brief moment, the pleading face of a child hoping his accusers would forgive his wrongdoing.

'They'd have sent Joe to prison! And the poor lad wouldn't have survived a place as brutal as that, types they have locked up in there. The things they would have done to him if they found out he was in for ...' Stan shook his head, more tears leaking down the ravine-like wrinkles in his cheeks. 'Being queer then wasn't what it is now. People were disgusted by it, they feared it, thought it was an abomination. Men got locked up for life. I couldn't let that happen to Joe. Not that sweet, innocent lad. I just couldn't.'

A realisation had crept into Mrs Brown's face. 'Stan, are you saying that ... that —'

'I killed him to save him from that,' Stan confessed.

Will and I exchanged a dark glance. Sensations of shock, regret and sadness churned inside my chest all at once. Will, too, looked surprised by the unexpected motive, but the look he was giving Mr Crouch still held a measure of distaste.

The harrowing revelation was too much for Mrs Brown. The kindly housekeeper pressed her hand to her mouth and emitted a wave of small, anguished sobs. Stan's emotions spilled over in response to seeing the impact his confession had had on his closest and only remaining friend.

'I was saving the lad, Elspeth!' he sobbed. 'I was saving him from a life of hell. I might have hated what he'd done, what that monster had turned him into, but I knew he didn't deserve punishment as brutal as prison.'

'But killing him, Stan!' cried Mrs Brown. 'Murder!'

'I thought about killing Crowley instead. But his goons, Dennis and Midgely, were in on his plan. Those two would have gone blabbing to the pigs and I'd have looked like the guilty one, like I was trying to cover up what Joe had done by killing Crowley. And they were as warped as their leader, they'd have kept the lie going out of spite. Joe and I both would have ended up inside. And how would I have been able to protect him then? Joe had no friends, no family, just me. He might as well have not existed, way people avoided him like the plague. It had to be him.'

Stan extended his shaky arm across the table, looking pleadingly at Mrs Brown. But she snatched her hand away at once. The sobs that came out of Stan in reaction to this rejection sounded as if they welled up from a deep place inside his gut. His arm slid slowly back across the table.

'How did you commit the murder without anyone hearing the shotgun?' I asked, shivering in my rain-soaked clothes.

'No one was in the house that night. The family had gone away for a long weekend. I went up to his room when he was asleep. I crept over to the bed with my shotgun. He only saw me for a brief second before I grabbed a pillow, pressed it over his face and ...' Stan's face creased with guilt as it entreated for forgiveness. '... he didn't know what was happening! He died quickly and without any pain!'

The caretaker broke into heavy sobs, his shoulders juddering, snot and tears glistening on his upper lip. It was as if a dam had burst inside him and all the shame and regret was pouring out. I recalled once again the vision from the cellar that I had believed to be my own murder. It was exactly as Stan had just described it, except I must have woken up before I saw the part where he grabbed the pillow. I remembered the feeling of sadness. Was that Joe's emotion I was feeling? Sadness because he knew that the one person who cared about him was about to kill him?

'What did you do with the body?' Will had spoken, calm and authoritative, controlling the situation, though he looked paler and less steadfast than he was before entering the kitchen.

'I buried him around the back of the estate, empty patch of grass midway down the garden,' Stan sniffed. 'A few years later I planted the weeping cherry as a memorial to him, a few feet away so he wouldn't be disturbed by the roots. Nobody even came looking for him. Lad didn't have anyone worrying about him. Only me.'

Will shook his head in disbelief. Stan, wiping his eyes, looked over at the window and a wistful look grew on his face.

'I knew he'd like it out there. He loved the garden, it's where he would have wanted to rest. And he never left. Not really. I could always feel his presence. Especially around the anniversary of his death. It were his birthday that night. That was just a coincidence, because it happened to fall on the only night I could do it, with the family out, and the pigs about to come sniffing over Crowley's accusation. But it was the best birthday gift I could have given him, sending him to the safest place he could be.' Stan's face lightened with a fond memory. 'We had the best day — biscuits, cake and homemade lemonade. I showed him chicks in a wren's nest. He loved birds. He loved to draw them, he did.'

'And did they come looking for him? The police?' asked Will.

The smile on Stan's face shifted to an angry scowl. ''Course they did. That evil little git was true to his word. Once that one sets his goal on ruining someone he doesn't go back. Little bastard relishes it. Pigs came marching up here in pairs to arrest Joe as if he'd done summat as bad as rob a bank.'

'What did you tell them?'

'That he'd left and didn't say where he was going. And they had no reason not to believe me, no one to say otherwise, no family to draw any suspicion. I guess they didn't care enough about Crowley's accusation to dig any deeper or bother following it up because I heard no more from the bastards after that. Billy was angrier at that than anything else, revealing to everyone he'd been molested by the 'freak' for no payoff. The smallest bit of justice I got that was, watching him try and wriggle out of his own lies when he realised he wasn't going to get his revenge after all.'

Will crossed his arms. 'That was the end of it for Crowley?'

'Yeah, buggered off not long after to no doubt wreak havoc in some other poor sod's life. But it wasn't the end for me.' Stan's face turned dark with fear as he looked at each of the faces staring at him in turn. 'They live on, you know, after they die. They still have the ability to think, to want, to need. Joe was angry. He couldn't understand why I'd done what I did. He couldn't rest. He was always more active around the anniversary. I could feel him, sense the unrest. But I've never felt him as strong as I did this time. When you lot arrived it was the last thing I needed. A bunch of folk summoning the dead.' Stan's eyes met mine. 'You even look like him. And you've got the same sort of soul he had. You see things others don't. I've lived long enough to spot folk who have the gift when I see them. It's in the eyes, the way they see right through you, reading every part of you. I was so ruffled with stress I thought you were him for a moment, that he'd reincarnated and come back to avenge me. But you weren't that. You were the missing piece he needed to find his way back. People like your ghost hunting friends have come and gone over the years, but they've never been clever enough to work out what Joe was trying to tell them. That's what he needs. That's why he can't rest, why he's so angry. The lad's confused, he wants others to see what happened to him. He only knew how to communicate through emotion in life, and it's the same on the other side. With your help he managed to frighten me until I confessed. Be proud of yourself, son. Joe's got what he wanted because of you. The secret is out now.'

I glanced at the photograph of Stan and Joe Maguire, noting my resemblance to the deceased young man once again. So that's why Stan had been watching me with suspicious, loathing eyes from the second I'd arrived at the manor. No wonder he hated me so much, the thing reminding him of what he had loved and lost, of what he despised, and the thing that threatened his dark secret being revealed.

'Something doesn't make sense,' I said, looking at Mrs Brown as a memory from our conversation niggled at my mind. 'You said

Joe came back about a year after he first went missing, that someone saw him looking for Stan in the garden.'

'That was Aubrey,' said Stan. 'Young housemaid who worked here a few years. She had the gift, too. She didn't see Joe that day. She was looking at his ghost. I just told Elspeth that so she wouldn't get suspicious of my story.' Stan's eyes drifted to the window again. 'It all makes sense now. It's as if everything came together at the right time so he could find a way of getting what he wanted. Not like I hadn't had conversations with him before, tried to explain why I'd done it. But I guess he couldn't hear it. Everything changed last night after you lot and the witchy woman brought that cursed board in the house. You gave him the strength to come back stronger than he's ever done before. He began haunting me like nobody's business after that, making noises in the cottage, moving stuff. Scary how much force they have in death. He was as meek as a mouse in life, wouldn't say boo to a goose. That's why I nicknamed him Mouse. He loved that name. He couldn't spell a word to save his life, but he learnt how to spell that name, he loved it that much.'

Mouse. It was a nickname. I looked at Will, saw the recognition of the name dawning in his eyes. And now the indecipherable word, the one Joe's spirit had spelled when asked how it had died — MUDRGUNN — suddenly made sense too. Joe Maguire couldn't spell, but he had tried to: MURDER GUN.

'Thought my heart was about to burst out my chest I did, he spooked me that much,' Stan went on. 'Thought he was going to kill me, if not by force through sheer fright. Got me so startled I grabbed my shotgun and put a hole straight through the wall.'

'The loud bang we heard last night,' said Will, almost to himself.

'You're a murderer!'

Mrs Brown, who had been sitting quietly for a long time, startled all three men around her by shouting at Stan across the table, her Celtic complexion red with rage.

'I don't care why you did it,' she yelled. 'You took a young, special boy's life away from him before he'd had a chance to live it. You got rid of him the way you'd exterminate one of your boggin rats. You're not God, Stan, you don't get to decide someone else's fate!'

'You're right, he was special!' blubbered Stan. 'Too special for a life behind bars, being abused. Ninety eight years I've lived. And if one thing's sure after that much time it's that this world is a rotten place. It takes everything pure and turns it black. I showed the boy mercy, Elspeth. Can't you see that? I saved him from having to suffer, before the evil of this world tore him apart. Please, love, you have to forgive me. They'll lock me away and do what they want with me now, but I can't have you hating me too. You're all I have left!'

Mrs Brown watched in despair as her friend burst into more tears from across the table. You'd have thought releasing such a burden would have made Stan look younger, but sitting there, a hunched and devastated figure, he looked like he'd aged another hundred years.

I turned to Will, a sick feeling in my stomach. 'What do we do?'

'Leave it with me,' he said, combing damp strands of hair out of his face and pulling out his phone. 'You stay here and make sure he doesn't try and do a runner.'

Will left the room. I looked at the table and saw Mrs Brown sobbing into a handkerchief, mirroring her distraught friend. Both people were far ahead of me in years, yet in that moment they appeared like small children in need of a comforting arm around their shoulder.

Instead of playing adult, I stayed near the door, guarding it. When I heard Will's voice on the other side, I opened it a crack to see what he was doing. But then I heard the scrape of chair legs on tiles. The sound of feet rushing towards me. I turned and saw Stan coming at me, his eyes on the crack in the door, ready to make a run for it. I hardly had time to register what was happening, but I knew I had to do something. And I did. For the first time in my life I hit someone. I punched an old man right in the nose, knocking him straight to the floor.

## - CHAPTER EIGHTEEN -

# *The Attic*

SLEEP EVADED ME when I lay in bed hours later, when the police had been and left with Stan and the commotion had died down. My head nestled in the pillow, I gazed out of the window at an indigo sky twinkling with hundreds of tiny stars. But even its mesmerising beauty couldn't lull the errant thoughts, carry me to the blissful oblivion of sleep.

My writer friend, however, was not allowing the shocking revelations of the evening to keep him from rest, evident by the long snorts and whistles issuing from his side of the bed. And I'd thought sharing a bed with Kat was bad. Actually, that's being unfair. Will's snores were soothing in a strange way. Here was a man who had been willing to put himself in harm's way to help prove that the vision I had seen was real. He had possibly saved me from being shot in the face in that rainy garden. And for that I would be forever grateful.

My eyes drifted to the suitcase under the window. I hoped Kat, oblivious to the events that had unfolded, wouldn't be too annoyed come morning that she'd missed all the action. But then I'm sure scooping her rivals to what was certain to be a top news story in the following days would make up for it.

I rolled over and thumped the pillow. Outside the manor a distant wind sang to the night with ghostly howls and whistles. The spooky sound would have been enough to unsettle me a couple of nights ago, but exhausted and still reeling from the evening's events, it had an unexpected lulling effect, like an haunting lullaby that crooned to me as I reflected on my stay at the manor.

So I finally had the proof I wanted. Ghosts were real. And they haunted us as much as we haunted them with our guilt and regret. Just like Esther said, we keep the dead alive by being aware of them. And it seemed the closer the bond in life, the more turbulent the circumstances surrounding the death, the stronger the haunting. The haunting of Stan Crouch and Joe Maguire had a resolution. But would my own haunting ever come to a similar closure?

Esther's words when I'd bumped into her on my way to the bathroom made sense now. My need to know that Elliot was haunting me, that he still existed, was really about needing to know that he forgave me. If he had come back to help me then it proved to my broken heart that he didn't hate me for not jumping into the water to save him. Maybe I would never know if he had forgiven me. Or maybe not getting my own resolution was proof he hadn't. I was to be tormented for the rest of my life with the uncertainty as my sentence.

I was just beginning to drift off when I heard a noise coming from above me. I lifted my head off the pillow and listened. There was a scratching, scraping noise coming from the floor above. From the attic.

The first thought that came to mind was mice. Or maybe a nocturnal bird had got inside and was fluttering about trying to find its way out. But then I recollected the night of the first ghost hunt, Norman telling us Stan had warned the attic was strictly out of bounds. After the evening's revelations I was suddenly very curious, despite being apprehensive, about what the disgraced caretaker might have been trying to hide.

I groped for my glasses, slid them on, then pulled back the covers, creeping in my t-shirt and boxer shorts over to the door. I opened it a crack and wavered on the threshold. All was still and quiet in the house, just that howling wind beyond its walls. And then the noise again ... *scratch scratch scratch*.

I glanced back at Will, watching him slumber on. If I ventured out he wouldn't be around to help me, the way he did when he wrapped me in his dressing gown at the kitchen table, when he pulled me out of the cold and took me back to his room. God forbid any more dead bodies had been hidden around the place. I'd be screaming like a banshee myself if I went upstairs and stumbled upon a decades-old skeleton. Will slept on his front, one arm under the pillow, the other hugging it close to his cheek. His naked back was bathed in pale light, the bed covers just below the hem of his underwear. Few people would be so keen to abandon a bed that contained such a sight. But there was that irresistible pull again. The same pull that drew me down to investigate the cellar.

In the corridor, the sconce lights had long been extinguished and the central heating turned down for the night. The scratching noise grew louder as I crept along the carpet runner. When I reached the door that led to the attic and pressed my ear against the cold wood it had stopped. I turned the handle a little then cast a wary glance in the direction I'd just came from. It remained dark and quiet, guests fast asleep behind its panelled doors. Did I really want to go up in the attic, in the dark, with the cobwebs and spiders and God knows what else? Of course I didn't. But there was no resisting the strong urge compelling me to do just that. I opened the door and, steeling myself, climbed the steps.

The attic was musty and full of dust. Motes danced like glitter in the bands of moonlight flooding through the windows, prickling my eyes and tickling my nose. I waved it out of my face before it made me sneeze and searched around for a light, giving up when I realised there was enough light to make out most of the space around me. It was the largest attic I had ever seen, stretching the entire length of the house, and its beamed ceiling was high enough to make the space habitable had anyone wished to convert it into a living space. They hadn't. The dusty floors were covered in mountains of disused furniture and clutter. There were boxes brimming with ornaments and books, ornate picture frames stacked by the dozen, and there was even a heavily-scratched and flaking bed frame in one corner, one of those types you see in hospitals and orphanages. Two intricately carved torchères stood like sentinels guarding the door.

My toe hit a cardboard box and I refrained from cursing. I edged forward, the floorboards creaking underfoot. I regretted not wearing shoes. If there were any loose nails or sharp splinters protruding out of these boards, I'd be waking the whole house up if one of them went through my foot.

I found a clearing in the clutter and stopped to listen. I eyed nooks and crannies, hoping a rodent wasn't going to shoot out at any moment and cause a heart attack. But it appeared the scratching noise had stopped for now.

A pile of books, files and elastic band-wrapped letters stacked on top of a cardboard box caught my eye. I walked over and squinted at them through the gloom. There was a scrapbook with dogeared pages protruding from its leather binding on top of the clutter. A closer inspection showed it wasn't as dusty as the other items, as if someone had been looking through it recently. I picked it up, blew off the remaining dust and pulled open the strap. Inside were pages and pages of drawings. Drawings that looked like they had come from a child's hand. But I knew immediately they hadn't been drawn by a child. They had been drawn by the same person who had drawn the picture that had fluttered down and landed on the runner in the corridor. These were Joe Maguire's drawings.

I flicked through the portfolio. More stick figures standing in front of a large house with lots of windows: obviously Hilderley Manor. Who knew who the people were supposed to be. The drawings were decades old; they could have been staff or people who lived in the house at some point. I flicked some more. Sketches of birds. Lots of birds. Black ones. They were crows, just like the blessed beasts that encroached the exterior grounds. There were pictures of them pulling wriggling worms from long grass with their beaks. Perched on the tall gates at the bottom of the drive. It was clear to see Joe had a fascination with the animal. A chilling thought occurred. Had that been why the ebony creatures had pestered us from the moment we'd arrived? Did they somehow sense the mystery that was about to be unearthed? I continued to turn the pages. The caretaker's cottage was next. Then butterflies fluttering around daisies sprouting amid blades of grass. Each drawing was signed in the bottom right hand corner: MOUSE.

'You always were an inquisitive bugger,' a familiar voice said.

Every hair covering my body stood on end. The scrapbook closed with a snap and I twirled to find Elliot standing behind me. Not the flesh and blood version he used to be, but an almost translucent version, with a silver light gilding his outline. I lost speech and thought. The scrapbook slipped from my fingers and hit the floorboards with a dull thud. All I could do was stare in disbelief at the face that I remembered so well. The longish sandy hair tucked behind his ears. The kind grey eyes, the same ones that belonged to his sister Amy. The dusting of freckles across his nose.

This was no misty figure, no smoky cloud floating in midair, no barely visible wispy shape that could be mistaken for a smear on a camera lens or water vapour rising from the ground. I was looking at a real ghost.

I opened my mouth and nothing came out. Elliot smiled. It was a sage smile. The smile of someone who had been to another world, garnered secret knowledge and returned to share it.

'Don't be afraid,' he said.

His voice sounded different. It was still the sweet voice that had stayed in my memory all these years. But like the smile it held the weight of a being far advanced in knowledge and understanding. And it delivered a calming effect that made me feel relaxed, and warm, like I was being bathed in sunlight.

'Are you real?' I said, surprised to hear my own voice working again.

Elliot shrugged. 'You can see me, can't you? What's more real than that?'

'Are you my imagination?

'I'm whatever you want or need me to be.'

I shook my head. 'I don't understand.'

'You will. One day.'

I blinked. Maybe I was trying to blink him away. But he didn't disappear, remaining exactly where he stood, moonlight and dust dancing through his ethereal body.

'It's so peaceful here, Quentin.' He inhaled slowly and a smile tugged his lips. 'There's no fear. No pain. No regret. No anger. Just love.'

'Where are you?'

'I'm everywhere and I am everything.'

I always thought that if I ever saw him again I'd have so much to say, questions, things I had left unsaid. But now he was standing here, it felt like none of that mattered, that nothing needed to be explained.

'I can't stay for long,' he said.

I felt a sharp tug in my gut. I didn't want him to leave. Didn't want this warm feeling to go.

'I thought you were trying to warn me,' I said. 'But it wasn't you. I got it wrong.'

'You don't need me to protect you. You have all the guidance within you if you trust and listen.'

'Then why did you come back?'

'To give you a gift.'

'A gift?'

'The permission to let me go.'

I continued to stare at him intently.

'Don't let the ghosts from your past steal the joy from your future, Quentin.'

'But … I don't want to let you go. You were the only thing that made life worth living.' My lip trembled. A tear trickled down my cheek.

Elliot was shaking his head. 'It wasn't me that made life worth living. It was what you imagined we could be. But that story wasn't meant to be. Let go of the dream. And you'll realise everything is worth living for.'

More tears leaked down my cheeks. A pain, so familiar, ached inside my gut. 'But it hurts, Elliot.'

'You let the pain overshadow your love, you let it dampen your flame. But love didn't disappear when I died. You suffer because you think I only exist if I'm alive. But I exist in your heart. I exist here right now, in your head. I exist when you see a robin. When you see a butterfly. We exist together, all the time, no matter where we are. And we'll exist together when you join me. Find the place inside your heart that sees that greater love. Letting me go doesn't change a thing. I'm already gone and yet I'm still here. All you have to do is light your flame again and you'll see that.'

I blinked through the blurriness of my tears. Elliot's brow knitted with sadness. And yet the smile remained on his lips. This was the message he had returned to give me, just like Esther had predicted. And now he had delivered it, it was time for the final goodbye.

He became less visible suddenly. The same expression, a mixture of love and yearning, remained on his face. But he was fading. Fading fast.

'No!' I cried. 'I need to know that you forgive me! Elliot!'

I lunged forward, reaching out my arm to stop him leaving, and it went right through him just as he vanished. But not before I heard his voice, distant but clear enough to hear him say the words, 'There is nothing to forgive.'

I blinked at the cold emptiness in front of me. I knew I would never see him again. Because now that he'd given me his message there would be no need for him to return.

I crumpled to the dusty boards and curled into a pathetic ball inside the beam of moonlight. I wailed like I was five years old again, when life seemed unbearably unfair. I let all the pain that had welled inside me over the years — the longing, the guilt, the resentment — bleed out until I was wrung dry.

## - CHAPTER NINETEEN -

# *Chasing Ghosts*

BIRDS SANG A chorus of trills and chirrups high in the trees of the garden on our final morning. An approaching wind rustled the canopies and fleeting forks of sunlight came through the scudding clouds, illuminating patches of lawn, the neatly-trimmed hedges, the water fountain. You could see how well Stan had been looking after the garden in recent weeks, despite the leaves that were falling off the trees by the second, creating orange and gold crunchy beds wherever you looked. It was easier now to see how much the garden meant to him, that he remained so conscientious of his duties with everything else that had been bothering him. I wondered who would mow its lawns and tend to its flower beds now. Who might take up home in the caretaker's cottage.

Lost in thought as I stood in front of the weeping cherry, I barely registered the sound of Kat's footsteps drawing up beside me. She looked like an insect in an angular black coat and enormous sunglasses that reflected the autumn hues of the garden. Her hair and makeup, as usual, was impeccable, but her pallor indicated she was feeling the unwanted after-effects of her alcoholic binge.

'Funeral's over,' she said. 'It's time to go.'

'Just a couple more minutes.'

It felt disrespectful to leave Joe Maguire's graveside so soon. He'd lain here decades with only one person to visit him. There hadn't been any of the customary posthumous proceedings. No procession of mourners to show how much he had meant to people during his short life. No gravestone to mark his existence. No flowers laid by reverential relatives. I felt he deserved at least some formality before the police showed up and taped off the area to declare it a crime scene, before the forensics started digging until they had recovered every last piece of what remained of him.

Kat lit a Marlboro Light, folded her arms and blew out the smoke as she stared down at the leaf-strewn grass. 'So ghost boy's somewhere under there, is he?'

'Around about here, yeah.'

Her nostrils flared at the thought. 'It's going to be a big story.'

'I imagine it will be.'

'We're really lucky, you know, getting the scoop before the nationals hear about it.'

I feigned interest. 'Yeah. Looks like you'll get those readers after all.'

'Well, you could sound a *little* enthusiastic.'

'I'll be enthusiastic when I hear Joe Maguire is being laid to rest inside a proper grave and Stan Crouch is locked inside a cell for the rest of his days.'

Kat said nothing more. Perhaps my retort could have been a little less thorny. Kat wasn't being entirely insensitive. She hadn't, like I had, seen Joe's memories, felt his fear, his sadness, before a bullet was put through his head. She hadn't listened in detail to the story of what he had endured at the hands of Billy Crowley, heard his anguished sobs in that grimy cellar. These things were going to stay with me for a long time to come.

A sudden gale coming from the direction of the woods behind the cottage shook the drooping branches of the weeping cherry, scattering more leaves over the dewy grass. A magpie swooped down from the sky, hopped across the ground and began pecking at the moist soil for worms. Kat lifted a finger to her temple and winced.

'Hangover?' I asked.

She nodded.

'I hear water helps.'

I couldn't see her reaction behind the sunglasses, but I spotted her scarlet lips twitch into what I thought was a smile. We continued to stand there in front of the tree, like two mourning relatives in a graveyard. Water trickled in the fountain. A car door slammed at the front of the building. The magpie flew off, looking for somewhere else to find food.

'I owe you one,' Kat said. 'Will filled me in on what happened last night. You were brave. And I wasn't. I almost ruined it, acting like a coward. There wouldn't be a story if it wasn't for you.'

I lifted one corner of my mouth. 'Wouldn't say I was brave. I was bricking it under those covers, waiting for the maniac to come and off me. Will was the brave one.'

'But he isn't my partner.'

I glanced up at the lenses of the sunglasses. The only eyes staring back at me were my own bespectacled ones mirrored in their reflection. But I had heard the sincerity in her voice. Did it mean we were official partners now?

She winced again. 'I need painkillers. And coffee. Be quick, yeah? When we get back to Cricklewood, I'm going straight back to bed.'

She walked off, her step a little unsteady on the gravel. I watched her walk past the fountain until she reached the steps. She turned around and shouted, 'Oh, and I'll make sure Josh knows how well you did.'

I smiled a thanks before she turned around and began ascending the steps. But as I glanced back at the weeping cherry again, those words "if it wasn't for you there wouldn't be a story" lingered like a dark prophecy. Was this my life from now on? Seeing and hearing the dead, their memories, the horrible ways their lives were taken from them. I wasn't sure I wanted to carry such a burden.

I blinked at the dewy ground. It was time to say goodbye to Joe. I looked around for something I could leave as a gift. Considered some nearby flowers, but realised that would just be moving one part of his resting place to another. I touched the amethyst necklace on my chest. Debated giving away such a precious gift. Decided I would own more stones in my life. And I had a feeling Esther wouldn't mind, given my intent. I unfastened the necklace from around my neck then bent down and left it on the grass. 'It might not be much,' I said. 'But it helped me.'

The birdsong had ceased. The wind rustled the trees again. It could have been a whisper of a thank you. But that could have been wishful thinking.

* * * * *

Every ending has a new beginning, so they say. I was wondering what new beginning might be in store for Hilderley Manor after everyone had poured out of its front door, bags packed, coats wrapped tight to ward off the windy weather. The crows were nowhere to be seen around the front grounds. The birds are a symbol of mystery, not just death and bad luck as most people believe — another one of those little facts Elliot loved to share.

Perhaps they would find somewhere new to go now the mystery that haunted this house had been solved.

The ghost hunters, hauling their cases and boxes of equipment over to where their Range Rover was parked, waved their goodbyes. Ash and Matt, dressed like a celebrity couple in designer winter wear, followed them, Ash hurrying Cottonball into the passenger seat of Matt's sleek black Mercedes before the wind had chance to carry the mischievous fluff ball away.

I heard the wheels of Kat's suitcase being dragged over the doorstep. The sound was followed by a loud groan. 'Oh bugger. I left my watch upstairs.' With an exaggerated sigh she headed back inside. I unburdened myself of my rucksack and rubbed my arms against the breeze as I waited for her to return.

The boot of the Range Rover slammed shut and the Freaky Foursome, as Kat liked to call them, climbed inside. Matt's car sped across the gravel, Ash operating Cottonball's paw so it looked like the pooch was waving at me. Distracted, I didn't notice that a figure had materialised beside me. I sprang back, peering down to see Esther Hill, resplendent in a mustard-coloured wool coat, gazing up at me.

'A pity we must part,' she said. The shamrock green eyes looked more of an olive shade in the stark light.

I returned a genuine smile. 'Yeah. It was great to meet you.'

'Indeed it was.' She waved to Giles and the other ghost hunters as the Range Rover drove away. 'Even under the macabre circumstances.'

'You heard about Stan, then?'

'Of course I heard. I'm psychic, darling.' Her eyes roved cheekily up to mine and she winked. 'When I'm not being a nosy beggar, that is.'

She took a step back and gazed thoughtfully at the building

that towered over us. I did the same, hoping I wasn't going to see some phantom there she had suddenly spotted. 'A mercy killing,' she said with a mournful shake of her head. 'What a bittersweet finale to such a pleasant weekend. But the young man's soul can now rest. It was the resolution it was after. Mr Crouch, too, will find that releasing his burden will bring an unexpected peace, whatever happens to the poor chap.'

'You don't think he should be repenting his sins for the rest of his days, then?' I said, still cynical. I was finding it much harder than Esther to muster sympathy for the man who had cut young Joe's life short, no matter how 'merciful' his reasoning.

'Wishing suffering on those who have caused suffering never got anyone anywhere good. All it does is keep the wheels of karma turning. There is nothing stronger than a belief. And people do the most shocking things believing it is for the greater good. They are guilty of not knowing a better way if anything.'

Wind whipped at Esther's hair as her wise words hung in the breezy air. But she had so much lacquer on the halo it hardly shifted, just sort of trembled like a topiary bush. I tried to share the view, but it wasn't happening. Maybe it would come later, when the events of the weekend weren't so raw.

'I wanted to let you know you were right,' I said. 'I was looking for more than just evidence that ghosts existed. And I got the answers in the end.'

Esther's magenta lips widened into that beaming smile that refused to be diminished. 'And now you have them?'

'I've been lost, confused and afraid. I wasted my time punishing myself for something I thought I should have done, but in the end it didn't even matter. I can't keep living in the shadows, too scared to come out into the light because of what might happen.' I cocked a brow at the manor, thinking of more than just my own past and the things I had learned over my short but eventful stay. 'Chasing the ghosts of our past is a waste of time. They just end up chasing us until we've got nowhere else to look but the future. That's where I'm putting my focus from now on, on the future.'

Esther's smile almost reached her ears. I felt like blushing under her gaze. The wise woman who had picked me out of the group on that first afternoon and read me like a book looked proud of me. And yet, oddly, I sensed from a glint in her eyes she had known all along that my visit here would bring me such insights.

'Life's ups and downs are our greatest teachers, Quentin. I learnt a lesson myself during my stay here. I remembered that it isn't my job to interfere when fate has clearly decided its course. If we had returned young Joe's spirit to its place of rest, the events of last night wouldn't have unfolded. You wouldn't have had such a realisation. You *or* your companions. Never underestimate how many lives can be changed by a single seemingly insignificant event.'

I smiled once again in fondness at the endless wisdom that poured out of the very colourful woman.

'Well, I must be off,' she said. 'They have the most delicious fish and chips in these parts. I've been salivating all morning thinking about stopping off at this delightful little establishment I discovered on the journey up here. Do take care, precious. And don't hesitate to look me up should you ever feel the need. I am never far away.'

With a wink she drifted towards the Audi Hatchback that had crystals dangling from the rear-view mirror and a dream catcher in the back, glancing admiringly at a flock of noisy birds soaring high in the bright sky.

A familiar concoction of aftershave and smoke blowing on the breeze let me know that Will was standing behind me. I turned and saw a man fresh out of the shower, as late leaving the manor as he had been arriving, the motorbike helmet in his hand.

'Interesting weekend,' he said, dragging on his cigarette.

'Don't suppose you managed to find that inspiration in the end?'

He shrugged. 'A couple of things have given me a few ideas.'

I nodded, pleased for him. Then I felt the nerves that rose up in me whenever I was around him. The sound of Esther's tires driving away brought a brief but welcome distraction. We watched the car turn and head towards the gates. Cyndi Lauper's 'Girls Just Want To Have Fun' was playing from the car's speakers at full blast.

'Well, I guess it's goodbye then,' I said.

Will nodded. 'Later, squire.'

He walked past me, heading towards the shiny black motorbike parked with the handful of vehicles left in the parking area. A sudden rush of butterflies flooded my stomach as I watched him go. It was now or never.

'Will?'

He stopped and turned around. I cleared my throat. But the thing I was going to say didn't seem to want to come out now those blue eyes of his were looking at me.

He nodded at my blazer. 'Check your contacts,' he said, before turning around and continuing towards the motorbike.

I delved inside my pocket and pulled out my phone. I scrolled through the list of contacts. A new name and number had been added: *Will the Great*. I glanced up as he was fixing the helmet on his head and laughed lightly.

'I'd forget my bloody head if it wasn't screwed on.' Kat reappeared in the black coat and sunglasses. She gripped the handle of her case. 'Right, let's get out of this haunted hole.'

I grabbed my rucksack and threw it over my shoulder. But before I'd even taken a step towards Kat's Mini, my attention was captured by a procession of vehicles coming up the driveway. Kat and I stopped to watch them approach. There was an expensive silver car, accompanied by a police vehicle and a forensics van. Stan had been cuffed and taken away in the night after the police officers showed up. And now they were back to investigate the grisly leftovers of his wrongdoing.

I glanced at the house and saw Mrs Brown standing in the bay window, a shadow of the woman she was when we arrived, that apple-cheeked woman who had welcomed us in from the stormy weather. She watched the vehicles with a look of sadness, then her head turned and she caught sight of me. We exchanged looks that were filled with regret and sombre gratitude.

The vehicles pulled into the parking area as Will took off on his bike. A very tall balding man with a large stomach peeking out of his brown coat got out of the silver car. He slammed the door and strolled to the front door with the look of a man who was often disappointed with what life had to show him. A handsome policeman, following him, was speaking into a radio on his chest: 'Stanley Oliver Crouch, that's right.'

Mrs Brown had appeared at the front door, looking even more wan and exhausted in the daylight. The tall man flashed her ID. 'Detective Superintendent, Ray Higgins, madam.'

The men disappeared with the housekeeper into the building. Kat and I walked to the Mini. As she opened the boot, I paused near the passenger door, taking a final look at Hilderley Manor. The imposing roof terrace. The vines climbing the stonework. The innumerous mullioned windows. But there were no misty figures looking down at me this time. Not now justices had been righted and ghosts laid to rest.

## - CHAPTER TWENTY -

# *Ten Weeks Later*

I'VE ALWAYS LOVED snow, the way it brings people together as time seems to stand still. Living alone you notice those sorts of things. I might not get many visitors knocking when the temperatures hit sub-zero and the blankets of white flakes begin to fall from the sky. But knowing others are wrapped up warm inside their houses with their loved ones brings me a vicarious comfort. Today, though, my focus was not on the wintry weather outside my window.

I'd been renting the attic apartment at the top of a three storey Victorian off my parents for the last three years. It was self-contained, partitioned to create separate living areas; it was quaint, cosy and had a beautiful nighttime view of the commercial part of the town from its dormer window. But recently the period building, despite its modern renovations, had been acting a little too 'bump in the night' for my liking. And I wasn't just talking about the late night banging from the randy couple's headboard in the apartment below. No, it was time to upgrade to something a little less haunted, and, with me fast approaching thirty, a little less studio, more ... homely.

The new place was a sweet little cottage sitting on the edge of a local forest. For some reason the owner, a friend of Dom's, was in a rush to rent it out. He offered it at a ridiculously reasonable price for immediate tenancy. I fell in love with it on first sight: the aged beams, the wood stove fire, the windows that looked out at the flowery garden and the winding path that led to a wooden gate wearing a plaque of the cottage's name: Mugwort Cottage. As a bonus it was well away from the bustle and noise of other people. Perfect for an antisocial hermit like me. It was a place to make a fresh start. And, more importantly, now I was being paid for working full-time at the *Cricklewood Gazette*, I could afford it. I would be in there next week.

Moving was the current task at hand and the snowy Sunday afternoon provided the perfect time to get cracking on it. First on my list was sorting my clothes out. I made cup-a-soup, cranked up the radiators and got to work.

I opened the wardrobe. Shoes. There were few of them. Shirts, jumpers and t-shirts. There were many. And they all looked the same. Kat, forever going on about my dress sense, was right. I needed a new wardrobe. A new style for my fresh start in a new home at the start of a new year. There was a shelf above the clothes rail. I reached up and pulled out moth-eaten blankets, extra bedding … I spotted something else. Tucked in the corner was a dust-covered storage box I'd long forgotten about. I slid it out and carried it over to the bed. I sat down, blew off the dust and pulled off the elastic band that was keeping the lid secure.

Inside I sifted through various documents, keepsakes and mementos I had accumulated over the years: old letters from a penfriend, holiday photographs, my adoption certificate, passport … it caught my eye, between a photo of Belinda, Dom and me in Scotland and a postcard Grandma Ethel had sent from Windermere. It was the poem Elliot's sister, Amy, had given me at his funeral. I lifted it in front of my bespectacled face and read the calligraphic verses:

*When I Die by Elliot Dunne*

*When I die, don't visit where I lay*
*In mud and bones I do not stay*
*I am the **rain**, **wind** and the snow*
*The **robin**, the **magpie** and the **crow***
*I am the **full moon** that shines at night*
*A falling **feather**, so light, so white*
***Butterflies**, their flapping wings*
*I am all of those beautiful things*

I had read the poem numerous times, but it had never made more sense than it did now. If it had been months earlier, the poem would have undoubtedly brought me to tears. I would have pondered its meaning until a well of sadness poured over and the only thing left to do would be to cry myself to sleep. But that wasn't going to happen today. I stowed the poem back inside its safe place and resealed the lid, smiling. The future lay ahead, not the past. And I would go for a walk later, glimpse a robin redbreast as it landed on a snowy branch to watch me pass, its orange feathers reminding me that we are all warriors, capable of a strength we never imagined we could possess. I would feel the snow kiss me as it alighted on my crimson cheek. And I would glimpse a winter moon as it peeked out of a clear blue sky, a reminder that someone is always watching over me.

My phone beeped inside my pocket. A message. I pulled out the phone and checked the inbox. The message was from *Will the Great*. I read it:

**Our weekend at Hilderley Manor paid off. Already on the second draft of Portent. Head's flooding with ideas and haven't been able to stop writing. Fancy going for a celebratory drink when I'm done? Will x**

I smiled at the little kiss at the end and replied:

**Sure. Give me a call any time. Really happy the writing is coming along. Q x**

The phone started to ring immediately after I pressed send. Kat's name flashed on the screen. I answered.

'Just showed Josh my final writeup about the Hilderley Manor ghost hunt and guess what?' she enthused right off the bat. She paused for dramatic effect. 'He's over the moon with it!'

I smiled, feeling a genuine happiness for my partner. 'That's great,' I said, rising from the bed.

Kat talked more about the article as I went into the kitchen and poured more hot water into cup-a-soup. I carried it over to the window and looked out. Snow had started to fall, flakes of white dancing down from the powder blue sky. I blew steam as it rose from the cup.

'Obviously we couldn't mention the details of the murder case for legal reasons,' Kat jabbered on, 'but after the court case is done there'll be enough material to milk for at least two more articles. And he's he's even talking about a possible book about the case: A blimming book!'

It was hard to share Kat's enthusiasm. Anything to do with Hilderley Manor brought about a shudder and unwelcome memories. And there had been more than just those memories that had followed me home from that godforsaken place. But I will save those stories for another day.

'I've got a feeling about this, Quentin. I think I could be in for the top job after all.'

'Chief reporter. That's great,' I said, still staring out of the window.

'Well, nothing's real till it's real. But I really feel things are shifting around here. And in the right direction, finally.'

'You deserve it,' I said. 'You've worked hard.'

And I meant it. Kat had worked around the clock over the last few months. Annoying as she might have been at times, showing up at my place uninvited, making me listen to her ideas for hours, her fierce single-mindedness was a force to be reckoned with. She was an incredible reporter. A woman who I was proud to call my sidekick.

'There's still a bit a tweaking, then we're good to go,' she said. 'But that's not the only thing I wanted to talk to you about.'

I took a tentative sip of cup-a-soup. 'Oh?'

Excitement filled Kat's voice. 'You are not going to believe the job Josh has got planned for us in the next few weeks!'

Thanks for reading

The journey has only just begun …

# CHASING GHOSTS

BOOK ONE of THE QUENTIN STRANGE MYSTERIES

Look out for

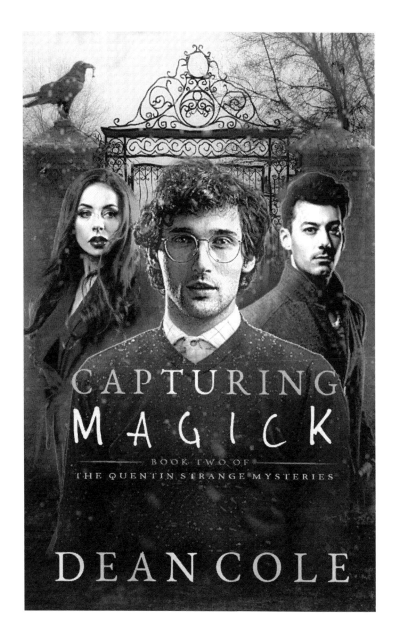

CAPTURING
MAGICK

BOOK TWO OF
THE QUENTIN STRANGE MYSTERIES

DEAN COLE

Book Two in The Quentin Strange Mysteries

# Capturing Magick

magick I. noun archaic spelling of magic.
1. the power of apparently influencing events by using
mysterious or supernatural forces

Revenge, black magic, murder. A cautionary tale of what can
happen when the human ego misinterprets the forces of our world.

# More books by Dean Cole

Charlie Stone has problems.

He's just found his boyfriend and his new BFF in bed together, and that's only because he failed to show up for his fortnightly back, crack and sack wax. Furious, he speeds away from the gates of his luxury home into the unknown. When he finds himself stranded on the side of the road in a remote village, his future looking bleak, his dreams wasted on a fairy tale that turned out to be a nightmare, he doesn't expect the handsome but shaggy-looking bookshop owner, Nathan Marshall, to come to his rescue. A Divine Intervention if Charlie ever saw one.

But the village is foreign land to glamour puss Charlie, who's more at home in the bustling city, shopping for the latest trends, getting his hair coiffed and nails buffed by best friends, glamour girls Trinny, Kylie and Sasha than he is trekking through muddy hills in jeans and wellies. And Nathan's never even seen the inside of a beauty salon, let alone considered having that tumbleweed on his chest waxed. How's a queen expected to survive in such dire circumstances?

Hope seems lost until Charlie discovers that an amateur dramatics group are looking for budding stars to fill in two of their starring roles at the last minute. Could the village offer more than babbling streams, scenic moorland and the smell of horse manure after all? Could it offer a chance for Charlie to claim back the dreams he thought were lost forever? And, more importantly, could an unlikely romance be brewing between this unlikely pairing, even when the dark characters from their pasts come back to make events very difficult for them?

A darkly comic look at love, death, dysfunctional family, emotional trauma and finding yourself. With a huge cast of characters, it's more than a romance. It's a story of self discovery.

# Preview

I SIT ON A PATCHWORK QUILT, LISTENING to the tinkling of cups being stirred downstairs. My hero stowed me here while he went to make coffee. I sigh as I stare down at my sodden bunny slippers and scrape one softly through the puddle they've created on the wooden boards.

Nathan—that's my hero's name—has a surprisingly cosy nest up here. It's as charming as the rest of the village. The walls are made of some sort of clay, thick beams run along the ceiling; there's a bookcase, a coffer and a lovely little stove fire. Every surface is bedecked with things that look like they've been knitted and sewn by old lady hands, or maybe elves. Across from me, my reflection stares back at me in the fogged panes of a Dickensian-style window, rain still falling in relentless sheets behind it.

'Take off those wet slippers. You'll get cold,' says Nathan, walking into the room with two steaming cups in his hands. He sets one down next to a lamp on the bedside table.

I do as he says and take off the slippers. When he sees my bare feet he pulls a pair of woolen socks from a chest of drawers and hands them to me. He settles into a rocking chair across from me as I pull the socks onto my feet. He's wearing clothes now. Black jumper, black sweat pants, and the flip flops have been replaced with woolen socks of his own.

'Make yourself comfortable,' he says, nodding at the pillow. So I do, lifting my legs onto the bed and scooting up to the headboard. I take a sip of coffee and the warm creamy liquid soothes my sore throat. I've shouted a lot today.

'Nice place,' I say.

'It's not much, but it's home.'

'It's charming.'

He lets out a small laugh. Beneath all that stubble I catch the glimmer of a dimple.

'What? It is,' I say. I take back my initial judgment of the place. It has old things. Things that have history. I don't have anything like that.

'To a city boy like you?' he says.

I frown. 'How do you know I'm from the city?'

'The flashy car. The clothes. That tan and haircut. Even your nails are perfect. You don't find many folks as polished as you around here.' He lifts a shrewd eyebrow. 'I suppose you're used to those penthouses with the glass windows overlooking the city and plasma TVs on the wall.'

I set my cup down and slide my manicured hands between my legs. I don't like being analysed, neither mentally nor physically.

'What's your name?' he says, taking a sip from his cup.

'Charlie Stone.'

'First two rules of surviving out here, Charlie Stone. One, don't tell strangers your name. Two, don't ever tell strangers your first and last name.' His mouth twitches into a smile.

I swallow and rotate my head towards the window. Rain hammers the glass as if demanding to be let in, and the canopies of black trees sway eerily in the distance. Where exactly have I ended up? Nathan coughs, and I jump.

'So, Charlie,' he says. 'Want to tell me how you ended up stranded out here in a pair of slippers?'

I stare into his eyes. I was right. In the soft light of the room there is a touch of hazel in them. As I look deeper, there's something else. Sincerity. And before I know it, everything comes pouring out.

'Oh, Nathan, where to begin? I've been so stupid! I gave Richard everything. Moved away from my family and friends to live with him. Abandoned my dreams of becoming a star to be a full-time man-wife. He promised me everything. Money, clothes, jet-setting to tropical places around the world. A fabulous life. I thought I was going to be like Gabriella from my favourite soap opera, The Lives of Housewives. You know? Marry a wealthy businessman and live the fairy tale life in a beautiful home. Going for brunch and shopping in the finest stores around the world. But it isn't a fairy tale. It's a nightmare.'

I'm aware that I sound a little melodramatic. It's entirely intentional, and necessary under the circumstances. It's having the desired effect. Nathan looks intrigued and concerned, his brow furrowed.

'Slow down,' he says. 'This Richard, he's your boyfriend, right? The lying, cheating whore?'

'Yes,' I sniff.

'And you actually caught him cheating on you?'

'With my friend, Nathan. My friend. And in our bed, too!' My face contorts as the image of Tyler lying on my silk sheets comes into my mind. My silk sheets! Who has a name like Tyler anyway? So last season!

'What happened?' asks Nathan, noticing his coffee is going cold and starting to drink it.

I let out a sigh that seems to carry all the weight of the world with it, a prelude to a long and detailed story.

'Well, I had an appointment at Powder'n'Puff this morning for my fortnightly back, crack and sack wax ...' I pause when I see Nathan's brow furrow. 'What? It's not my fault I was born with the hairy gene!'

When his expression doesn't change I realise he has no idea what I'm talking about. Has this man ever seen the inside of a salon? Judging by his hair, the stubble and that tumbleweed I saw on his chest earlier, I'm guessing not.

'Anyway,' I continue, a little flustered. 'I had a dodgy stomach from the moment I woke up, probably those whelks we ate at The Delauney the other night. So I called and told Sasha I wasn't going to make it. Then I went into the conservatory to read a magazine. Before I knew it I was asleep.

'When I woke up, I'd only been asleep for half an hour. I heard a noise upstairs. I got scared. Richard works days and our cleaner, Madelina, never comes unless it's a Saturday. I thought it was an intruder. I crept into the hall, ready to run out of the door. But then I saw Richard's clothes on the stairs, his shirt on the floor, his tie on the stair's rail. I heard giggling. I crept upstairs and peered through a crack in the bedroom door and that's when I saw them. Tyler was undressed under the sheets and Richard was in his boxers, straddling him. Tyler was giggling as Richard playfully kissed his neck …' I trail off, the memory too emotional to bear.

Nathan's eyes are fixed on mine. 'What did you do?'

'Went berserk, of course. I barged into the room and demanded an explanation. Richard was the most surprised to see me. I never miss an appointment at the salon so he would have been certain I'd be out all afternoon. As I'm sure you can imagine, Nathan, looking as good as this takes time.'

Nathan blinks but doesn't answer.

'He must have planned the whole thing,' I say bitterly. 'Taken the afternoon off work. Picked Tyler up from his boyfriend's house. Because there's no way Tyler would have walked. He lives over a mile away and doesn't drive, and he's so lazy he orders a taxi just to go to the corner shop.'

'The conniving buggers,' mutters Nathan. 'Tyler has a boyfriend, too?'

'Mmm hmm,' I say, secretly liking the fact that Nathan called Tyler a conniving bugger. 'Tyler's boyfriend, Emmett, works from home. He's one of those psychic mediums that have popped up all over the city, reading tarots for champagne socialists and stay-at-home housewives with nothing better to do. I knew he was a fraud. How can he be psychic if he doesn't even know his boyfriend's cheating on him? That's why Richard and Tyler chose to desecrate our place. They didn't even go to a hotel.'

'What did you do then?' asks Nathan.

'Well, I have a short fuse, so of course it was going to get ugly. Most of it's a blur I was so angry. But I remember that Tyler ended up with a bottle of aftershave and a can of shaving cream on his head, I slashed two of Richard's suits with a coat hanger, I broke a three-hundred pound vase and threw my favourite dildo through the conservatory roof.'

Coffee explodes out of Nathan's mouth.

'Of course, it could have been much worse. If I hadn't been so emotional,' I sigh. 'Richard and I have a difficult history. He's cheated before so violence is a part of our life. But it's usually with guys he meets in clubs or his regular rent-boys. Never my friend. It's against BFF law!'

Tears threaten to fall out of my eyes again so I grab my coffee and start drinking to quickly distract them.

'But, why would Richard want to cheat? He has a good looking boyfriend like you.'

'That's very kind of you to say, Nathan.' I smile. 'And I've often wondered the same thing myself. But you have to understand what it's like in our world.'

'Our world?'

'My world. His world. The world of image and money. Richard grew up in a rich household and then inherited most of his wealth, so he hasn't had to work hard for anything he's got. Not like most people have to, anyway. The problem with someone who's had it so easy is that he's never satisfied. When you've never had to fight for the things you've got, how can you appreciate them? No matter how many cars or houses he acquires, Richard's never happy. It's not enough that he's forty nine and dating someone half his age. If there's someone younger, sexier, more attractive on offer, then he wants them. And he can have them. He just buys them. His rent-boys. Sluts like Tyler. But they're just after money. Deep down I loved Richard. I thought I could make him change. But they've betrayed me. All of them.'

And now I am crying. I pull my knees into my chest and sob like the poor baby that I am.

'But, I don't understand,' says Nathan. 'Why would you be

with a man who treats you with such disrespect? Is it for the money?'

I stop crying and sniff as I look over at Nathan in the rocking chair. His eyes are a little less softer and there's something else in them, too. Is that an accusative stare?

'You can't blame me for wanting a better life! I was only nineteen when I met Richard. Naive. Stupid. He flashed his money around and told me I was beautiful and special. He enticed me. He said he would look after me. Anybody that young would have been impressed by that. How was I to know he only wanted a trophy on his arm, someone who'd be there every day when he got home to massage his feet, a thing to keep up the appearance that he was someone who was wanted and adored. You can't judge me until you've been there yourself, been in the predicament I was in.'

'I didn't mean—' says Nathan, but I interrupt him.

'You don't know what money's like. It tricks you, corrupts you. It's like drugs. Addictive. You buy one thing and get your fix, but after that it just makes you want more. It offers you a sense of security, until you start to see that it's really just a never-ending trap. You finally accept that it's never going to make you happy, but you still can't live without it.'

I'm angry at my sudden outburst, at Nathan for thinking I'm just a money-obsessed doormat. So I ball my fist and thump the bed, hard. But it hurts, and all that does is make me start crying again. The sobs come out harder this time, snotty and unattractive.

'Hey, hey.' I hear the creak of the rocking chair and the pad of Nathan's feet coming towards me. 'I never meant to upset you.' He sits down on the mattress and curls his arm around my shoulder. It feels good to have human contact right now. Really good.

'Ugh!' I shout, flinging my head back dramatically, my eyes clouded with tears, my nose streaming with snot.

Nathan grabs some tissues off a nearby shelf. 'Here, use these,' he says, rubbing my back like he's burping a baby. Which is exactly what I feel like right now.

I blow my nose and dab my tears. 'I know you didn't mean it.' I look up at him through bleary eyes. 'Look at you. You're like a man puppy with your shaggy hair and those big round eyes. You've been so kind and helpful, taking me off the road and bringing me up here. Even giving me your socks to put on my feet.'

He smiles. 'Are they warmer now?'

'Yes, thanks.' I straighten up a little. 'Wait a minute. This hasn't all been some plan to get me into your bed has it?'

He laughs. 'Well, if it is I'm doing pretty well so far, seeing as you're sitting on it.'

This cheers me up a little and I allow myself a smile, wiping my nose with the tissue.

'Listen, it's late,' says Nathan, checking his watch. 'Why don't you sleep here tonight and we can call someone about the car tomorrow.'

I glance around the room. 'But there's only one bed.'

'I have a sleeping bag. I'll kip on the floor, you can have my bed.'

Part of me knows I should protest and offer to sleep on the floor, but this bed is comfortable and it's been a long day. 'OK,' I say.

'Give me the keys and I'll make sure the car's locked up. Best not to take any chances with a flashy motor like that, not even out here.'

I pull the keys from my pocket and hand them to him. He slips into a pair of boots at the door and disappears down the stairs.

As I stay huddled on the bed, hearing the tinkling bell ring downstairs, it occurs to me that Nathan wasn't uncomfortable at the suggestion he might have been trying to get me in his bed. He's pretty rugged and masculine, and although there are plenty of gay guys like that, I hadn't suspected he might be one of them. Until now. What are the chances of being rescued by a gay hero out in the middle of nowhere?

Life does work in mysterious ways, I think, spreading out on the bed. I look up at the beams on the ceiling and close my eyes to the sound of rain drumming against the window.

But it's interrupted by another noise. Angered voices. Shouting.

I leap off the bed and run to the open window. That's when I hear his voice. Loud and full of rage.

'Charlie!'

My eyes go wide. Richard has found me.

Printed in Great Britain
by Amazon